THE MAGNETIC GIRL

THE MAGNETIC GIRL

a novel

JESSICA HANDLER

HUB CITY PRESS
SPARTANBURG, SC

Cover and book design: Meg Reid
Cover Illustration by Jeffrey Nguyen
Proofreaders: Kalee Lineberger

Alan Michael Parker, excerpt from "The Invention of
Money" from *Elephants and Butterflies.*
Copyright © 2008 by Alan Michael Parker.
Reprinted with the permission of The Permissions
Company, Inc., on behalf of BOA Editions, Ltd.,
www.boaeditions.org.

Library of Congress
Cataloging-in-Publication Data

Handler, Jessica, author.
The magnetic girl / by Jessica Handler.
Description: Spartanburg, SC : Hub City Press, 2019.
Identifiers: LCCN 2018031294 | ISBN 9781938235481 (book)
Subjects: LCSH: Hurst, Lulu, 1869-1950—Fiction.
Entertainers—United States—Fiction.
Psychics—United States—Fiction.
GSAFD: Historical fiction
Classification: LCC PS3608.A69985 M34 2019
DDC 813/.6—dc23

LC record available at https://lccn.loc.gov/2018031294

This book is a work of fiction. References to real people, events, establishments, organizations, or
locales are intended only to provide a sense of authenticity, and are used fictitiously. All other characters
and all incidents and dialogue, are drawn from the author's imagination and are not to be construed as real.

186 W. Main Street
Spartanburg, SC 29306
864.577.9349
www.hubcity.org

When the lightning was invented and the tree that was standing was struck sorrow was invented. Love was invented to give us something to do with sorrow.

ALAN MICHAEL PARKER,
excerpt from "The Invention of Money"

For my mother and my sisters, magnetic girls all.

FALL

CHAPTER ONE

Cedartown, Georgia:
October 1883

OBJECTS HAD ALWAYS JUMPED INTO MY POCKETS, which is why I didn't think of what I did as stealing. Whatever I took from one place to another was merely my attempt to help a lost thing find the right home. A button on the schoolroom floor by the wood stove, the pearly white shine so different from the chapped, dry floor beneath it that the only right thing to do was to rescue that smooth disc. A button the size of my fingertip, escaped from the tight row of its companions along Ada Shoals's faultless back.

Mine now, and safe, you little button. This treasure joined my collection inside a wooden box that had at one time held spools of thread. I lined the box with a scrap of brown velvet I'd lifted from beside the scissors at the dry goods store. I kept three different glass-topped hairpins in the box, too, along with a playing card that showed a drawing of a mischievous fellow sitting Indian-style, waving a heart over his head. I also kept a glass medicine dropper. The rubber bulb was empty now, but it still squeaked when I pinched it. Once in a while, when I held the tip of the medicine dropper to my nose and inhaled, I could smell the bitter ghost of my brother's medicine. My mouth watered when I did, a feeling that could nearly transport me back to a time before everyone forgot me.

I helped other things besides the button. An earthworm writhing in the hot dirt, practically calling out to the cool grass that it couldn't reach. The worm was silent, of course, but I understood how solitary it felt. I crouched down and used a twig to lift the anguished creature. The worm lay crosswise over the twig, brownish-red flesh struggling in the air for something solid to cling to. Quick, before it fell to the ground and perhaps bruised itself—could an earthworm bruise?—I delivered the thing to the soft green strands, a wet place where it could burrow into the dark earth and find comfort.

I hadn't meant to hurt my brother.

The year I turned six was Leo's first, and I hardly ever let him be. I pestered Momma enough that she taught me to hold him without her being right there behind me. I listened like she was talking Gospel truth.

"His little neck is like a green branch, Lulu," she said. "But his head is heavy, so we have to help him hold it up."

She handed my doll brother to me, and he was warm and solid, and I was so very careful. One hand stayed cupped behind his head, the other under his bottom. Leo's eyes were gray like a winter sky. He looked right at me. That was the first time a gaze punctured my soul. When Momma said, "Very good, Lulu," and took him back to her breast, I held his fingers, unwilling and unable to fully let him go.

Momma rarely let me watch Leo alone. When she went to the woodpile or got the water boiling in the yard for the wash, I held him close, fussing with his dress or jiggling him in my lap. I told him intricate, imagined stories about how school would be when he went for the first time.

"Someday, Leo," I said, "you'll go, too, and the teacher will be proud that you're my brother. You'll already know how to read, like I do, and she'll clap her hands for you being so smart. 'Smart as Lulu,' she'll say, and you'll be a boy who won't play rough or bring home dirt on your clothes."

Fascinated, Leo reached for my hair. Besotted, I let him.

On a beautiful, bright warm day when I was alone with him for the few minutes Momma stepped away, the urge to show off a bit of the world overtook me. A swarm of birds had landed like a glittering black cape on the field, their bickering as good as laughter.

Want to see. My brother, five months old, spoke inside my ears.

"See the birds?" I asked.

Leo grinned, clutching at the motes of dust in the sunlight as he tried to seize something he couldn't hold.

I picked him up as easily as snapping a pea from a pod and lay him over my shoulder, so he could look out the window. His chin rested perfectly against my collar. I stroked his warm back and schooled him about how birds ate worms and insects.

When they've had their fill, I said, they fly away.

I lifted him then, my hands around his middle. I held my brother high above my head so he could thrill, like I did, at the sheath of wings rising past the window. My baby brother quivered, a movement so new to my hands that I pulled them away.

Leo fell, alone, untended. He hit the kitchen floor with the sound a mattress makes falling from a wagon, a padded, simple, singular thud.

I screamed and swallowed the sound at the same time, silencing my terror for my brother and the fear that Momma would come running before I could undo whatever harm I had done.

Leo screamed, too, panicked from his fall, my childish arms no consolation. When I scooped him up, his face was wet with my tears and his own. I tried to look in his eyes and hold his gaze, but he looked away, furious and broken. I held him to my chest and rocked him. I rocked us both, six year old me and baby Leo, a single being seeking solace.

And ever since that time, objects found their way into my palms, my pockets, and of them I made neat rows inside my wooden box that had once held the thread that stitched our clothing. With the very sharpest things, the hairpins with tops like jewels, the lone sliver of glass slim as a sewing needle, I pierced myself before I set them aside. I never felt pain when I slid a sharp tip slowly and carefully into the meat of my thumb. What I felt was satisfaction, a question answered before it had been asked.

My father collected things, too. He kept stones in a pile on our parlor mantel. Before I was tall enough to reach them on my own, he would lift me and let me move the stones, reshaping the pyramid to a square and back again, or placing a black stone—hematite, he said, iron ore—at the top, then a milky-white one—quartz—in its place.

The stones were cool to the touch in summer, so much so that I would drag a chair to the deadened fireplace to reach them. I held the flat ones to my face, closing my eyes against the bright sun flaring at the edges of the drawn drapes. Small round ones I placed in the V-shape between my fingers, spreading the skin and letting air into the humid spaces. The stones stilled my mind and gave me rest. When I heard Momma calling me, I arranged the stones back into formation before dismounting the chair and pushing it back into place, my heartbeat thudding in my ears. The stones weren't to be touched unless Daddy was there. The stones and the furniture went back exactly where'd they'd been without my thinking about it. I always had a map in my mind.

On a day when I was fourteen and loading kindling onto a cart, a fox ran toward me like a black-footed bullet. I didn't shout. A fox will avoid people if he happens on them, but this one, hurtling toward me, had to be diseased. Leo lay in the shade on a blanket beside the cart. In a single motion I set the kindling down and pulled Leo onto my back, all the while holding the fox in my gaze. When I crouched, the animal was at my eye level. The fox froze, a front paw in the air as if he were about to speak.

Which was what I wanted.

I lowered my eyelids halfway. The sounds of birds and the rustle of leaves faded. The sunlight paled. The world closed in around me, Leo, and the fox. I felt my brother's heartbeat against my own, and I patted his hand while I willed him to stay still.

I counted my breaths, feeling my own bumping heartbeat. Not until it slowed and steadied did I stand, my gaze still linked to the fox's. With Leo's weight against me, I backed away from the motionless animal, stepping carefully until my heels touched the bottom step of the porch. Then I turned, my heart racing, and shut the door behind us.

When I looked out the window, the fox was gone. Nothing out there but our mother's purple irises, and past them, the half-filled cart of kindling.

Back then I believed that I was magic. My power appeared as a bodily urge, like needing to use the privy or sucking in my stomach to button up a dress that no longer fit. I loved my secret talent so much that I gave it a name: captivation. I sensed more than most people, too, without using words. I was the only person in my family who understood my brother when he spoke, although Momma tried her best.

Leo was my center. In his eyes, my most secret faults were forgiven. And I wanted to change his life.

Not long before the incident with the fox, my body had turned into something I couldn't control. My feet tangled when I walked. My bones ached in my sleep, thickening inside my flesh. Sometimes they scalded like steam, other times they cramped with ice. The easiest place to be was home, where I didn't hunch my shoulders or bend my knees to keep boys' faces from looking straight at my collar buttons or the dress seams at my bosom.

Momma had quit seeing anything truly special in me by then. She went out of her way to remake me in her image. She'd wet her hands and make a hailstorm of little hits on the top of my head, trying to get my thick hair to lie flat and smooth. She tugged at my sleeves and my skirt, covering what my dresses could no longer hide. She wanted me to be someone I wasn't. I had been big as long as I could remember. At fourteen, I could look my father in the eye, and he was six feet tall. Momma told me I was done growing, but I didn't know how she could be so sure.

"Be gentle, Lulu," Momma said every day like a reflex, so often that I'd stopped considering the meaning. Collecting eggs from the chickens meant holding the warm shells in my open hand, my fingers curled up to make a shallow bowl of my palm before I lay the delicate eggs in a bucket. That was gentle. Cleaning house, I shoved the table to the wall under the windows, so I could sweep under it easily. I dragged it back into place with one hand. When Momma came in, she eyed me funny and fussed with the chair cushions like she was looking for something to do. And she scolded me to be gentle.

When I started school, girls' hands in mine felt insubstantial when we played Ring-Around-the-Rosie in the schoolyard, and I never was sure how tightly to grasp. One girl would wince and draw away from me, another kept her hands at her sides. Eventually that ring of girls no longer opened to include me.

"Go with the fellows, you tall tree," a town girl hissed. "There's where you belong."

Across the schoolyard, the boys ignored us. That very minute, two boys were brawling in the swept dirt, dust swirling around their flailing arms. The other fellows circled them, shouting encouragement.

I could win that fight without trying, but who'd ever want to sit with me in the schoolroom after I'd pushed one fellow onto his rear and pulled the other one to his feet?

I had been a town girl once, when Daddy clerked at the hardware store. Momma and Daddy and I lived upstairs. Leo hadn't been born. What I remember is that inside our home, the curtains fluttered in a breeze that I tried to catch in my hand, and when I walked on the sidewalk with Momma, the sun made the world too bright at the edges and hard to see. The fresh-cut pine smell from the boards in the sidewalk made me want to inhale all the air all at once.

I taught myself to read before I turned four, pronouncing words from the sides of grain sacks and the labels on medicine bottles at the store. Saying the black and gold lettering's alchemy aloud, I practiced my words. "Hoofland's Bitters for the Liver," I said. "We sell everything from horse shoes to hats." For the longest time I believed the store only sold objects that started with the letter "H."

A few months before God brought Leo, we packed up and moved to a big white house and acreage outside town, where Daddy said a man could be himself and not feel like other people and their *avarice*—he spit the word in a way that frightened me—shadowed him at every turn.

Not long after my terrible mistake with Leo, my brother was one day speckled with an angry red rash. For two days and a night between he cried so hard I thought he would explode. The doctor came with a Vapo-Cresolene lamp that Daddy kept lit day and night. The lamp didn't do anything but tear our throats with the smell and make everyone's eyes sting. Poor Leo must have hardly been able to breathe right under it.

Although he'd made attempts at talking and could almost sit up on his own, when his fever broke, he made only sad little squawks of dismay, a sound like a bird trapped in the eaves. He spooked me. If I could hold him like I had before, I would have gladly shared some of my already oversized height and heft, but Momma banned me from getting near him.

Even from my station at the doorway I could see how he kept his neck bent like he had a crick in it. I couldn't tell anyone what I knew about the reason for his sickness. I tried once, twice, but the words gagged me until I nearly blacked out from regret.

The doused lamp went into the barn, where it hung blindly from a nail. The light was gone from Leo's eyes. His arms and legs flopped, and I cursed myself for ever having let myself think of him as a doll. Momma said that because of his fever, Leo's mind would never grow up.

My love had done this to him. Sick and silent with guilt, I held Leo's head up with my arm when Momma left the room, and I begged his forgiveness. He and I both knew that if he were ever going to be a regular child again, the responsibility would be mine. I leaned over him and brought my face close to his. His gray eyes didn't fix on anything.

"Leo," I whispered.

My voice sounded like a branch scraping rusted metal. No nursery songs came to mind, so I tried hymns. They were all about death and leaving this world, so I quit, with him so close to having done that very thing.

"Look in my eyes," I said.

Leo smacked his lips but didn't look at anything.

"Leo," I said, low and slow in a voice that didn't sound like mine, or our mother's, or our father's.

His body jerked. I jumped back, then eased myself close again. I waved a hand over his eyes. He followed it. Maybe he could only see close up. I held my breath and half-lidded my eyes. His gaze drifted away as my hand made a full transit across his face, my palm like a full moon.

"Leo," I said. "Help me fix you. We've got to finish before Momma or someone comes in."

He opened his mouth like he was about to squawk. Now or never. Leo watching and seeing, Leo talking, that was my due to him, a payment that would make everything right again.

"Look at my hand, little boy," I said, my palm inches from his nose. Leo's eyes wandered. Nothing would come of this. My brother would be broken forever. He stiffened and tried to push himself over with the little strength he had. I didn't want him to roll over, not yet, and he knew it. He gave up trying to change position and returned his sight to my palm. I drew my hand back slowly, thrilled to see him follow my motion. When my hand was before my face, I drew my hand away, and let his gaze settle on mine.

I saw my brother. My brother saw me. And he smiled.

Our parents wept when I showed them what he could do.

"He can watch me move, Momma," I said, after I'd called her in to show how he watched my hand. He and I did our trick a half-dozen times, and instead of tiring, he made a sound that I knew was a laugh.

Momma wiped her eyes on her sleeve and reached for Leo. His laughter had become a whistle in his throat.

"Next time you handle him, watch that he doesn't choke," she said.

She spanked him between the shoulders, and when he'd quit whistling, she lay her hand, gentle, on my cheek.

When she told Daddy, his smile was crooked, a broken window shade.

Leo and I grew into opposites. He was delicate, I was ungainly. At fourteen, I walked like a dray horse, according to my mother. Leo was eight. We could look each other straight in the eye and know right away what the other was thinking. His walk was tentative. He supported himself with his hands against a wall. His legs gave in more often than not. To an observer, Leo would be the weak one and me the strong, but they would have it backward. I was weak inside.

Without Leo whole, I would never be enough. Our parents looked at him and saw an empty space shaped like the man he could never be.

CHAPTER TWO

Tennessee: July 1862

WILL WAS NINETEEN THE FIRST TIME HE GAMBLED. Almost all the soldiers did, waiting for a skirmish. Short on pay, Bill Lee and Harmony played every chance they could. They bet buttons or stones when they had to, laying out IOUs worn and bent at the edges like a tomcat's ear as collateral for the day when the paymaster's leather folder would be full.

"Seven," Bill Lee said.

Will watched them play.

He had been sitting on a stump, cleaning his Winchester with a cotton rag. His grey wool cap lay on a different rag he kept for the purpose of protecting the hat's rim from dirt. His blond hair was filthy. He hadn't had a decent wash in a long time. His scalp itched.

"Can't make seven on your come-out throw," Harmony scolded Bill Lee.

"Go on and watch me, asshole," Bill Lee said. His heels were in the dirt, the dice curled in his fingers. Bill Lee always seemed to watch everything closely, as if the world held a secret code that he would find if he peered close enough. He'd have made a lousy devotee: Will had known him to bird-whistle a warning call when he saw movement in a distant tree line.

Bill Lee shook his loose fist and rolled two dice onto a plank. The ivory squares, yellowed like old molars, rattled across the surface, the first one rolling head over heels and landing with the four side up. The second die followed, a lagging twin, until it stopped near the raw edge of the plank. Three up. Seven.

"Owes me again," Bill Lee said, not bothering to look at Harmony. Bill Lee took a cone of notepaper from somewhere in his jacket, unrolled it, and jotted a note with a pencil stub. "Asshole," Harmony said.

Will finished cleaning his rifle. Needing something to do while he studied the craps game, he had cleaned it twice. He set the weapon down beside his hat and wiped his greasy palms on his trousers, stiff with sweat and smoke.

"Y'all interested in showing a man the game?" Will inquired. "Not much for gambling, but I figure I might could play and keep busy."

Bill Lee and Harmony, each in a throwing crouch level to Will's knees, looked up at him, a silent duet. Although they'd been side by side for months, the men formally introduced themselves.

"Harmony Any Last Name's as Good as Another, Knoxville, Tennessee." Harmony was red-headed, thin, and hard-muscled like a whip.

Will shook Harmony No Last Name's hand. The fellow held on an extra second, a salesman's grip.

"William Hurst, Tennessee," he answered, turning to Bill Lee.

"William Lee Borden. My ma calls me Billy, but I spell it like two names." He grinned in an ear-to-ear little boy's smile, a beam of sunlight. Like Will, he was blond, but had stayed nearly a tow head although he looked to be near thirty. His eyebrows were white-blond, and his lashes, too. Bill Lee had a roll of fat around his waist even after months in camp, and Will wondered if the man hadn't stashed some chow in his rucksack and secretly nibbled away on jerky or chunks of dried apple when no one was looking. Will's stomach pinched.

"Set down here and we'll get a game on. Learn while you earn." Bill Lee patted the plank beside him.

Will knelt, and Harmony put the dice in Will's outstretched palm. Cupping his hand around the dice put Will in mind of the trick his mother had taught him. Fold your right thumb into your right palm so it can't be seen. Bend your left thumb so the nail touches your left pointer finger. Now press the back of your right thumb against your left nail, turn your hands around, pull them apart real quick, and presto! A thumb split in half!

For an entire afternoon, Bill Lee and Harmony taught Will the game. Roll like this, light, like you're letting a baby bird fly loose from your hand. Feel the dice under the tips of your fingers as you warm them in your hand: imagine they're a lady's titty. Look at him blush. He don't know what that feels like! You've thought about it, for sure. When they're ready to go you'll know it, don't think about it, just feel it—sling 'em out there on the wood, easy does it. Don't look away, watch how they fall.

Will's childhood attempts at prestidigitation came back, but he'd never been effortless. He had craved the attention, the winning and walking away with the secrets, the money, and the power. He'd never had the knack to master the trick itself. He lacked his mother's patience.

The three men played until it was too dark to see. Bill Lee could have gone for his lamp, but by then chow seemed the wise choice. Harmony leaned the plank upright against a dogwood tree and pocketed his dice.

"I need to eat, if you'd call that shit food, pardon me," Harmony answered. He made a show of rubbing his almost concave middle. His hip bones pushed sharp edges against his trousers.

Like a father teasing a child, Bill Lee reached down and ruffled Will's hair.

"We'll pick it up tomorrow. Looks like we still ain't going nowhere."

Bill Lee and Harmony headed into the dark together, one of

them hawking and spitting on the ground. Will smoothed his hair down, then flexed his fingers before he took three flat pebbles from his pocket. Practice makes perfect.

The three of them played craps for a week. No orders came to move camp. Cannon fire shuddered in the hills. Refugees rolled by in a line of carts coming from one settlement, going to another. Children waved at the soldiers, who waved back. The soldiers with children at home went to their tents afterward, writing letters or staring at the grime of their canvas tents. Someone shod a horse. Someone else sewed torn trousers. They expected to pack up within a few days. In the meantime, Will's throw got lighter and faster. Once in a while, he won a game, but his IOUs piled up quickly under the fist-sized chunk of stone by Harmony's rucksack.

While they played, Harmony tried to preach his beliefs to Will.

"The human body is made up of fluids," Harmony began one afternoon, watching Bill Lee prepare to roll the dice.

"Fluids you piss out," Bill Lee muttered.

Harmony, entranced with speaking his catechism to Will, ignored him.

"We have tides in us, rolling like the ocean. Magnetism is its name. Magnetic fluids."

"Seven," Bill Lee said, a risky come-out. He shook the dice and looked heavenward. Bringing his gaze back down to earth, Bill Lee threw. Harmony was silent for the throw.

The dice landed six and six up. No seven.

Will held out his hand for the cubes. Harmony started up again.

"The motion of the planets pulls our internal tide like the ocean's tide. The planets pull on our fluids, and our nerves react. It's science and nature combined."

"You yap this shit all the time," Bill Lee said. "You're getting on my nerves, and that's my nature." He worked this like a variety amusement act.

"The body has its poles, oppositional. Fluid goes back and forth evenly if a man's in balance." Harmony stopped and looked at Will, who had not yet thrown.

"You ever been sick?"

Of course he'd been sick. Who the hell hadn't?

"What kind of sick?"

"In the head," Bill Lee said. He was drawing in the dirt with a stick, figure eights and waves.

"I've had the grippe, I've had stomach trouble, I had an infected finger one time got drained and cauterized. I've been..." Will stopped himself here, still surprised by his reticence. Ten years had passed since his mother's failures.

"What. Been what?" Bill Lee was interested. Harmony said nothing, patient.

"Morose. I've been morose," Will said. He'd slipped up and given Harmony precisely what he needed. Will could have kicked himself. "That's a sickness," Harmony said. "All these illnesses," he pressed down hard on the word, making "ill" weigh more than the next two syllables—"are natural magnetic fluids out of balance in your body. Your magnetism was disturbed, and you were out of alignment with the planets."

"Roll the damn dice," Bill Lee said.

Will looked at his hand, surprised to find the dice still there. He hadn't shaken or rolled or given a thought to what he'd call to try and take Bill Lee's money. They were playing for actual dollars today. Confederate money wasn't worth much, but the idea of it was better than buttons. Time passing without him knowing irritated him. Always had.

"So how did I get better, then?" Will asked. "Planets come down and make me well? According to my ma they did, but she wasn't one to allow a doctor." That was more than enough said.

"Somebody went and put some money on the doctor. I'll bet he had a damn fine horse and lived in a mighty nice house." Bill Lee surrendered to the conversation.

"Your fluids got balanced," Harmony said, serious as a preacher. "You're a lucky man. Some people need help with that, but you can do it alone, it seems. Some got it, some don't. People who've got it strong have been known to kill a rabbit just by laying their hands on the animal. Magnetism comes through them and kills the thing right where it sits."

"Sounds like an easy way to get dinner," Bill Lee said.

Will rolled the dice around in his hand. What was that riddle, what's lighter, a pound of lead or a pound of feathers? A trick you had to think about. A pound of feathers would have to be so much bigger than a pound of lead. Everything you thought you knew could be an illusion, until you applied reason. The bones of a bird are hollow. The shimmer over a flame is a gas.

"I have the gift of observation," Will said, giving in to the litany he'd been raised with. "It's the way to heal and to lead our lives. We spend our infancy and childhood observing. A babe does nothing but observe and learn from what he sees. Where's Mama? Mama is the first planet around which the baby revolves. Our gift of observation, even if we are not sighted but can touch and smell and hear, allows us to make men of ourselves. That's nature, as planets and tides are nature. Observation of our nature—our magnetic fluids conducted by our nerves from electrical pole to pole in our bodies— is the natural path to righteousness."

Harmony would be gaping, he knew, but Will wouldn't let himself look. Bill Lee? Same, most likely.

His mother had taught him this, and she was dead, and she had been dead since he was a boy. He'd quit fantasizing about her alive somewhere, having merely run off to avoid what she called the *death-like appearance*. Her patients came to her looking that way, she said. And she cured them, one or two uncertain visitors in a month at first, then twice that many in a day, every day. Even Sunday. *You want to thank God for your pain*, she would tell them on those days. *God's given you a message and brought you here.*

There had been an earthquake when she was a baby, she'd told him once. All the world shaking as if Cerberus, the dog of hell, held our planet in his mouth. And look what came of it. Nature's magnetic fluids scattered and sprayed and came to rest in her, bringing with them the gift for healing.

Her health diminished until she died. That was the simple

explanation in this real world. She didn't go to Summerland, the afterlife from whence her spirit voices came. Her trembling hand on an acolyte's cheek, her distorted vision gazing into a devotee's future (the wardrobe door shaken by his father's hand hidden behind, the curtains blowing on cue by his own paper fan waving from where he crouched beneath the sill outdoors) led to retirement from the hands-on trade, but the relief of human suffering remained her focus. Once bedridden, she put her talents to the page, producing a guidebook for those who would follow in her footsteps.

The book was all he had left of her, and if he tried, he could hear her voice when he read the words. *From expression comes splendor,* she'd written. Hardly, he answered back. What splendor is there in abandoning the house in town, or a father dried up and useless without his wife, or sitting out here, day in and day out with nothing to do and nothing waiting at home?

She excluded the idea of defeat from the book. Will had never seen the acolyte spurned by a lover and come to his mother to heal her heart. He only heard the rumors afterward: how his father had cleaned the bloodstains from their parlor floor, how his mother buried the knife the woman used to try and excise her own heart.

"All people will ultimately reveal themselves as fools," his mother said.

Will crouched and warmed the dice in his palm, calming his thoughts. Sunlight was warm on his back. Sounds of the world around him vanished: no bird songs, no throat clearing from Bill Lee or Harmony. He slipped inside himself, at one with the rhythm of his own breathing and his heartbeat. An image of two double-spotted dice floated into his vision, a stereopticon card overlaying the real view of the planed pine board neatly placed in the black dirt.

A planet's brightness or its position in the night sky told his father when to plant and when to harvest, if a winter would be cold or mild. Electricity was an experiment in Europe, a factor in the telegraph, but not a magnetic liquid surging through a body. Will made no plan. He exhaled the word "four" in a whisper that he didn't hear but knew he had said aloud. Then he threw, and his dice came up three and one. He rolled again with more precision than he had the day before. Two and two. Bill Lee whistled approvingly. Harmony nodded.

Maybe his mother applauded him from somewhere in the ether. Maybe she waggled her fingers, and the Mesmerism she claimed moved his dice into a winning figure. Will rocked back on his heels, and the outside world opened up to him again. A catbird chirped a series of quick sounds, and somewhere distant, a horse whinnied. Will stood.

"Gentlemen, you finally owe me."

Harmony clapped Will on the shoulder.

"Congratulations, my friend, and welcome. Welcome to a new world, where poverty and the life of the lesser man is no more, where money is yours for the taking."

INTELLIGENCE HAD COME IN saying that Union troops were headed in from the West. Within a day, the cannon fire was audible. Will, Bill Lee, Harmony, and their fellow infantrymen waited for the order to charge. Bill Lee treated the pending skirmish like a bad joke. The big man dug trenches like a thresher, working his own and more than thirty feet of others' until, without warning, he pitched his spade toward the horizon. The implement flew like a spear, raining dirt as it went, and Bill Lee stormed off to his tent.

"Fuck it," he said. "When they come, I'll be in here. I've been waiting so long I'll kill a dozen of them with my bare hands. I don't need a damn gopher hole."

Harmony worked a trench crew, untroubled, cleared roadways through the brush for wagons, caissons, and, he told Will, ambulances. "We'll see plenty of meat wagons, Mr. Force of Will," he said. "Look around you at the regiments coming in. We're going to see the elephant, alright, and it's about damn time."

The elephant was battle; a huge, lumbering thing you couldn't see around once it was in front of you. Will fully intended to see battle and emerge unscathed but for some romantic, painless scar, and vigorous tales unsuitable for mixed company. Months of relentless

busywork, waiting, moving camp, and more of the same had worn
the fight out of him. Add to that the weeks of playing craps, and he
was nothing more than a homeless man weighted with debt.

A trickle of sweat at the back of his neck rolled into his collar,
taunting him to wipe it away. A cannon boomed, and the stink of
gunpowder clung to the morning dew. When the cry to "charge"
came from down the line, he wanted to vomit, but like a machine,
like Harmony, Bill Lee, and a sea of men, Will ran forward. As if
choreographed to a musical score, men fell ahead of him and behind.
A man tumbled from his squealing horse and landed on Will,
knocking him into the dirt. Will struggled to rise, pushing the man's
weight away just enough to get to his knees. The man's face had been
blown off: only a dark beard sticky with blood and an eyeball loose
as a toy on a string marked it as a face. Will retched and ran, struggling to hold his rifle.

He tried to spot Harmony in the churning mass of men around
him, but everyone had become the same man. The earth had opened
into a pit filled with writhing bodies. Men and horses raced into the
vortex. The air itself was blue with smoke, and blood caked Will's
arms and hands, and he could do nothing but run and shoot wildly,
aiming his rifle at the fragments of sky that appeared through rafts
of smoke.

Running blindly, Will somehow doubled back toward a road. There,
away from the line of artillery, he saw the ambulances Harmony had
teased him about. Will was soaked with blood. He could certainly
pass for someone critically wounded. An ambulance could carry him
to a field hospital, to a town, to somewhere not here.

Running toward salvation, he tripped over a root, wrenching his
ankle and tumbling face-first into a wet burlap sack. Pushing himself up on his elbows, Will saw he had fallen into an artilleryman's
jacket, the grey humped and torn over the body of a young man,
dead but still warm. Will collapsed across the newly dead stranger,
the man who would save his life.

When the attendants came for the dead soldier and the scattered
wounded and dying around him, the blood that Will had smeared on

his own flesh had gone tacky and dry. The late afternoon air smelled like iron filings and buzzed with sated flies. The attendants hurried in their work, although the fighting had moved on. With one man holding arms and another legs they hoisted corpses into the ambulance. Like relay racers, they tended to the wounded, wrapping tourniquets where they could, applying clean rags to the oozing caves that had been stomachs or thighs, then carrying the moaning men on litters to a second wagon. Grown men sobbed and called for their mothers and wives. Will called for no one. An ambulance attendant crouched over him and told him he'd be all right. They were taking him to a field hospital. Will assessed the medic through one eye; about his age, and earnest. Even in a sea of blood, the fellow shone with the bright light of doing good works. Will laid it on thick, biting his lip nearly through and wincing as he nodded thanks. When the attendant moved to lift him onto a litter, Will's deficit of injury nearly gave him away. He'd forgotten to cry out. The suspicion in the attendant's eyes brought Will back to the gamble, and he put all his weight on his twisted ankle, screaming in pain as he allowed himself to fall again in the dirt.

Will slumped into the ambulance as the attendants loaded two, three, and a fourth moaning, blood-soaked comrades around him like so many cobs in a corn-crib. When the ambulance jolted and began its rattle down the road, overtaking the dead-wagon, Will unwound a relatively clean bandage from a man who looked dead. He held the cloth over his mouth and nose, filtering the stench. Rolling along the path that Harmony had helped cut, Will closed his eyes and dreamed of a city's streets, and of debt's dead weight shed from his back.

CHAPTER THREE

Cedartown, Georgia:
October 1883

OUR HOME WAS A SUNK-IN PLACE, WHERE GREEN hills rolled like lumps in a blanket under a sparkling blue sky. From our porch, I studied the road to Cedartown, which either was born or died at our property, depending on how a person considered it.

The Cedartown Appeal was my atlas. In that newspaper I saw glimpses of the world beyond our dead-end road: cotton prices, train schedules, advertisements for Cheney's lung expectorant, and closeouts on knit underwear. I read the train timetables more closely than any school book. Cedartown to Palestine, Tredegar, Singleton, all in Georgia, until the end of the line, Pell City in Alabama. Eighty miles in just half a day. Electric wires webbed the skies of New York City, strung overhead like the work of massive spiders, wires that came loose from their wooden poles to spark fires in the streets and roast a little boy unlucky enough to grab the living cord. In New York, Mrs. Vanderbilt dressed for a ball in a gold and silver electrified gown and called herself "The Electric Light."

In the South Pacific, a volcano rained black smoke onto a place called Krakatoa. In America, the men who ran the railroad companies were getting together to decide how people told time. They sliced the nation into zones from the Pacific to the Atlantic. Six o'clock in the morning in Georgia would be three o'clock in California. Time and distance folded like paper.

I wanted to leave our close hills, but where would I go? If I had all day, I could walk into town, but I couldn't picture myself telling the clerk the name of a city, buying a train ticket, and handing over money I didn't have. How would I decide if I should go to New York City or Atlanta? I could choose a closer place, like Rome, Georgia, or Chattanooga, Tennessee, but I had no answer to what I would do when I got there. School, church, the barn, and the field were where I belonged, even less for Leo. We had a sister, too, but she was under a stone, born, baptized, and buried in a day. There was nothing here for any of us, and yet here we stayed.

Imagining myself out in the world meant leaving Leo. That thought made me want to wrap my arms tight around our square white house with its peeling white paint. Momma said that no one with any class should act like they were someone's renter, but the house wasn't ours. We leased it and worked the land for the family of the man who had built the place fifty years before. The oldest members of his family were gone to the beyond, the newest ones gone somewhere else earthly. Those hills and the land we worked kept me hemmed in during the winter when I ran with the kitchen bucket to the cistern, my coat over my shoulders, sleep gritty in my eyes. No matter how cold I was, I always stopped to watch the hills, gray-green and speckled with snow, crows drifting across the silver sky. In summer, I watched the hills through the wavering heat of the afternoon, perspiration holding my dress tight to my skin.

If I left, I wouldn't have to hear one person say I looked like a possum in a dress, the way I'd overhead a fellow remark at the post office. He'd looked me up and down when he thought I wasn't aware. If I left, no one would whisper behind their hands when I came into the schoolroom, calling me a tall tree. Captivating a person, not a fox, would make a moment when no one could shame me. So, on a Sunday, when Mr. Campbell pointed his finger at me for Sunday School recitation, I tried it.

"The tongue of the wise useth knowledge aright: but the mouth of fools poureth out foolishness," I said.

Behind me, Early Trumball belched, then whispered, "Excuse me."

"Train up a child in the way he should go," I continued.

Calling out a miscreant with choice Bible words had entertainment value, and I hoped Early got the message. As I spoke, I lowered my eyelids, filtering the daylight into a warm blur that let me focus on soft, round Mr. Campbell at the front of the room. Half-lidded, I brought him into bright relief, and then concentrated only on his eyes. My recitation grew distant in my ears, replaced by the thrumming of my blood coursing through my body. I kept my gaze locked to Mr. Campbell's until it was clear to me that a nearly empty room was behind his eyes. A room inhabited only by me.

At the last line of my recitation, I cut my gaze away to the windowsill, and let him go.

Mr. Campbell staggered, knocking a piece of chalk to the floor. As he ducked to fetch it, the back of my neck crawled. My head swam, and I sat without him telling me to. I nearly missed my seat, landing half on and half off as I went down too hard. Even though the stove was not lit, my collar and the backs of my knees were uncomfortably damp.

THE FIRST TIME I WENT alone to my father's study was the next Saturday afternoon. He had books that Momma wouldn't have in the parlor, books with stories about somewhere not here.

"Nothing a lady would choose to spend her time with," she said. No copies of *Godey's Lady's Magazine* or the Cedartown *Appeal*, or a novel like *The Victories of Love*. She found his books dull. Almanacs. Shakespeare. Histories of the Ancient World.

Momma had gone with Daddy to town. I convinced Leo that he wanted a rest, and after he lay on the divan I hemmed him in with a blanket and busied him with his wooden soldier. I promised myself ten minutes with my father's books. That number that seemed right before a neighbor or a tradesman happened by of a Saturday afternoon and noticed through the window an unattended boy, an absent girl. I arranged a line of chairs around the divan to protect my brother like a cage.

Undoing my boots so my footfalls wouldn't distract Leo from his toy, I crept away, thrilled by my planning. At the study door, I turned the handle quickly, and slipped into the room. The door hinges didn't squeal, the frame didn't scrape—a grant of permission, at least from the room itself. The single window streamed a burst of sunlight onto the bookshelves. My father arranged his books tall to short. His ledgers squared to the far edge of his desk calmed my racing heart. In this room, all was as it should be, perfect and controlled. I wondered what my father believed when he watched the field and the fringe of trees from here. Did he pretend, like I did, that we owned it all? His presence clung to the air, a scent like sour teeth and flatiron starch. Five years had passed since he had asked me to help with his accounts for the church or the store, me reading numbers back to him as he flicked his pencil tip against the pages of a ledger. When I had been very small, I drew pictures in the empty spots in those almanacs and histories, happy in his company.

I hadn't helped him count since the day Leo fell.

I listened for Leo's conversation with his soldier. Even the distance of two rooms between us was a laxity on my part. No cry of frustration from dropping the man to the floor, out of reach and out of balance, no shouts of glee as the soldier fought a blanket or a weak fist.

The books, spines out, seemed to have their backs turned to me, but those books who didn't want my company would be the ones to tell me what a train ticket looked like and how a person chose a destination. If that person's brother wasn't imperfect. If she wasn't a person who kept silent about the day she dropped him, the day he hit his head. Leo, in the parlor, was silent. He might have fallen asleep, solider in hand.

Turning out the Bulfinch, the Shakespeare, an almanac or two, I came to a book with a red leather cover. Involuntarily, I pushed my thighs together as if my body had made that color. The book's title was *The Truth of Mesmeric Influence*. Below that, in somber black letters, the author's name. Henrietta Wolf. A book by a lady writer. Surely a novel, but why tucked away here I couldn't fathom. Momma likely hadn't read this one. I would beat her to it.

To my dear reader—the first chapter began. Being the dear reader, I rested for the moment in my father's chair.

I am capable of affording testimony. The atmosphere around my head was not like smoke, nor fog, but a kind of sunrise or glare directed only at me.

I thought of how the sunlight over the sidewalks in town made my eyes hurt when I was a little girl. Like me, this author suffered under a glare that no one else saw.

I turned a page.

She wrote of curing blindness in an elderly woman, of hearing words articulated clearly before the speaker had opened his mouth, of being overcome by a heat wave in a chilly room. Like me, devastated by a wilting heat after I'd captivated Mr. Campbell.

Cautioning myself to be gentle with the brittle paper, I turned page after page, devouring her words like a meal.

She had been *imprisoned by aloneness*. So had I. Her empathy moved me to tears. *Sufferers are many*, she wrote.

In the parlor, Leo was searching for me. As if I were at his side, I saw him elbow himself up from the pillow, and crane his neck to find me in the doorway. His *come get me* rustled in my ears. *I'll be right there* formed in my mind and flew toward him.

I needed to know if Henrietta Wolf had stilled a wild animal or made a teacher stumble at his chalkboard. The book wouldn't fit in my pocket or palm like a pin or a button. I couldn't bear to leave *The Truth of Mesmeric Influence* behind. Henrietta Wolf knew me deeply. We were dear friends already, and I had read only a few of her pages. She understood suffering and silence, and her words were a gentle hand over mine. I know you, they said. Stay with me and I will show you who you are. I pushed the Bulfinch and the almanacs together to cover the empty space where the book had been. Lightfooted and light of heart, I hurried to my brother's side, *The Truth of Mesmeric Influence* a prize against my ribs.

That night, I carried my lamp to my bedroom and unwound the book from the cocoon where I'd hidden it inside a woolen scarf in my bureau. Freed at my table, Mrs. Wolf described how Aaron in the Bible used hypnotism to turn a rod into a serpent. She hadn't seen it herself, but she knew how it was done. *A behavior of stillness and rest is effected by the transference of human energy,* she wrote. *So much knowledge accumulates every day that not a single book can hold the whole truth. In a month, in a year, what will the genuine practitioners learn and share with their dearest ones? The Mesmerist's mystery exerts a force over his subject.*

When Leo followed my hand after his fever broke, he was able to do so because I had captivated him with my human energy. Mrs. Wolf described back to me what I could do and what she could do, and she called herself a Mesmerist.

There was so much more to learn. Had I known everything she could do—that I could someday do, too—on the day that he watched my hand, I might have cured him right then.

The whole body may be filled with a churning magnetism that recipro-cates the gift of human energy.

That swirling in me was why I had to poke holes in my poor ruined mattress. I was filled with magnetism that I had to release. Every time I worked a pin into the underside of a finger, I wouldn't breathe—I couldn't—until I'd broken the skin without raising blood. That tiny disturbance of sharp metal into dull flesh was a relief, a victory. Blood would have been a failure, proof that I was merely human, clumsy and made of shame. Magnetism stirred in me, seeking exit.

At first, I had worked the pin into the pad of my finger, but I'd learned that moving it across the narrow column of fat at the place where the joint met the palm was better. This hurt less and left no tiny torn piece on the tip of my finger, a defect signaling weakness.

The sight of that silver pin, so sharp and bright at the tip showing blurred and yellow-pink inside my own skin calmed what I had no name for until Mrs. Wolf named the feeling. *Magnetism. Human energy.*

When I was done, I eased the pin out as intently as I'd put it in, watching that I didn't break the skin but for the entry and exit points. I rendered the pin innocent by wiping the metal against my dress and returning the tool to the sewing box from where I'd taken it.

No one knew this, of course. Not even Leo.

One more day, I told myself. One more day and I'll put Mrs. Wolf's book back on the shelf. One more day before Daddy notices a gap in the height of his books, before he looks for a red cover that couldn't belong to the father I knew. While I read, I slid the point of a glass-topped hairpin through a waxy callous at the base of my left ring finger. There was no need to watch.

A WEEK PASSED. Even though we were well into autumn, the air hung summer-heavy. I sat by the kitchen door hoping for a breeze, peeling potatoes, tossing the skins into a bucket, and dropping the exposed white lumps into a bowl in my lap. The glare of hot weather had begun to hurt my eyes. Thunder in the distance meant relief.

I knew I couldn't captivate my cousin Dale. She never would look straight at me.

Dale attended the same girls' academy in Tennessee that our mothers had. They were sisters, and until they'd married, did everything together. Like them, Dale studied Shakespeare, Scripture, homemaking, and Latin. She sang in an unstable soprano that sounded like a bucket being pried from ice. And as often as possible, Momma invited her to visit.

"She's the kind of young lady we don't see enough of lately," Momma told me every time she sent an invitation.

Everything I did, I did better than right. Counting the stitches as I sewed a hem, I made twenty-four, twenty-six, then twenty-eight, each exactly the same. Always evens, too. No stopping at an odd number ending in a seven or a nine or a one. Even numbers and balanced sets tended to keep me from wanting to jump out of my skin. Same with movement: even numbers. Churning butter was a task where Momma's "be gentle" didn't apply. I counted to myself in twos, fours, eights. Collect the eggs, sweep the house, do my school-work when I had it. Tell stories aloud to myself and Leo when I didn't.

When I did, Daddy told me to hush up. He read the newspa-per aloud to Momma, who could read, of course, but liked to hear Daddy while she did her needlepoint in the evening. I sat on the piano bench and spoke quietly to myself about horses who could dance and boys and girls who sailed across the ocean on a slice of toast.

"Listen to your Daddy," Momma told me. She didn't look up from her green thread. She was making a parrot in a jungle.

My story kept on inside my head.

"Quit moving your mouth like that with no sound," Daddy said. The *Appeal* was in front of his face, but he could see me.

Tell me the story again, Leo said, inside my head.

The last time Dale was here, she twittered at Leo. I wanted to slap her for aiming a laugh like that at such a little boy, and her without the sense to see that Leo wasn't right. Dale dropped fussy French phrases into the most average conversation. She wasn't right either, talking in a language none of us but my mother understood.

Momma had sent Dale and me into the woods to pick scupper-nongs. Away from my mother's judgmental eye, I plucked the green grapes from their vines. The fullest grapes radiated pressure from within, like skin swollen by a spider bite.

"Dale, look, a grape like a swolled-up finger," I said, presenting her with a fat grape.

As I expected, she recoiled, which prompted me to bite down on the swollen-fleshed grape, squirting green muck and pale brown seeds in her direction. The grape's skin was sour and unpleasantly slippery inside, with rough scabs on the outside, but she didn't need to know that. The mess didn't touch her—I hadn't intended that it would—but fell onto the dirt, no bigger than a bird dropping. Dale curled her lip.

"Mmm," I said, possessing my field, my grape vines, my peeling house. "Just like popping a good blister."

Dale's shriek didn't gratify me the way I'd hoped it would.

While Dale approached us on a train from Tennessee, I waved flies from potatoes and worried that she'd find my book wrapped in a scarf atop my wardrobe. My paring knife skipped and peeled a strip from my thumb.

Sure enough, when Dale made herself at home in the chair beside my bed, she settled her too-many clothes into left- and right-hand stacks, smoothing the tissue paper between each fold. I didn't own five dresses to wrap in paper. She kept a broad-brimmed straw hat in a patterned hatbox, and I was certain I'd heard her whisper 'goodnight' to the hat the last time she visited. I'd have wished the hat sweet dreams too if it were mine, the way it complemented her petal-white skin and sat just right against her hair. Her hair was black as mine, but smooth and shiny as a crow's wing.

I helped her unwrap three dresses from their paper, but the heavy weather made my head throb. I wanted to unbutton my dress and walk around in my cotton chemise and stocking feet, stomping like the dray horse I was, just to annoy someone. Her. Me. The sky drooped like soiled diapers. Faced with a week in Dale's company, I tossed out a story.

"The last time the weather felt like this, we had nuts from the hickory tree in the yard come flying in the front room," I told her. This wasn't a complete lie. There *had* been a rainstorm and strong winds. When the front door blew open, nuts scattered off the tree and rolled into the house.

Dale picked strands of her hair from a brush and made the not-listening listening sound. "Mmm-hmm."

I flung myself wide across the bed, circulating the stuffy air.

"Electrical tree," I said, delighted by my inspiration. "Electricity flew them in, knocked them around like hailstones. Then they stopped cold and fell to the floor. Me and Momma swept them out, even though they were still sparking."

The last part wasn't entirely a lie, either. We had raked the nuts out the door, lifting the edges of the carpets to find the strays.

"Keep any?" Dale asked, shaking out a purple and blue checked skirt. "You know it's 'Momma and I.' Don't act ill-bred or you won't get the right kind of *paramour.*"

Fooling her was deliciously easy.

"I'd love to hold an electrical nut in my hand, see if it's still got a jump in it," I said.

She clicked the trunk shut.

"What do you know about electricity anyway, way out here? We saw electric lights in a drawing of Paris up at school in a lecture about great cities of the world. They make streetcars go without horses. They're bright as the sun, electric lights. You can't look right at them or they'll burn out your eyes. On the avenues of Paris, they burn all day and all night and never go out."

I didn't know the first thing about electricity other than what I'd read in the newspaper. The Wizard of Menlo Park was going to do in America what Dale said about Paris. The editor's column in the *Appeal* claimed that electricity was an artificial light more brilliant than a thousand suns, and it was dangerous. A person could burn to cinders from touching it. Consider that boy in New York City, fried on a wire.

Propping myself up on my elbows, I waggled my foot at Dale.

"I *should* have kept one! You're right, that would have been a thing to own. Hold a nut up to a light in France, maybe it would dance again."

I would have liked to see an electric light. I hadn't yet seen one. No one I knew had. Dale alighted on the bed and made the not-listening sound again.

"Do you have my shawl? I'm sure I set it right there on the chair."

I didn't say anything about the shawl. Instead, I told her that I'd heard from one of the girls at school that electricity is an example of God's power on his earth. I'd heard no such thing, it just seemed like what Dale wanted to hear, and I wanted her to not sit so near to me.

The hot dry treetops glared like cut tin. Wind stirred the field across the road, making the trees scrape against each other like giant matchsticks.

"You know that the Devil isn't far under our feet," Dale said. "Below this house, below the fields. Mama told me that years ago there was an earthquake in Tennessee, and the newspaper back then said that if the earth did open for good, the Devil would be free to walk among us."

Dale got up and probed through her stacks of clothing while she talked. Finding no shawl, she fussed with her skirt. A stray lock of hair came loose from the twist at the back of her neck, and she threaded it back into the bundle with the thumb and middle finger of her free hand.

"Uncle Will's people were from Tennessee, weren't they?" she asked.

As good a story as the Devil would make, the only thing below my feet was the floor, and below that, another floor, and then earth, and roots. Around the roots, copper and iron threaded through the insides of rocks. Daddy said so and proved it with his cairn of polished stones on the parlor mantel. Veins of copper and iron ore ran through those stones. The copper tugged gently at the iron, and according to him, the iron responded, bowing toward its true mate, copper. These two together, Daddy said, made the power of a magnet.

"Are you listening to me?" Dale asked. "I'll find the shawl after we eat. We have to go downstairs and help with supper."

"Did they find him?"

Dale had her hand on the doorknob.

"Find who?"

"The Devil."

"Hush, you." She shook her head and shut the door behind her. Her footsteps tapped down the hall and receded down the stairs.

"Well amen, then," I said, but only to the door. My washrag swung slightly on a peg, mocking Dale's pull on the handle. I reached into my blouse and extracted the shawl she had been looking for. I shook it out, folded it into a little square, and lay it neatly in the hatbox.

The sky was sickly green by the time we sat down for dinner. My ears popped, even though I worked my jaw and tried to shake my head clear like a rained-on dog. When rain fell while the sun shone, people always said, "the Devil's beating his wife." I couldn't imagine who a Mrs. Devil might be, or how she and the Devil might have courted.

Momma dished up second helpings of ham, squash, bread, beans, and pickled tomatoes, a warning in her smile. Eat all of this. For Dale, we would show no struggle in planting the food or keeping it alive, no strain in portioning it out for the table. When we were alone, Momma tallied up prices like they were my fault. A sack of corn cost one dollar sixty cents, and five pounds of dry beans a quarter. A gallon of kerosene cost the same as five pounds of beans. Money was scarce as blood from a turnip, she said. On a rare night, we ate possum.

"Once you've had possum," my father liked to say when he had his plate, "you won't go back to squirrel."

He had it backward: squirrel was all right. Some nights we ate cornbread and syrup, and I gave Leo a sweet rag to suck so he could think his belly was full. He knew better but pretended along with the rest of us.

With Dale at our table, the chat was about a fellow over by Aragon who'd stopped his wagon to have a smoke and burned up his bushels by accident. Daddy was sympathetic to the man's loss. Momma called the disaster the fellow's own fault.

Dale cleared her throat and patted her mouth with her napkin.

"Uncle Will, do you plan to open more acreage?" She was breathy and childlike, a fluttery Dale, not the cousin who last year had screamed about a grape.

Please hush, I warned her in my head, but she couldn't hear me. Sitting across from her, I couldn't reach under the table to pat her arm and take her attention away from the disaster she was igniting right here at the table.

She wouldn't make eye contact. I couldn't get to Dale. I cut into my ham, wishing it were her flesh, or mine.

"I would think by now you'd just go ahead and move back to town. I mean to say that you ought to give up," Dale said.

My forked shrieked across my plate. My cousin, with her perfect hair and womanly shape, had shot flames from her mouth.

"Living out here while the town's going on," she continued. She might as well have spit ash. "Momma says Aunt Sally will fade away from indigence."

Momma paled and didn't speak. Rude as anything, Dale pointed to my mother, in case we hadn't understood who her Aunt Sally might be. Maybe the floor had opened, and Dale was the Devil.

I wiped Leo's chin and put a sliver of ham into his hand. I was teaching him to eat with his fingers in the interest of dexterity.

"More water, please," Daddy said, tapping the rim of his glass. He spoke as if Dale hadn't said a word. Momma stood to get the pitcher from the sideboard. She had to have been relieved to turn away.

Dale had spoiled dinner, and she was pleased. She was so pleased, in fact, that when I sat back from helping Leo with his ham, she looked straight at me, claiming a win. That was my chance, and I took it. I stared right back into her pale eyes. The sounds of Daddy pouring his water, of Leo chewing, of Momma's anxious picking at the tablecloth faded into a dull hum. Dale wanted to pull away, but I held her like I did that fox and Mr. Campbell. Not until my father safely stood to leave the table, patting his stomach with an elaborate motion, did I let her go.

That night Dale took the pillow, leaving me with the edge of a blanket under my cheek. With her in the bed I couldn't lie corner-to-corner the way I liked. With her in the bed, my feet hung off the end into the open air. Dale was the guest and taking up space was her prerogative. She fell asleep fast, mewing like a kitten. Beside her, I watched the starless night. My mattress stank, and I wished for Dale not to smell the sickness in it.

Momma's father had lived his last months as an invalid on this mattress. He had died on it. When I became what Momma called a "little girl getting her big girl's bed," she pulled out the worn feathers and stuffed the mattress with empty feed sacks. She swaddled the stained mattress in oilcloth, since I was, after all, still a little girl. The mattress never entirely lost the stink of illness. When the sour smell got too bad, I rolled to the farthest edge and lay on my side, putting as much of me off the mattress as I could get.

Dale's bedroom wouldn't smell like old waste and varnish. I

imagined her bed as soft and wide, with crisp sheets that smelled like perfume. I inched closer to the window and pushed it up for some fresh air. Blue and white streaks lit the distance. Outside was alive with a heady odor like fading sparks.

I'd been stabbing at that hard-edged mattress with pins for months, harder than when I slid a needle into my skin. When the sharp pin broke through the cracked fabric, my mouth watered from the anticipation and release. Small rips at the pinholes would expose my deed if anyone saw them, so I held the sheets under the soapy water when I helped with the wash. Wooden clothespins on the line covered the growing rents in the fabric.

Stabbing a pin through the thick cloth and feeling it pop through to the burlap inside satisfied an itch behind my knees and along the edges of my teeth. The relief in pushing through the mattress's resistance, probing its depths, and that discrete little sound of completion when I pulled the pin away quelled my craving to scratch, or bite, or scream.

Dale didn't seem to feel so mislaid in her life. Everything was dresses and cake to her. She slept beside me. My uncovered feet shone a dim blue with each lightning flare outside. Downstairs, my parents slept, and my brother slept. I rolled onto my stomach. Dale wheezed in her sleep, a deep sucking sound. Lately, what I wanted and what was right weren't always the same.

A flash of lightning lit my bedroom walls. When the skittery brightness vanished, my hand crept toward the nest of hairpins on my bedside table. I found the one I liked best: a pin with a little metal fan at the top. That delirious moment when the sharp tip in my hand perforated the blunt mattress was so near. Lightning flashed once more in the heavy air, and thunder rolled as I counted ten. Ten miles away. In my mind, I watched the lightning strike a dead tree in a dry creek bed, starting a fire that would die out harmless and alone.

The pin made a hollow pop when it ruptured the mattress. I sucked in my breath and held it to calm my racing heart before yanking the pin free. That made another pop, a backwards sound.

Dale jerked upright.

"What was that?"

Caught in a private act, I froze.

"There must be a bug or some snake in your house," Dale whispered.

She slid from the bed. I lay the culprit pin on the table, blessing the dark before I lit the lamp and rose to shake out the quilt. Dale searched beneath the bed and around the curves of the wash basin before she went for the wardrobe.

"Bugs with horns or claws," she whispered.

"Like needles," I whispered back, grateful for the darkness hiding my hot face.

Dale poked the walls with my buttonhook. No vermin emerged from the cracks.

"It was just the storm," she sighed. Her face was flushed, the collar of her nightgown awry. She seemed disappointed.

"Well, thank heaven," I said. "I was thinking a bug would bite my leg."

In bed, Dale fell immediately to sleep, but I couldn't rest. Captivating a fox or a person was an aptitude, certainly, and I'd hidden my secret—*human energy stirring*, as Mrs. Wolf told me—by letting Dale's imagination run away with her. She'd figured the sound I'd made was scuttling vermin, and I didn't say otherwise. I'd stabbed that pin right beside her because I had to, and she wasn't the wiser. I wanted to throw off the blankets and pace the room, but I didn't want to have to talk to Dale if she woke. I lay still and shut my eyes, ready to stroll the aisles of a store in my imagination, choosing whatever I liked, peeling bills from a bankroll stuffed into a beaded purse. I bought a string of pearls, a red velvet dress with a bustle, and a matching hat with a white feather that complemented my jewelry.

A flash of lightning blasted the imaginary store to bits. In the depth of darkness that followed the bright light, my hand moved to my table. A hairpin rolled under my fingertips. Forcing myself to breathe slowly, counting the ins and outs in twos and fours, I slowed my heart's banging until it was a rhythmic song of comfort. I was going to stab the mattress again, and I couldn't stop myself.

My skin felt tight. I crept my hand beside Dale's head and lifted the pin not two inches from the pink folds of her right ear. I plunged the metal through the mattress's heavy ticking and lost myself in its disappearance in the packed fabric inside. My heart raced, then slowed again. I eased the metal up and out with a single movement of my wrist.

In the hills outside, thunder rolled and faded away. Dale tugged on the blanket, and the fabric slid from my legs.

"Oh, Lord," she said, sounding small as a child. "Oh, Lord, promise us that we heard the voice of one of your tiniest creations."

The Lord didn't answer.

I dropped the hairpin beside the bed, swinging my feet hard to the floor at the same time to hide the ping of metal. Dale slid on all fours onto the rug as a door banged below us. My father's heavy footfalls ascended the stairs. His lamp's weak light fanned out under my door.

"It has happened again," Dale said in a monotone. The pungent scent of her fear made me want to bounce on my toes, but I caught myself. I'd need to act scared with her.

"What has happened again?" My father's voice boomed through the closed door.

Had Dale and I been younger he'd have busted the door down, but we were nearly grown women, too mature for a man to enter a bedroom without permission. I grabbed my dressing gown from the peg and handed it to Dale before I checked my nightdress, making sure everything was buttoned up and pulled down. Dale lit the lamp and checked her reflection in the window glass. I glanced at my hand, still feeling the hairpin between my fingers.

With that empty hand, I opened my bedroom door.

Daddy stood in the hallway, a monument in a blue nightshirt. Momma came up behind him with a lamp. Dale wailed as soon as she registered my father's fury.

"A bug. Some giant bug or a living thing under the bed scared me out of my skin! And sparks flew around, big as thumbs!"

What had actually happened meant nothing to Dale. I'd made her believe she'd seen flaming thumbs in a room lit only by distant lightning. I wanted to try again that very moment and watch her face as I pushed and pulled my pin. I wanted to watch myself create the idea of flames where there were none.

Some kind of train was leaving the station, and I took my chance on that train. Yes, I said, there had been terrible, unnatural, sounds that woke us. I described shoving the furniture aside in search of insects or squirrels going about their vermin business. Dale began to moan like a pipe organ, and Momma charged past us, sniffing my bedroom's air in all four directions. I quit talking to watch her.

After a minute, she spoke. "It's atmospheric," she said.

I grabbed Dale's hand, partly for effect, but more because I was dumbfounded. Momma had plenty of opinions, but I'd never known her to fail to spot deceit.

Momma sniffed the air again. Daddy's face was stone.

"What frightened you wasn't vermin," Momma said to Dale. "Particularly if you saw floating lights."

"We saw them. Floating lights." Dale repeated herself, nodding vigorously.

We'd seen no such thing. She'd conflated the aftermath of lightning into something present here in the house. I had made that happen. Anxious, I tugged my hair, a habit my mother hated.

"The storm has washed our home in electrical energy. Odic Orbs like the ones you saw are electrical," Momma said. "They are the power of magnetism alive in this room."

The floor might as well have opened under us. I had a sudden urge to hang onto my mother's skirt, so she could pull me along behind her when she walked away, our game when I was small. But she left the room without me, nightdress swishing, Daddy following with the lamp.

"God's with us, right now in this room," Dale murmured. "It's His power, alive all around us, bringing the glory of an electrified city into your own home!" She spoke as if she were in love.

From beneath the scarf in my wardrobe, Mrs. Wolf's book applauded me, its pages like so many hands. *From expression comes splendor,* she said. No one heard her but me.

CHAPTER FOUR

LIGHTS HYPNOTICALLY BLUE PULSED BEHIND MY closed eyelids, inside the farthest reach of a soft black cave. They were like the soul of a flame, and I wanted to capture them in my hand. If my head hadn't hurt so much, I might have laughed. The lights receded and returned at their own will, their glowing blue a fixed pinpoint in a miasma of splintering pain.

The headaches had started to come on once a month sometime last year; at first tentative and not every time, but by now I could expect them the third week of every month, along with the rags that I washed out in private, the pain like rodents gnawing my hip bones, and a relentless need for sleep. Sleeping, I dreamed of sunflowers turning their pocked faces to the sky. I dreamed of starved, blighted ground absorbing water as fast as it could flow.

The worst headaches kept me in bed. I couldn't stomach the cup of broth or tea that Momma brought upstairs. Toasted bread might as well have been tree bark on a flowered plate. Momma learned quickly not to waste butter on the bread. The oily smell made me weep with disgust.

At first, Momma lay cold cloths on my head. They were too heavy, and when she left I tossed them to the floor. I tried to dress but reaching for my clothes made me want to run for the basin. I buttoned my dress unevenly and left my hair prickled like an angry cat's back. Shaken by the effort, I lay back on the bed. Cold, I pulled the covers up. Hot, I peeled them back.

"Momma," I wept, but my wail emerged in a whimper.

"Momma," I tried again, gathering effort.

Momma was downstairs. Daddy had stayed away, made nervous by the physical demands of femaleness.

"Rub my back," I whispered to the empty room. Momma's cool hand and strong grip would help, but she didn't hear me. I inched my arm behind my head and pressed my fingertips into the rigid muscles at the root of my neck. My headache receded, but the blue flame danced vividly in my sightline, the color somewhere between indigo and cobalt, the texture a mix of satin and velvet.

Electricity pulsed in the air between my body and the world beyond. I slept.

When I woke, night had fallen. My curtains and the window over the wash basin were open to the air. Momma must have come in. I heard the sounds of supper downstairs; low conversation, a chair scraping the floor. Leo laughed, a dish clanked.

I went to the open window. Hands on the sill, I leaned my head against the wooden mullion. I was muscle-sore and drowsy, but my head no longer hurt, and my stomach was still. The air drifting in over my hands was warm from the day and smelled like cut hay and wet dirt. I caught the distant rich scent of manure, and the remainder of cooking smells: fat and boiled greens.

What if the view out this window wasn't darkness, but streaked blue with electrical light? How far could I see with electricity? If I rode a streetcar with blue light crackling out of wires overhead, how far would I go?

A WEEK HAD PASSED since Dale's departure, and *The Truth of Mesmeric Influence* was still in my room. I read every night and went about my business during the day as if I weren't learning far beyond my school work. Still, Mrs. Wolf occupied my thoughts so much that one morning I nearly stepped on Daddy's boot when I backed out of the chicken coop.

"Missy, you and I will speak privately," he said, flat. "Put the eggs in the kitchen. You have five minutes." Anger shimmered around him.

He turned and stalked into the house, his back rigid, his hands balled into fists. I never took a book from your shelf, I could say. I'd been so careful putting everything back and covering the slim empty space on his shelf. This might not be about the book at all.

The walk to the back door, up the steps, and into the kitchen helped me count off what else might cause his anger. Right foot down; Leo was with Momma, so there was no neglect there. Left foot down; Mr. Campbell might have found the courage to tell him what I'd done in Sunday school, but Mr. Campbell wasn't the type of person to admit something he didn't understand. With each step a new idea arose, with the next, the idea was discounted. In the kitchen, the eggs went into a bowl, and I covered them with a cloth. They'd go into bread dough later. I left the kitchen door open. I could always run.

My father's chair creaked in his study, and he called my name.

Wishing I were so small that my steps were silent, I went to his doorway. He didn't look up from his ledgers. The way he sat, I could see his blond hair thinning on the top of his head, and I wanted to look away. He kept writing in his ledger. When he finally looked up, his mouth was set in a tight line. My stomach sank.

"Give it," he said.

For a long second, I tried to convince myself that I didn't know what he meant. But I knew. On the shelf, the space where *The Truth of Mesmeric Influence* had been was blank as a missing tooth. If I spoke up and pointed out that the very fact that I'd picked that single title from the shelf meant that it was destined for me, Daddy would have laughed.

"My book, Lulu." His voice was steel. "Leo certainly didn't take it."

I hated when he dug at Leo.

"*The Truth of Mesmeric Influence* is mine, Lulu. You know I don't go in for that stupidity, but that book belongs to me and it's not here. I didn't lose it and your mother doesn't care for it, which leads to the obvious deduction that you took it."

Daddy slapped a ledger shut, a smack I could feel on my face. All I could say was that I was sorry. I *was* sorry. I wished that I had stayed blessedly beside Leo that afternoon, untroubled by a cousin, or myself, or anything at all.

He took a sheet of paper from his desk drawer and pushed it toward me. He pointed to his bottle of ink and his pen. His pocket watch ticked. I was on the high end of a seesaw in mid-lift, bracing myself to slam to the ground. Daddy sighed. He acted as if I were a child incapable of forming clear sentences, untrustworthy in my intentions. His word for what I'd done was "took." Not my word. Mine would be "borrow."

"You'll apologize to your cousin," he said. "Right here, you'll write a letter to Dale explaining how you made her act the fool and how sorry you are to have upset her."

She'd come in here a fool, and a vicious one, too. That wasn't my doing. Daddy had never said one word to her about her rude remarks at supper the night I did what I did with the pin. A person who didn't know him would think he'd forgotten it, but I didn't see how he could have.

"Write." He pushed the paper toward me. "Dale left out of here sure we were experiencing the work of the Lord first-hand. You need to set that girl right and not have her telling a lie before God and everyone."

"*Dear Dale*," I wrote. This was as far as I got for several minutes. Dear Dale.

Dale would show this letter to girls I'd never meet. They would pass it among themselves, and who knows where gossip would take it after that. I'd be the butt of their jokes, and I wouldn't be there to captivate those girls and make them mine, even if only for a beautiful minute.

"I am sorry to tell you this but there was no work of the Lord from my hands in our house in Cedartown when you were our guest. I am afraid that I let my poor nature get the better of me."

If I could only tell those girls, "Oh, I was only playing a trick on Dale. She's so easy to fool, bless her, that I couldn't help myself," they would laugh sweetly and rest their arms across my shoulders. They'd invite me to their homes, where the walls were freshly painted and the cushions plump, and we'd take a refreshing jaunt in the buggy after dinner.

"Momma said that what happened in my bedroom came from electrical orbs, and I regret to tell you that I neglected to speak up and so let my mother make a false statement. There was no electricity or work of the Lord. The scarf was also my doing."

No, I'd never leave here. I would watch Leo all his days and marry some fellow who'd never been anywhere and had no wish to travel. I'd set up a home with him, and itch for the rest of my days for the freedom that came from doing what no one else around me could do.

"I pray that you will understand and forgive me, and I remain, Your loving cousin Lulu."

I blotted the letter and handed it to Daddy. He would make me change it, probably more than once as a lesson, and then carry it into town during the week to mail.

He took the letter and leaned toward me across his desk. Instinctively, I leaned away.

"When you were six," he said, "I found you outside before dawn. I was on the way to milk the cow and nearly tripped over you sitting on the porch steps. You told me that you wanted to hear the sun come up. You had gotten yourself dressed, even tied a ribbon in your hair, and there you sat."

I remembered. He'd gone pale when he saw me.

"I wanted to holler at you," he said. "Get up, be useful, go fetch some water or feed the dogs, don't sit like a stone, but you *were* sitting exactly like a stone, looking to the distance, one hand on each knee, your little back straight as a board."

I remembered thinking that when the sun rose, he would hear it, too.

"When you finally did move," Daddy said, "you asked could I hear it. I heard birdsong, and I'm sure the cow was shifting around in the barn. You were close to crying, Lulu, and when I reached for you, you pushed me away."

I remembered the torn-open feeling when I understood that no one else knew what it felt like to be me.

"Your hands were hot as melting candle wax that morning," Daddy said, shaking his head. "I only wish I'd been honest with myself on that day about the power that you and I can wield together."

With this small recognition, waves of stories poured from me. I told him about reaching into Dale's trunk in the moments she'd turned her attention to her beloved hat box, and how I wadded up her scarf and shoved it into my blouse just for fun. I told him about captivating the fox and saving Leo from the animal's attack, about Mr. Campbell, about how Mrs. Wolf wrote that I could learn to undo the damage done to Leo. I told him about how when I learned to do that, time would go backwards to the days when we were happy, and no one looked at me as if they couldn't remember why I was there.

Daddy rose and turned to the bookshelf. I talked faster, distracting myself from the gap where *The Truth of Mesmeric Influence* should have been. He picked through the books on his shelf, pulling one out, sliding it back, examining another. First, the leather-bound Bible, then worn almanacs that dated back to 1866, the year he came to Georgia from Tennessee. One after the other, the collected words of Shakespeare, two hymnals. Daddy spoke quietly, his back to me.

"Yours were careless actions," Lulu," he said. "You say you can stare into someone's eyes, make them believe one foolish thing or another that they already had buried in them, but that's not real power."

What did my father know of power, of the beauty in stopping time? Because of the book that all but jumped into my hands.

"Why do you have a book about Mesmerism?"

"Why I have any of my books isn't your concern," he said, selecting a slender cloth-bound volume from his shelf.

"While you were writing, I got to thinking. You seem to be allowing yourself to become a liar and a thief. However, in the right hands, those same skills can be shaped into a gift."

"Thank you," I said, because I didn't know what else to say.

"You've got a gift," he repeated, "and all gifts are God-given. Even the thief and the gambler are skilled at their trades, although we know that their duty is to overcome sin and turn to good works."

"Yes, sir," I said. Had the Devil risen out of the floor right then, I would have offered him coffee.

Daddy smiled, the real, wide smile of the days before we moved to the farm, the days when we were four whole people. He passed the book over to me. The cover showed a turbaned man whose eyes were drawn to look like they glowed. Lightning shot from his brow. *Modern Marvels of Alchemy* paraded above his head in gold and black lettering. He was foreign and malevolent, and he was magnificent.

"This is what you've made an attempt at doing," he said. He looked at the turbaned man on the book cover as if he were a long-lost friend.

"Science, Lulu. You're going to learn *science* in the evenings, not some made-up hoodoo. Science is the tool with which we will forge your gift into a beneficial influence."

He looked at the turbaned man again.

"There's not a single excuse why some woman in Ohio with a stick has to hog the whole vista of public distractions. God has clearly given us a mission."

The floor had opened, and I was glad for my chair.

Daddy rose from his chair and came to stand beside me.

"It's no shame for a man to ask for God's help," Daddy said. He stroked my hair, making me flinch. I never enjoyed the feeling of being touched.

"Mrs. Wolf writes about healing, Daddy," I said, working hard not to shake off his hand. "She helped souls recover from their troubles."

Daddy crouched at my side and I was six years old again, waiting for the sun to rise, for both of us to hear the sound. For the briefest moment I feared my father would weep.

"Lulu, when I was a boy, I fell under the spell of a charlatan who held me spellbound. But I loved that person who preached that if a person is in balance, the fluids in his body travel evenly around their conduits. If a man should be unfortunate in these conduits, he falls ill, or he loses his loved ones. He becomes a victim of poverty."

When Daddy stood, his knees cracked.

"Those magnetic fluids between the poles must be balanced, this person said."

"Because he read Mrs. Wolf," I answered, certain.

Daddy laughed.

"This person believed themselves right, and I swore so, too, but I was a little boy then. What I've learned since is that the common person will believe anything if it's wrapped up in bows. Those of us who value our honest character are asked to be vigilant in approaching the slender line between devotion and deception."

Daddy had never spoken about his past. His parents were dead, he had no brothers or sisters, no aunts or uncles. The delivery of this story alone was extraordinary. I would get no more today, maybe ever, and I averted my eyes, uncomfortable for us both. Outside, a crow called. In the kitchen, Momma chattered to Leo while she banged around at the stove. I should be there, keeping him busy, listening to him. Leo didn't like being talked *at*.

"God has sent a message to me through you, my oldest child," Daddy said. "It's become your duty, Lulu, to study up on this gift you have. Through your hands, if we remain vigilant and honest, He will bring our reward."

My hands. I thought of dinner: biscuits, gravy, and greens.

Ribbed, pointy-tipped okra, their pale spines tearing my fingers when I picked the pods from their stalks. Our wagon needed new seats and springs. And though Leo no longer needed his terrible coal-oil lamp, he would always need help.

"I prayed for the power to help ease our financial strain," I said. From the ever-widening crack in the floor, the Devil chuckled.

I had not prayed for this at all.

My voice rang out in that close room.

"I prayed for a way to help us all."

"You're a good girl, Lulu," my father said. "You're a good sister to Leo. Poor little boy, he'll always be a child, and who will be here for him when your mother and I are in Glory? Just you, and you'll be a fine sister to him no matter what becomes of our baby boy."

Thinking of Leo's future was agony. Until that moment, no one had outright said that he would end up in my care, but no one had to. My brother, who squeezed my heart dry, was the single reason I could not truly picture myself in the world beyond Cedartown. How would a man who couldn't walk on his own and whose speech made no sense to strangers earn his living on a farm or in a city? Leo wouldn't ever be able to do his business in the privy on his own.

"Mrs. Wolf says Mesmerists have a duty to use their powers to cure disease."

Daddy toyed with my letter.

"Mrs. Wolf was deluded," he said. "It's a sorry thing that my own good hard work can't lift this family higher."

Daddy held my letter up, the sunlight flashing the page bone white. And then he tore the letter in two.

I grabbed at it, but he held the paper out of my reach.

"You can paste the letter back together and I can carry it to the post office for you, but you know how that will look when your cousin reads a letter made of scraps. That's evidence of your trying to renounce an honest statement and then thinking the better of it. Inconsistency."

He slipped the two halves of the letter between the pages of *Modern Marvels of Alchemy*.

"You can borrow the book," he said, not looking at me.

Mrs. Wolf's book? My heart jumped into my throat, but I stayed silent in case I'd misunderstood him. Mrs. Wolf so clearly wrote about love and charity, about the *reward in our work* when she began to mesmerize.

"The Mesmerist book," Daddy added, as if he'd heard my thoughts. "Consider it a loan of light entertainment."

I was dismissed.

Now that *The Truth of Mesmeric Influence* didn't need to be hidden, where would I keep it? Leaving the book out on a table the way I would a school book or one of Momma's novels seemed discourteous to Mrs. Wolf. Exposure to the ordinary trials of life could leach the information right out. After some reordering of the glass-tipped hairpins in my box of keepsakes and protecting the fingernail-sized window panes of mica chips by covering them with a square of fabric, the book fit into box, if I put my found buttons in each corner. The top of the box wouldn't quite lie flat this way, but I had made a safe and sound bed nonetheless.

Who was Mrs. Wolf? There was no illustration, no lithograph anywhere in the pages, but I could hear her voice when I read. My mother's voice clanged like a fork striking a metal bowl. My own voice was low, and sometimes I spoke so quietly that teachers asked me to speak up. Mrs. Wolf's voice was musical, I was sure. She was an alto singer, a sound like breath blown across the top of a bottle.

She wrote, *Miss Elslag, returning from her place of worship, was struck to the ground by lightning. The shock rendered her dumb, with the ability to speak only the words yes or no when asked.*

She could have been telling me my own story. *Miss Hurst, lying in her bed during a lightning storm, was struck by the fury inside her. Her inexplicable emotions made a connection with the transference of human energy we Mesmerists know as Magnetism.*

What had happened to Miss Elslag? Momma was calling from downstairs, so I lay a glass-tipped pin against the page to hold my place, and put *The Truth of Mesmeric Influence* into its bed.

After supper, Momma plucked the forks and knives from my hand before I could clean them.

"Go and see your daddy," she said. "He's got big plans for you tonight." She cupped my chin. "I'll wash up. It'll give Leo something new to look at."

I tried to pull my face from her grip.

"Don't you know?" she said, sparkling. "You're a great, great gift to us."

I nodded, my chin still in her vise. I held my breath to block the thick stink of mouths and teeth on the dirty fork tines. When she let me go, I ticked Leo's ribs to make him laugh, and hurried to my father's study.

He was waiting for me with a pocket notebook and a fresh pencil. He smiled to beat the band, which made me want to look behind me to see who he was really smiling at.

He laughed.

"Lulu, teaching you will be easy as pie. You've already seen for yourself how ready folks are for humbug if they don't recognize what's happening to them."

Dale must have been ready for humbug—she was the one who'd thought up the vermin and fireballs big as thumbs. I took a seat across from his desk and tucked my fingers into my palms to keep from picking at the arm rest.

Daddy flipped open his notebook and cleared his throat.

"Your average person, if he figures out he's been humbugged, won't make a peep about it because he doesn't want to admit he's guilty of *falling* for the humbug," he began.

That was true. Mr. Campbell hadn't looked straight at me since the day I'd captivated him. He knew I'd done something, but he would never own up to it. Each time he avoided my gaze my stomach fluttered. I'd won a game that he hadn't agreed to play.

Daddy reached beneath his desk and pulled out a broom. The straw had been stripped from the business end. From beside his desk, he kicked out a long past useful wooden chair. Someone had cut down the old chair's legs. He pointed to the chair, and without questioning him, I went to sit in it. The thing was cut so close to the floor that I nearly had to squat. I felt more oversized than usual, as if

I were a grown baby. With nothing else to do, I reached upward for the destroyed broom.

"What good is this if it won't sweep?" I asked.

"Exactly what you're doing," Daddy said, mimicking how I held the broom. He extended his arms out before him, making the wooden stick the crossbar of an "H."

There didn't seem to be any other way to hold the broom, but fooling with the thing made no sense, and I set the broom down.

"This gift you have, making innocent people believe, is unusual in a young person. I've seen it work, and I've also seen it fail," Daddy said. He began to pace. "Your cousin believed she saw electricity right here in our house, but I knew, and so did you, that all she saw was lightning out your window. Your sticking her with that pin gave her the go-ahead to surrender to her secret beliefs. All she needed was permission, Lulu."

Jumping up and running out of the room was a bad idea. But he was acting like Dale, loading significance onto one stupid thing I'd done. Startling my cousin or staring into someone's eyes until they lost their way wasn't me giving anyone the go-ahead for what they privately wanted.

He talked on, flipping through a notepad.

"In your lessons with me, you will learn to manufacture the impression of great feats of strength," he said. "Not hoodoo. Nothing more than understanding how people find what they desire in the simple aspects of life they observe. Also, we'll learn some basic action of the fulcrum and the lever."

"Sir Isaac Newton's laws of motion," I volunteered, always the good student. Mrs. Wolf already said as much. She'd written in the first few pages of her book how the *mesmerized patiently observe Newton's method*. Did Daddy know that his ideas were so similar to hers?

"Your power resides in timing," he continued. "Your success will be directly related to how you guide others in observing you. This, in turn, arises from how you observe them."

Daddy was spellbound by his own voice, a preacher at the pulpit.

I said, "Yes sir."

Please calm down, I prayed. Please lower your voice. Please stand still. My collar was damp, and I couldn't catch my breath. Drowning might feel like this. My wet palms scraped my skirt, and I picked at a stray thread. Anything to focus. Back when I'd been baptized, I'd panicked under the water, but we came right up into the sun. This time, there was no welcome rush of fresh air. I shifted in my seat, sinking in his words.

"Why do you think that iron furnace runs night and day outside of town?" he asked. "The railroad men learned about the iron in our soil, and they came in and built pig-iron furnaces."

We were going out of this room now, lifting up and away from me. I inhaled, clearing my head, but Daddy snapped his fingers in my face so closely that the air popped.

"Iron filings get attracted to one end of a magnet, repelled from the other. That's where timing comes in. You've got copper and iron right here under your feet. I've told you how they act on each other. In the mind of the regular person, why couldn't you also have the draw of a magnet in you? You've grown up right here, walked the same soil that I've tilled."

"Copper is in your pebbles," I said, thinking of his collection of stones, so nice to the touch.

Daddy applauded. I was getting close to whatever he wanted me to catch on to, but I couldn't quite grasp it.

"Copper wire is in the battery, the telegraph, and those lights in France your cousin was crazy for. I *read*, Lulu. The scientific types call copper a conductor. Copper works magic on iron, Lulu."

Suddenly, I knew.

"You want me to pretend I'm Magnetic," I said.

"You are our Magnetic Girl." He beamed, sweeping his hands in an arc above my head.

How a person would act magnetic I couldn't fathom. Pretending I could conduct electricity wouldn't do anything but make me look stupid. People I didn't know would laugh and point, just like people I did know. They'd joke to each other about how tall I was, not caring that I could hear them. They'd talk about how my hands and feet were big as bread loaves. I only wanted to be Lulu Hurst, the girl who captivated—Mesmerized—her brother until he could walk and talk and stand tall on his own. Then I would be the girl who could leave.

"Magnetic reminds people that you're the conduit for the copper and iron in the earth. If 'Magnetic Girl' doesn't pull people into our parlor," he said, laughing at his joke, "we can always call you the Georgia Wonder."

My mind squeezed out single words at a time. This must be how Leo felt when he tried to talk clearly.

"Parlor?" I asked.

"There's no whoop de do or immodesty, no hazards to anyone's health or character. We'll be here in our home, same as with any friend or neighbor coming to call. A more appropriate setting than Sunday School, with you attempting tricks on your teacher."

Captivating was no trick. Sometimes captivating stopped the world.

"Why did Momma say the noises were electrical?"

Daddy laughed. "Your Momma listens too much to her friend Mrs. Hartnett. That poor lady's addicted to her *Banner of Light* séance paper."

He snatched at the air like he was catching fireflies in twilight. I'd done that same thing when I was little, reach out and cup my hand around a lightning bug, put it in a jar. I'd do this until I had a jar glowing with trapped life. The living lantern by my bedside cast a thin, otherworldly light while I drifted off to sleep. In the morning, the bugs lay dead from their futile attempts to escape. The green, bright smell they'd had when I caught them had turned to the damp stink of rotten potatoes.

"People like Mrs. Hartnett will tell you that electrical particles swim in the air, and that's exactly the kind of person who wants to see The Magnetic Girl."

Daddy offered the denuded broomstick to me again, holding the center, the ends pointing to the floor and ceiling. With nowhere else to put my hands, I took each end. He moved the stick as if he were turning a wheel until he had arranged the broomstick parallel to the floor.

"You will make this lifeless broomstick appear to have a heartbeat and the writhing fury of an Indian cobra snake, power enough to knock a man off his pins. The goal is to raise the question 'is this merely a household implement, or does this innocent object surge with life?'"

"It's just a broomstick, Daddy," I said.

"This is no longer a broomstick," he said. "This is a fancy walking stick: ivory-handled, made of gleaming, polished wood."

It was still just a broomstick, but his voice resonated like an echo and I bit my lip to keep from laughing. He didn't know that talking took away the concentration I needed to captivate.

He pushed toward me, his hands wide on the broomstick. Afraid he would snap the wood and stumble, I did the first thing that came to me: I grabbed the stick near the center to hold it steady. He pushed toward me, harder. We were playing a game I'd never seen, my father and I, with the broomstick as the prize. He was trying to snap it across the middle, and my job, clearly, was to push back and keep the broomstick in one piece.

My arms were straight out, palms on the wood and open toward my father's chest when he released the broomstick. Without his resistance, I tumbled to my knees.

Daddy leaned against his desk, hands in his pockets. My spine rattled from my tail bone to my jaw. He'd let me fall on purpose. He'd *made* me fall. The broomstick was still in my hand, useless. I rolled it away from me across the floor and got to my feet.

"You let go," Daddy said, accusing me. "You let go and allowed the electrical power coursing through that broomstick to throw you to the ground."

My palms burned.

"You're thinking I've lost my mind, but I promise you I'm sane," he said. "What's just happened is *my* demonstration of the Magnetic Power *you're* going to demonstrate on others. You control the cane.

They get knocked back by what they believe is its lively spirit."

He seemed to think I could knock anyone into a cocked hat any old time. Dale's scarf was nothing, and the two people I'd captivated were a baby and a childish teacher.

"You don't really believe people will accept the idea that there's power in a stick of wood when all they do is let go of it?"

He looked right and left, elaborately pretending to check for eavesdroppers. And then he winked.

"It doesn't matter what I believe. What matters is what *they* believe."

He waggled his fingers at my nose.

"You carry Odic fooooorce."

He sounded ridiculous, and I laughed. We were nearly the father and daughter I believed we would be on that morning a decade earlier, on the porch before the sun rose.

Over the next week, we practiced every evening after supper. We worked on what Daddy named "tests," a more serious word than "tricks" or "acts." A much more scientific word than "captivating," but that word was my own, and I kept it close to my heart.

My primary job was observation.

"Present yourself as if you were wide-eyed, not judging, not thinking, like a newborn baby," he said as he shaped my arms into a cradle as if I were rocking a baby.

My holding an invisible baby suggested the terrible mistake I had made, the one he didn't know. I went rigid from stifling my own fear.

"What does a baby do?" he asked, without seeing me. "A baby reacts. He is merely a vessel for what he sees and hears."

The imaginary baby squalled to be set down gently, far away from me.

Daddy made a mark in his notebook.

"In a manner of speaking, you are a baby. What you observe in the person opposing you in a test will determine everything you do. In time, you'll come to know what a person will do before he does it."

I thought I already knew. Dale's scarf proved that, and so did Mr. Campbell's straying from his task as he led pupils in recitation.

Daddy bought a new *People's Regulator* notebook for our practice sessions, and by the second evening the pages were curved from his pocket. On each page he wrote our practice date, and the numbers one to ten along both margins to rank my effort. He drew lines across the pages that slanted upward to the ten, calibrating strain. They spiked like a mountain peak if I failed on a first try. On my best days, the lines were flat and even, a well-maintained road from one side of the page to the other.

From my father, I learned to hear the way a room sounded all of its own; the creaking of a closed door, the drift of air through an open window, the shifts in tone as four walls settled on their foundations. I learned that my thoughts crowded me out of the natural state of a place.

The same broomstick returned. I practiced holding it steady between us, an equator at chest height. My father and I pushed equally toward the other, my hands at the center of the bar, his a few inches outside mine. As I pushed forward and the smallest bit upward, always matching my force to his, our balance was in my control. I learned to recognize the shiver in my stomach in the split second before he tried to outmaneuver me by pushing harder with his right or left hand or leaning away. Alert to his movements almost before he made them, I secured us both in our stances and rarely lost my footing. I grew quicker and more confident with each try. I had the broomstick trick easy from the third day, but we worked it until he was satisfied that I was more than lucky.

And then we worked with a chair; different from a stick, with a confusion of right angles that made it hard at first to figure out his intentions.

"Hold it up here," Daddy said, pressing his forefinger to my heart.

I did as I was told, the chair protruding from my chest like a weird appendage. At my side, Daddy laid my arm across the seat, curling my fingers where knees would go. He moved my other hand to the top of the back rail. Hugging the chair to my chest made me shuffle somewhat in my balance. Daddy assessed my predicament and placed his hand alongside mine on the seat. Helping me stay steady, he lay his other hand along the slats. If the chair were a baby, he'd have burped it. This made me laugh, and my laugh got him going, too.

"Try and put the chair down, but don't let it go," he said.

To set it down I'd have to quit holding so tightly. Bending my knees brought the chair down some, but Daddy pressed the seat and I staggered forward. Leaning forward from the waist like an open knife elicited the same problem.

"Can't happen," Daddy said. "Not without you falling over."

My arms ached, and letting go of my hold, I put the chair on the floor where it belonged.

"Think about what would happen if you were on my side of the chair, and the person where you're standing now was sure your Magnetic Power kept that chair from sitting like it should."

Become the aspect of revelation, Mrs. Wolf said.

"You keep him off his balance, Lulu. Out-think him."

And then Daddy sat in the same chair, with his back to me, rude as anything. As I stood there wondering what to do, that twist in my stomach warned me of his intent to move. The anxiety crawling across my shoulders told me the same thing.

He rocked the chair back onto his rear legs, and before I could think I clutched at the posts and righted the chair, but I went too far. My father's feet hit the floor in front of him with a slap, the back legs of the chair lifting before he rocked the whole thing backward again, setting the chair squarely on its four legs.

He hopped out of the seat gleeful as a boy and turned to reach for me. I stepped back, searching his face for some clue as to what I'd done to make him so happy.

"Lulu, you lifted me straight off the ground." He didn't seem to know if he wanted to embrace me or clap me on the shoulder.

"Sir?"

All he'd done was tilt a chair far enough backward to take a spill. Instinct had taken me, and I'd kept him from cracking his head. I shut my eyes against the image of what could have happened then, and what had already occurred.

"Never mind how I know this," Daddy said, catching sight of my relief. "I know it is all."

He'd already opened an old wound when he told me about the fellow he'd admired as boy. That wound had closed again and closed for good. Whatever blood he'd spilled in telling me about his past was a mistake, and he wouldn't open that scar for me again. I didn't want him to. That dark hole was filled with questions and answers, but if I tore it open, I'd know my father as the boy he was, and as the man the world saw. I would know him as more than a father. I couldn't stomach the intimacy.

"Lulu, don't hide from this," Daddy said. He hugged me, pressing my face into his shirt. Bristles of hair stung my cheek.

"Open your eyes and see that you have a gift," he said. His voice held all the confidence in the world.

"How do you get lifting out of falling backward?" I asked when he released me. One eye opened, then the other.

"Science," he said. "And guiding the way a person observes what's truly taking place around him."

Daddy tipped the empty chair backward. I envisioned a seated fellow lazing on a porch, his feet propped on a railing as he watched the day amble by. Until Daddy shoved the chair forward onto its two front legs. Any fellow in that seat would have split his lip on the rail where his feet had been. Before my invisible spectator could recover, Daddy rocked the chair back and set it down innocently on four legs.

"I weigh well over two hundred pounds," Daddy said. "With me in chair, it didn't fly so far forward. This is a story of balance, Lulu, of fulcrum and lever, and how for the moment when you've got a fellow in a chair in the place between leaning back and tipping forward, he believes he's lifted, an inch or two or maybe more. And you, Missy, you believe it, too."

We practiced a day or two or maybe more. When my arms were straight out and rigid and my father was seated ahead of me in the chair, I couldn't lean the chair backward far enough. When my knees locked, I couldn't tilt the thing forward at all, and the trying strained my stomach muscles and slid my feet out from under me on the rug.

Daddy's pocket watch ticked loudly from his vest. He needed to wash. I made myself listen not to my thoughts, but welcome instead the soft cushion of quiet around my breathing. My heartbeat grew louder, and the room around me slithered away through a pinhole.

Something circulates in the background, Mrs. Wolf wrote.

I pulled, and the chair groaned, and then it rose, back and up and easy, the front legs hovering an inch or two above the floor, the back legs balanced on their edges. I held my father there, suspended, in the moment of finding the apex between far back and far front. In that single place, there was a real and true lift, at the top of the triangle of man and kitchen chair, rocked back, then forward, by me.

Daddy's shout broke open my padded world. Blinking and dizzy, I massaged my raw hands. His grip on my shoulder was hot, and I heard his laugh, but he might as well have been on the other side of a glass. Momma ran in, confused, but Daddy spoke words that stretched and bobbed and made no sense. Momma applauded me, her smile beautiful. And gradually, with his hands on my arms and hers around me, they came through the glass, and my feet were on the ground and my parents were so very happy.

"Newton, Lulu," he said. "Fulcrum and lever in action."

My heartbeat roared over his voice.

He wanted to work this test until I got it smooth. I was too flustered, he said.

"Yes, sir," I said, waiting for my pulse to return to normal.

SUCCESS AT HOME WAS the first step. When I was ready, people would come to the parlor to watch. After that, he said, I'd play the Magnetic Girl in a theater a few times. Enough to lift the loan from his shoulders, as I'd promised.

"Consider that fox you say you held in your thrall," Daddy said. "Who needs a dumb animal when you can hold a roomful of strangers the same way?"

The lines he drew in his notebook became tight wires with every test, every time.

"Think of how proud Leo will be," Daddy said.

The straight lines in his notebook were my gift to my father. For myself, I only wanted to captivate and practice the power Mrs. Wolf applied to her visitors: the Mesmerist's *kindness toward the unwell.*

CHAPTER
FIVE

MY FATHER CHOSE A SUNDAY IN NOVEMBER FOR MY parlor tests. All the guests would be men. Women frighten easily. Just look at Dale, he said. She was a prime example. Men protected ladies, and if men believed what they'd seen was too alarming for ladies, more men would want to come see what the fuss was about. Eventually the ladies would get their way.

The fact that Mrs. Wolf, when she was alive, was a lady—as was I—didn't escape my notice. In her writing, she hadn't seemed frightened at all. Momma was a lady and she didn't rattle easily. But Leo would, after all, someday be a man, so I might as well practice on men. Still, I didn't see why I couldn't captivate a wife or mother when I did a test.

After church, I waited in the wagon while Daddy invited Mr. Rogers, up from Atlanta visiting family, and Mr. Shepherd, the husband in a young couple Momma had deemed "charming" because they were new and he was in business with the Iron Furnace. I picked dirt from my boot heel and watched my parents stroll with Colonel Furman, who owned The *Appeal*. Nearly everyone who had fought in the war was called Colonel, no matter what their rank. My father was called Colonel by some. Drummer boys were old enough by now to get themselves called Colonel, and I guessed that was all right.

I was only half-listening to Leo chanting *Eeny, meeny, miney, moe,* because I was watching Daddy shake Colonel Furman's hand. Momma and Mrs. Furman pecked cheeks. When they were done, I swung around to join Leo's game.

Leo picked his nose. I didn't have a handkerchief ready, so I ignored him.

"Play eeney meeney," I said. "Whoever's faster wins."

Leo waved his arms at me. *I'm fast.*

I held both my palms out flat for him to smack. I always let him win. Giving myself over to my brother relieved me of myself and the world around me, always too full of atmosphere. Odors clogged my nose and throat and stuck to my palate like bad glue. At church, a woman's perfume, days old and gone sour. The stink of rancid wax in a man's ears, a boy across the room who had cleaned fish. In school, I heard thoughts that weren't my own, but I told no one. One day I heard "clean the slop jar" from the teacher. I jumped, thinking that she'd somehow been in our house to watch me in the night, but she was busy writing on the chalkboard. The sting of a hangnail could shrill like a bugle from a fat man driving a cart. These were truths that I only told Leo. Every time I did, he squeezed my hand.

Daddy helped Momma up to her seat, and untied Jack the mule from the railing. When he came around and put his hand on my shoulder, my stomach clenched.

"Looks like we'll get a good crowd, missy. Colonel Furman's looking forward to joining us, so we just might get you in his paper without even trying."

His relief telegraphed through his touch, alarming me. He hadn't nailed everything down before now. I'd agreed to captivate strangers before we knew if anyone would show, and now a newspaper reporter would write down everything I did. *She's practiced, this doesn't come as naturally as she wants us to think*, he would write. *More importantly, she's keeping a secret from her father.*

I could fall out of the wagon. A broken arm would mean I'd be no good. If I fell on my face, no one would want to look at me. But then the newspaper would tell how I'd disappointed the crowd my father had worked so hard to gather. The writer would say I was a coward, and my parents wouldn't disagree.

I yanked my hands away just as Leo's palms came down. Up front, Daddy called 'ho' to the mule. The wagon jostled into the road, and I watched the people gathered in the churchyard slide away.

In the house, Momma didn't say a word about dinner. Instead, she hurried to her wardrobe, perky as a girl. She returned with tissue paper draped over her arm, the same as Dale packed between her clothing. Momma rummaged in the loose paper and my heart stammered. Beaming, she pulled from the wrapping a deep blue skirt, a white blouse, and brand new, un-darned, black stockings.

Afraid of seeming vain and unserious, I'd put off asking what The Magnetic Girl should wear, but here was Momma with a new outfit and without her usual words about how my clothes never fit me right and how mannish I looked when I walked. Momma had worn store clothes, but I had never.

She rolled the skirt out and I held the blouse to my shoulders.

"I think it's beautiful," I told her, because it was. The clothing must have cost a fortune. The skirt was elegant, the shirt very fine. When she pressed the skirt's waistband to my ribs, the hem pooled at my toes. For the first time since I was little, my clothes covered me.

"These are on credit," she said, shaking out a length of pink fabric.

While I held the blouse against me with one hand and the skirt with the other, Momma looped the pink sash around my waist. She tied the ends into a bow at my back, then came around to look me over. The pink bow tagged me as a little girl. If the girls at school saw that sash they would hiss their disapproval, the sound of a gust of wind through their pursed lips. Condemnation of the sharpest kind.

"One more thing," Momma said. "Let me see your hands."

I extended one hand, letting the blouse's shoulder go limp.

"You can't have paws like a farm hand," she said. "People need to believe your fingers are direct channels to electricity."

She gestured for my other hand while she produced from her pocket a delicate pair of scissors and a jar of scented cream. She answered my question before I could ask it.

"I had these from before. When I was a girl, we took care of our looks. None of this hard labor turning our skin into saddle leather."

She didn't look up as she snipped and dug at my fingers. A particularly sharp cut, and blood beaded around my nail. Shamed, I stuck my jabbed finger in my mouth. I had too much to do to stand there with my hands in my mother's control. The skirt needed hemming, and she'd given me permission to rest before tonight instead of helping with supper. She wasted a good part of that free time rubbing cream into my cuticles, my knuckles, and over the backs of my hands.

"Momma, stop!" I pulled away when she scooped another dollop from the jar. "I'll be too slippery to grab hold of anything, and then what will happen?"

Whatever calm I'd tried to hold onto ran right off with of the fear of chairs skidding from my hands and canes poking some fellow's eye. I wiped my slick hands on a kitchen rag.

"You'll be glad of the clean-up," she said.

Guiltily, I gave her back one hand, then the other. She had made my nails almond-shaped and smooth. They didn't look at all like my own. Keeping busy fixing supper, reading aloud to Leo, even pulling weeds from the vegetable garden would have calmed me, but I couldn't do any of these with the polished stranger's hands at the ends of my wrists.

I was too pent up to rest. I'd come so close to making mistakes before: those straight-armed failures behind the chair, the pulled muscles in my arms as Daddy turned the broomstick until I could feel the balance without thinking. Momma could have found my box of objects any time. Daddy had turned away from my attempts to captivate him.

In my room, I went for Mrs. Wolf's book, but I couldn't concentrate. Betraying her, I went to the window. Half a dozen men lounged in the yard. Some leaned against their wagons, others crouched in the grass. One leaned over his horse's neck and spat, mucus landing in Momma's flower bed. I pulled the curtain back. There wasn't anyone I recognized from town or church. How had they known to come here? Anxious, I tugged the curtain closed, but not before one of the fellows looked up and waved. I was trapped, curtain in my hand. The fellow slapped the shoulder of the man next to him and pointed at me. Seeing them through window glass, I told myself they were store dummies.

The skirt lay with the white shirt and ridiculous pink bow across my bed, in the same spot where I'd held my breath before reaching for a pin during a lightning storm. The clothing was the image of an empty girl. I couldn't begin to imagine what she had cost my parents. That empty girl could fail, too. I stepped out of my Sunday dress, leaving the faded floral pattern, the browning perspiration stains under the arms that I could never completely clean away, the wrists too short, and the band of added hem in a heap on my floor. With a deep breath, pulling my stomach in and ignoring the taunts of "tall tree" that never left my mind, I stepped into the blue skirt.

A few minutes before five, Momma knocked on my door. Even without a clock, I always knew the time.

"Let me get an eyeful," she said, looking me up and down. She went to the basin and splashed water into her hand to plump my bangs. Then she started her little patting motions on the crown of my head. I turned a full circle for inspection. I'd checked myself in my hand mirror from every angle I could manage, although I knew what the guests downstairs would see: that Colonel Hurst's daughter was tall for her age at five feet eight inches. My bosom had just recently grown to a small shelf. I had my father's broad smile and direct gaze, and my mother's brown eyes and dark hair.

"Well, you're just dashing," she said. "All the big bugs are in the parlor. There's more than I expected."

"Who are the fellows sitting in the wagons?"

"You saw them?" She straightened the curtains and eyed her lawn and her trampled flower beds.

"Yes, ma'am. I didn't expect—"

"I didn't either," she answered, dropping the curtain. "Let's go downstairs."

As if I were a little girl, I let my mother take my hand.

MY FIRST LINE WAS "How do you do?" Colonel Furman from the *Appeal* sat front and center on the divan. A gawky fellow with a notepad sat beside him: a reporter with his editor. I swallowed hard and kept going. The fellow from the Iron Works perched on the red brocade chair where most nights Momma worked her needlepoint. The rougher fellows from the lawn lined the wall like a stand of pines. The room was stuffy and smelled like sweet hair pomade. Daddy lay his hand on my shoulder and I leaned into him, not enough that the guests could see, but enough to calm myself as we headed into more than a practice. And then, not enough so guests could see, he pushed.

"My name is Lulu Hurst," I said, loud and clear. Alone.

I never disliked the sound of my voice, but I had worked out just how to say this phrase. The words were easy, but I wanted the lilt of a genteel lady. I took what Dale tried to do in her breathy, halting way of speaking, and outshone her by half. *My name is Lulu Hurst. I am The Magnetic Girl.* I practiced on the chickens. *How do you do, Mrs. Hen?* I spoke to the slop bucket. *Beg your pardon, Mr. Bucket.* I thought of Mrs. Wolf's words. *Mesmerism is a near relative to sleepwalking.*

Colonel Furman stood and extended his hand to me. I took it, but in the interest of acting ladylike, withdrew my hand quickly. My grip was too strong. Momma said so.

"Shall we begin?" I asked, smiling directly at him before turning to my father. I'd practiced the smile, too, sneaking up on myself in the speckled hallway mirror, trying look welcoming and confident. Here in front of the house's best feature, the carved banister on the staircase, my smile could only look good.

Daddy had arranged the parlor for the tests. A plain wooden chair sat before the piano beside an urn with a single silver-handled walking stick. I'd never seen that walking stick before, and now wasn't the time to ask why I'd never had the chance to practice with it. Daddy began applauding, a lone and strange sound in that expectant room.

Cautiously, the guests began to applaud with him.

"My friends, welcome to our home," he said. His voice was loud, and he sounded happier than I'd heard him in a long time.

"You're our honored guests tonight, the first individuals outside my own precious family to witness the mystery of wondrous power that has come to reside in my own child's hands."

Two latecomers entered. A man by the door held his finger to his lips, hushing them. My father kept going.

"Last month, a simple lightning storm over our Valley—indeed, directly over our house—became a greater phenomenon than weather. My daughter Lulu found magnetic strength at her command. Objects scattered at her approach, flying as if thrown by invisible fingers. Our furniture jumped like crickets. The storm drew the magnetic power of the copper and iron beneath our feet into her veins, rendering her The Magnetic Girl, a mere child from whose grip no man can tear away."

He paused.

"Believe me, I've tried."

The joke was new. Someone laughed, then someone else. Panic crawled up my limbs like mites. Too many people were watching me. Cornbread from dinner rose up and clogged my throat, and I choked the clot back down. I wanted to jump up and down and escape the panic strangling me. I clasped my hands at my chest to keep myself from tugging my hair. A giggle escaped, the sound of my nerves.

The clock on the mantle ticked. I'd never felt faint before, but the room throbbing at my edges and the lack of feeling under my feet was surely how fainters feel. Don't keep them waiting, Daddy had warned. The faster you go, the less they'll see. Pushing my way through my fear, I spoke, and my voice surprised me. Mine was as loud as his in this crowded room.

"Who will be my first volunteer?"

A man whose beard looked like things were living in it sat on the flowered carpet, looking for all the world like the fellow on the playing card in my lost-things collection. His hand shot up in the air. From the corner, Momma exhaled too sharply. A grown man sitting on a parlor rug irritated her.

"Come hold this chair, sir."

Worried that I sounded dull as a reciting pupil, I smiled harder. He unfolded himself and bounded over. He might be a simpleton. I directed the beard to lift the chair from the floor and hug it tight. Everyone laughed.

This would be no different from practicing the test with Daddy. Easy as pie. Standing beside the man, I put my right hand flat against the lowest back rail of the chair, and my left on the chair's empty seat, as my father had with me. Together the bearded fellow and I held the chair above the carpet like a trophy.

"You can set the chair down now," I said for everyone to hear. While I spoke, I fixed my gaze to his. I could smell him, horse and sweat and something I didn't want to think about. I put my mind to the sensation of my hands on the chair and the tension forced into the wood from our four hands, his clutching the poor old chair to his chest, mine appearing still. If his breath made me wince or lice wriggled in his facial hair I couldn't notice. The chair was everything. The chair, my position, and my timing.

Look at me, I thought, imagining writing my words on the page of his brain. *Look in my eyes. You poor thing, you're afraid. I won't hurt you. I know you believe me. Your friends are watching you, just you. Grip tight, tighter. Push down while you rearrange your balance. Correct yourself, and I'll mirror you so slightly no one will see. When you least expect it, I will let go.*

When the chair shot from his grip, the force flung the whiskered man against the piano. The keyboard cover slammed down like a jaw, the piano clanging with the impact. I jumped against the wall, knocking the framed magazine picture of sheep in a pasture against my shoulder. The bearded volunteer brushed himself off and held his hands in the air.

"An electric current passed through that chair," he shouted.

Son of a gun. I bit my lip to keep my mouth shut. He carried on.
"I felt a ripple. A burning sensation."

Some of the men in the room hooted. Momma was at my side
with a handkerchief, but before I finished wiping my brow and my
hands, Daddy fetched the urn with the walking stick, and then set
the chair before me again. Mr. Rogers rose from the divan, and the
room quieted.

"Miss Hurst, will your magnetic power tell us all my age?" he asked.

I could only smile, frozen. We had never practiced a question and
answer test, although given time to corral my wits I was sure I could
come up with something. Daddy cut the silence.

"Mr. Rogers, we don't go in for Spiritualist hijinks, even if that's
the thing down in Atlanta. My child is no mere Mesmerist, telling fortunes and pretending she can see the beyond. No sir, we are
Christians and so are you. I know because I met you this morning
at church!"

His chit chat set everyone at ease. Some of the men laughed.

"I understand, sir," Mr. Rogers said. He held his hands up in apology. "No harm meant."

He was my schoolmate Sarah's cousin, and he turned twenty-eight
last month. She'd told everyone about the dinner he'd thrown for
himself. Oysters. Beer. Mutton. A meal I could only imagine. I slid
my foot forward just enough to catch a rear leg of the wooden chair
in front of me. My hands rested across the back rail. Anyone would
believe I was just pausing here while my father and Mr. Rogers con-
versed. Before Mr. Rogers could take his seat, I watched his face
change as he heard a scraping noise. Man after man looked up and
down, at the ceiling and at one another. The bearded man who I'd
knocked into the piano looked peeved.

Scritch. Scritch. Just as they did, I looked right and left. Silently,
I counted. The sound repeated itself twenty-eight times before it
stopped.

"That's my age," Mr. Rogers shouted. "I turned twenty-eight last
month."

Murmuring rose around him. I felt like I could fly but kept my hands atop the chair. Let them think the very air in my house could speak.

"Can you tell me the time?" Mr. Rogers asked the ceiling. He enunciated carefully, as if the mysterious counting didn't quite understand English.

I laughed, masking the sound as a sneeze.

Mr. Rogers—and all the rest of them—were as easy to fool as Dale. She believed the lights and sound came from God. And now here was Mr. Rogers believing the same of the ether. Daddy was right. People want permission to be humbugged.

This time, I rested only one hand on the chair. Someone might look in my direction. If one of the fellows had the luck or insight to watch my feet, I was done for. I tugged at my hair while I calculated. A fellow looked closely at me but seeing nothing more suspicious than a girl fiddling with her bangs, went back to chatting up his pal.

We had started at five on the dot: Daddy wouldn't have had it any other way. Considering the talking and the joke and the chair test and then the blow-up with the piano, I figured ten minutes had passed. Willing the crowd to keep up their murmuring, I clenched my right foot inside my boot. My big toe cracked, as I'd hoped it would. My boot, my skirt, and the carpet muffled the noise some, but the sound was clear enough if a person listened. After the crack, I tapped my heel twice. With the big toe crack, that made three. I paused, observing the audience. They'd gone still as waxworks. Daddy hadn't moved either, but a storm cloud gathered in his eyes. Six, then seven more pops and taps, with me moving my hand from my hair to my face and casting nervous glances around the room, mimicking my audience's search for the source of the sound.

By the time I hit ten, the arch of my foot ached and my toe felt broken. Mr. Rogers checked his pocket watch. Looking sick, he passed the watch to Colonel Furman, who nodded gravely.

"The hands show ten minutes after five," he said.

The room erupted. The *Appeal* reporter scribbled in his notebook, hollering questions to any man he could get close to. Surrounded by pushing, jabbering men, no door was close enough for me, the stairs too far, the cool sweet dark outdoors blocked by shouting strangers. When Momma appeared at my side, I leaned into her arms, inhaling her vanilla scent and listening to the crowd.

Someone called us shameful for keeping a girl Hercules to ourselves. I hid my face in my mother's shoulder. I was no Magnetic Girl, only a risk-taking girl courting disaster, daring to outsmart a roomful of people.

The Mesmerist's slumber apace, Mrs. Wolf wrote. Like a sleepwalker, I let myself be guided away from the urgent voices in the crowd. I didn't look at them or say goodnight. No one would have noticed if I had.

Midnight came and went. I huddled on the divan, where I'd been since Momma finally shooed the last guest out. I'd vomited twice in the kitchen, and now a basin sat at my feet. My bones felt broken. Jaw, I thought, trying to settle myself by naming each hurt place. Shoulder, elbow, wrist, fingers five four three two one. Outside, night birds whistled and called, simple and pleasant after the roaring skirmish in our house.

Daddy paced. He stopped, faced me, and started his circuit again. I thought I might vomit, but exhaustion crushed me flat.

"That wasn't in our plan." Daddy spoke quietly, thinking.

I wanted to tell him how a person can plan one thing and then it becomes something else, but I was empty with a capital "E." Toying with the rough wool of my skirt, I mourned how guiltless the clothing had been when it lay empty across my bed a millennium ago.

Momma spoke. She worked her needlepoint, but her eyes were on me.

"You hadn't been introduced to that gentleman, had you?"

Mr. Rogers asking his question was pure accident. If I hadn't known about his birthday, I wouldn't have taken the chance. Summoning all my energy, I answered her.

"Mr. Rogers is a cousin of Sarah Hines at school."

My voice was a croak.

"She told me he was coming up from Atlanta to visit. His birthday was a big frolic there a few weeks ago. He turned twenty-eight.

When we met him in church I figured he must be Sarah's cousin."

I could have made fools of everyone. I could have caused a disaster. I didn't think.

"You didn't think," Daddy said.

"What about telling the time? The clock was behind you. Were you using your Mesmerizing power to read a fellow's pocket watch across the room?" His sarcasm stung. Ever since I'd learned to tell time I'd been able to sense what the hour was. It was just one of those things.

"We started at five," I whispered.

He pinched a dead leaf from a potted plant and pointed to the window. Momma tucked the blanket around my toes in their black stockings. My foot still cramped, a souvenir of how far I'd taken our tests.

"That time-telling's not going to pass muster, Lulu. You need to listen to me and do as you're told," Daddy said. "Not once did we study on table rapping. People need to see the Magnetic Girl is above simple tricks. We do this the right way here and we can move on to bigger things."

The right thing to do would be promise that I wouldn't do it again. But if another time came when was as sure as I had been tonight, I'd go right for it. Quick thinking and my own resourcefulness had taken the evening up a notch, even if it did leave me worn out and in pain.

"Our guests are in their homes right now," Daddy said. "They're talking about your power. The Magnetic Girl has given our friends a peek at something, and they'll want another look. They're going to tell their friends. Colonel Furman and his reporter guaranteed a story about you in the *Appeal*."

But what if I'd waited too long to answer the man's questions, or gotten the answers wrong? Weariness swallowed me. My parents' voices blurred like mosquito's whines. Words like "diversion" and "obfuscation" nosed through the darkness that gathered around me.

"They're going to want to see Magnetism, and not one thing more."

My father spoke from far away.

I woke disoriented. In my dream, clouds of disembodied hands extended dollar bills while men and women murmured, "thank you." I tried to thank them in return, but my father reached past my face to collect their money. His hands closed my mouth. Dollars passed my face in bunches, the paper crackling like sparks.

The fire had been banked and my parents had gone to bed, leaving me tucked under a blanket on the divan. The evening's commotion shimmered like a ghost in the sleeping house. I could almost see that bearded man sitting on the carpet, unaware that I would knock him into the piano. The air was crowded with the shouts and gasps from the moments after I'd told Mr. Rogers's age and the time.

The house shifted and sighed in the night. The world, alive, reassured me. Faster than anyone, and sharper, too: that was me. Daddy figured that if he praised me, I'd get lazy. *Watch me*, I thought. *Watch me save you, Leo.*

CHAPTER
SIX

IN THE MORNING, THE HENS RUSHED ME AT THE COOP like always, pecking my shoes. Tossing their feed downwind ran them away from me. From where I stood, I saw Daddy in the field, his shape from this distance not much bigger than my hand. I used to wish I could bring him to school with me, a miniature version like he appeared now, tiny protector and concealed voice of pride. Every answer I made correctly in the classroom—every answer I gave in school was correct—there he'd be.

"You're a smarty, Missy," he'd say. He'd glare toward the makers of mooing noises and whispers of "treetop," silencing my schoolmates before the teacher could. That pocket-sized father could have stayed hidden under my hands.

My hands moved furniture, he told people. My hands conducted electricity.

Mrs. Wolf disdained fakery. *When an audience witnesses the atypical upon a stage, the crude among them perceives something other than*

Mesmerism. Daddy felt the other way. The only thing that mattered was what a person believed, he said.

Chickens clucked and purred around me, spellbound by their meal. Daddy's idea of an audience behaved like these birds. Throw dry corn on the ground and know what they would do every time.

They would eat.

People would believe.

When I went to put the feed away I found Leo sitting by the barn.

"You haven't talked to me all day," I said. I blotted the dirt on his cheeks with my sleeve.

How come I didn't get to watch? Leo scowled.

"Quit trying to look like Daddy." I sat beside him in the dirt. "I'm playacting. Like Sarah Bernhardt, or the holiday pageant at church."

Leo narrowed his eyes at me.

So why all that commotion and people hollering in the parlor?

"I'll tell you, but you have to promise you'll never tell. No one, you hear?"

Leo grinned.

"I can make extra money for you to have nice things. We could buy Momma something extra-nice for her birthday."

Leo shook his head.

That's not it. People were shouting.

"I didn't do anything bad," I said. "I did like that time with the fox, except I tell people to hold onto a cane or a chair, and then I make them think Mr. Edison's gotten his hands on the thing."

My brother's little-boy smell made me want to cry and hold him and run away all at the same time.

"I'm going to learn how to fix you," I said. Just saying so was painful, an admission of guilt.

Leo leaned away.

"I *am*," I said. "You have to trust me."

I am not broken, Leo said.

"So you can run," I kept on. "And speak so that everyone will have to listen."

Leo busied himself with his pant leg. I took his right hand and unfolded his pointer finger. We'd made oaths before, pressing our fingers together and promising not to tell that I'd given him a spoonful of cake batter, soft and easy to swallow, or shaped his fingers around a stick of chalk and guided his attempt to make an "L" on the cover of a schoolbook.

"You're only going to disappoint him," Momma said the one time she caught us writing. When she'd left the room, I pressed the chalk into Leo's hand and we tried again.

I had already taught him the thumb trick Daddy showed me. Hide your right thumb into your right palm. Bend your left thumb and first finger so the nails touch. Now press the back of your right thumb against your left thumbnail, turn your hands around, pull them apart real quick, and presto! A thumb split in half. Daddy laughed enough to spit the first time he saw me do the trick. His saliva had spattered my cheek, and I didn't wipe it away. I would have had to undo my hands from their disappearing-thumb shape, and nothing was worth losing the love in his eyes or the airborne feeling in my heart.

With Leo's hand in mine, I bit my cuticle until it bled. With a hairpin, I nicked the pad of his thumb. A red bead glistened on his white flesh.

"This is the magnetic fluid that beats in our hearts," I said gravely, and Leo nodded, serious in our trust. I pressed our fingers together and felt our blood travel between my veins and his.

Blood shared, I wiped our fingers clean and scooped my brother up. Time to go in.

AT SCHOOL, GIRLS WHO had never willingly spoken to me weren't laughing behind their hands. They swarmed me in the schoolyard, begging, "Show us," and offering as walking sticks thin branches twisted loose from bushes. *Can you throw Early Trumball's fat granddad? Can you tell me how many biscuits my brother ate this morning?*

I accepted the twisted stick Ada Shoals waved in my face. She had never looked twice at me before.

"I'll go easy," I told her. I wouldn't go easy one bit. Before I could say the same instructions that I'd given the bearded fellow in our parlor, Miss Cochran ran from the school shouting. You must never. You may not. Rough behavior. Unladylike. With the teacher so close and her disturbance so extreme, there would be no chance even to pretend a test with Ada. I gave her back the stick.

They watched me all day, girls and boys both. I felt a wonderful pull in the surety that they wanted my attention, my friendship. For the first time, I had something they wanted. I watched my hands as if they belonged to a different me: hands writing on my tablet, turning a page in my book, or settling over a worn spot on my sleeve.

Miss Cochran glanced my way and opened her mouth to speak. I fixed my gaze on her, lowering my eyelids until her figure blurred. *The Mesmerist's greatest goal is to commune with the deepest intentions of those who seek to be Mesmerized,* Mrs. Wolf wrote. *She knows the seeker's intent often before that seeker recognizes the very same.*

My schoolmates' laughter roused me. A field of green and yellow plaid loomed in my face. Miss Cochran stood too close to my desk, smelling of onion.

"You might spend some time considering that your attention belongs on your school work," came from above the plaid dress and lunch pail odor. I leaned my head away so I could breathe. Miss Cochran's face loomed above me like a dinner plate. The laughter had stopped.

"Yes, ma'am," I said, my voice too loud in the sudden quiet.

Miss Cochran wiped her hands together as if she were cleaning, dismissing me.

"Magic Girl must need her rest, sleeping in school like that," she said, swishing to the front of the room.

Sarah Hines's hand flew up. She never volunteered anything.

Miss Cochran nodded in her direction, and Sarah rose, her pale neck quivering against her red hair.

"It's 'Magnetic Girl,' ma'am."

Sarah's thin voice grew stronger.

"Lulu's called that now. Not 'Magic,' but "Magnetic.' It's different. My cousin went to her house and he said so."

She sat, and it was my turn to gape. Sarah smiled at me, full on. I grinned back, a real one.

MY ROUTINE ON THE walk home was to count my steps, a calming habit like tugging at my hair. Thirty steps from the school door to the road. Seven pines in a cluster on a hill to my left. Always I stepped out to the road with my right foot first for luck and did the same at the rise in front of our gate.

There, my heart nearly burst. Thirty-two people clustered around the front porch.

A crowd like this could mean someone had told the police. *There's a father in there planning to relieve fools of their sense*, they'd say. *There's a daughter who says she'll go along with it for her own reasons.* No policeman would believe me if I explained why. No excuses, he'd say, the glint of his badge blinding me. *You won't be able to use your magnetism to save your brother if you're in jail.*

I could keep walking or cut through the woods and slip in through the kitchen door, but there was no use. My home was unreachable. The crowd leaned on the fence, their backs to me. I counted them once, then twice, wishing I could pop them away like soap bubbles. A man ground his spent cigarette into the earth. A boy sat astride the front gate, but no one made a move to pull him down. And yet this is what I'd asked for when I'd counted out a man's age in our parlor and taught a fellow to hold a chair and forget he'd lost his balance.

Time to run. I set my books on the grass. I'd been holding them so tightly that my empty arms floated upward.

Momma came out the front door puffed out like a hen, bobbing her head at the strangers. She smiled and made shooing motions. Someone spoke and she laughed.

My first thought was, *She's telling them about the Magnetic Girl.*
They already know, was my second.

Sarah Hines's speaking up for me was the first sign that the way people thought of me was changing. Every person who saw The Magnetic Girl would tell another. Daddy was right. Sinking to my knees in the grass, I took in the folks who would be my next audience, and for Leo, I thanked them.

With my touch, sufferers will ascend from the depths of their misfortune, Mrs. Wolf wrote. Her face wasn't on any page of *The Truth of Mesmeric Influence,* but I would know her if we were to meet. And she knew me. She understood my responsibility every bit as deeply as I did.

I practiced every free minute I had. Collecting eggs in the chicken coop, I timed my paces from an imaginary theater curtain to my father's side on an imaginary stage. I tried my smiles for the public in window glass, shifting one way and another to judge different angles. Shaking out rugs on the porch became my friendly wave toward an imaginary audience. The trees heard what I'd say to admirers. With a frying pan, I mimed standing across from a fellow and telling him how to hold a cane.

But if a crowd wanted more, then what? Like chickens at their feed, they'd peck at me until I was nothing. I'd fail a test sooner or later. That was just how life worked. Pushing and pulling and lifting weren't what I'd set out to do. I could only truly captivate, and I'd failed that too, more than once, with Daddy and nearly with Dale. Unladylike. Ungentle. That was me. What ran in my veins was blood, and blood only.

I kicked at a chair and it went over. A weak thing, weak as me inside.

BEFORE BED THAT NIGHT I took *The Truth of Mesmeric Influence* from the keepsake box. Paging through it under lamplight, I sought Mrs. Wolf's guidance. We were so much alike, Mrs. Wolf and me. Long before I was born, she had expended this same great effort. Did she feel—had she felt, I had to remind myself, since she was certainly long dead by now—the same doubt?

The answer was barely ten pages in.

My weeks have been overflowing with hard work and effort the likes of which are new to me. But my labor is filled with joy, for my hands are learning to transmit the powers that can change lives.

"But how did you endure?" I whispered to the book. My friend remained silent.

CHAPTER
SEVEN

Cedartown, Georgia:
November 1883

DRIVING JACK THE MULE, WILL CONSIDERED WHAT he'd choose to teach his daughter. His mother's unnerving ability to concentrate—sitting for as long as an hour as if she were furniture—had re-emerged in Lulu, along with eyes brown as strong tea, and a willful, prohibitive silence. He'd not inherited one thing.

For days after his mother died, his dad wept and prayed with a devotion that left Will feeling cheated. Will went back to the field after a day of mourning, and his father followed not too many days after, shamed into action by his son. Will, at ten, at twelve, at thirteen, inspected his fingers while he picked a splinter from his hardening flesh or scrubbed his hands clean for church. He imagined those same fingers coaxing from his believers their unyielding faith in him.

Instead of an acolyte's face, he laid his touch upon a plow handle.

His mother's book was the only physical souvenir of his childhood. As a grown man, he made it his business to speak against the foolishness she had enjoyed. Faith healing and its allies, Spiritualism and Mesmerism, were varied threads of one cloth. He'd recently seen in the paper a story about a woman in Ohio who started fires by pointing a stick at dry tinder. He read this aloud to his wife and children after supper one night.

"Spiritualist entertainments insult God and man," he told them. It's abhorrent to act as if the dead communicate with us through creaks and bangs in furniture. The dead say nothing.

Celia Hartnett considered herself an intellectual rather than a faddist. People like her referred to magnetism as "Odic Force." Once, when he was in earshot, Celia had read aloud to Sally from her second-hand copies of the *Banner of Light*, with announcements of lecturers promoting the "Sublime of the Ages," and messages from the spirit world. Staff Sergeant so and so or Cavalryman this and such, believed by his people to be lost at war, lived on in Summerland. Celia read aloud as if Sally were hard of hearing, stopping to explain that Summerland is the residence of our dear ones watching us as if through glass.

They're not in any damn Summerland. They're dead, rotted on the battlefield, long gone to worms by now if they weren't lucky enough to lose only a limb or smart enough to run away.

He snapped the mule's lead. Lulu would have no trouble convincing idiots like Celia Hartnett that she commanded special powers.

Lulu would be the oxygen feeding the fire burning in America's imagination. Magnetism, spirits, and the stubborn belief in the vaporous phantasm of electricity was everywhere if a person knew how to look for it. That was a thing he knew as well as his own name. In the minds of innocents, every living thing, including swine, rhododendron, and babies, was a vessel for electromagnetic fluid. If the fluid got out of balance, the bearer of the fluid grew ill. In the hands of a Mesmerist, the application of a magnet to the afflicted body caused the fluids to agitate. When they settled, the ill person was restored to health. A magnet's force could be passed like a solid rock from hand to hand if a person were skilled enough to control it.

He spoke Celia Hartnett's beliefs aloud.

"Odic Force," he said, conversationally, directing his words toward his mule's brown rump. "Odic foooorce," he moaned again. The phrase sounded ludicrous: ancient and severe.

In the squeaking of his wagon wheels Will heard his mother's doctrine.

Not even a hundred years ago, a physician and scientist in Austria treated the finer people of his day with animal magnetism. He rearranged the flow of magneto-fluid in the body. He made a blind man see, had a little boy select a particular tree in a forest, and the boy was so over-whelmed by Mesmeric Force that he fell right to the ground in front of the tree. The Queen of France followed the Doctor's teachings.

Will fought the nausea cloying his throat. When he'd enlisted, he been nearly free of remembering her. He thought fighting would shake off his mother-love, but there in his regiment he found her beliefs coming from the mouth of a fellow his own age.

"Anton Mesmer made Mesmerism," said that fellow, Harmony. Who names a person such a thing, and him covering up his last name? Will shook his head, dislodging the image.

My gift is in bringing Dr. Anton Mesmer's curative to the country people, the folks who aren't Queen Marie Antoinette or our own Ben Franklin. Mesmer had a pet canary that woke him every day with its sweet song. The doctor could manipulate that tiny creature's fluids with a stroke to its feathered head. When the man himself died of age, the bird starved itself, never sang nor ate, and soon flew to Heaven to meet his master.

His mother and Harmony both spewed that bull crap, but they tinged it with science. "The sun and the moon, the day and the night, they're twins in natural balance," his mother had said. Ben Franklin was Mesmer's advocate while he was Ambassador to France. That kind of factual information was worth something to the skeptics.

Electricity was pure science. Telegraphs did not whisper words from the dead. Real newspapers—The *Banner of Light* was hardly legitimate journalism—did not print messages from Summerland. A marvelous thing, information that traveled from battlefield to newspaper office through a clicking machine. Whatever moments of reward Will enjoyed with a set of dice were flickers of good luck and his own talents of observation. No spirits. No magnets.

The men at Fortune's threw on a table, not the dirty ground. They presumed a higher caliber of gaming. The first time he'd played, the sun blasted through the open doors, and the ice-cracking sound of sawing wood and shouts of men working in the lumberyard out back made soothing music. A movement at the corner of his eye made him look up from the dice in his hand, and he startled at the sight of blond hair atop a tall, featureless figure filtering the light in a mother-shaped cloud. The sounds of labor evaporated.

"We have tides in us, rolling like the ocean," came from the cloud. "You're a lucky man."

But the sky that day had been cloudless. To distract the other fellows while he recovered from his hallucination Will told a story. A woman cured of incapacitating nervousness by a Mesmerist passing a magnet over her body, up from her feet, around her head, back to the floor again. Magnetism. The fluids in her body had tipped out of balance. The power restored her health, and it drove her just a little wild.

"Tried to get friendly with the Mesmerist," Will said. He had no idea if that were so.

"That magnetism mess is everywhere," Hartnett offered. He leaned his chair back and watched the ceiling while he talked. "My wife's got an aunt down in Atlanta takes that *Banner of Light*. Has since before the war, got mad as hops because she couldn't keep up with her spirits when she refugeed to her husband's folks' place. Them fools believe all kinds of spook-house garbage, but now Celia's believing in it too, and her aunt sends the paper up when she's done. Celia wanted to hold a magnet over my finger when I got it wrenched up in a vise. I talked her out of it."

Hartnett dropped his chair legs to the floor and jolted forward with the impact, punctuating his statement.

"I ain't never let on to y'all about my wife, hear?" he added. "Roll the dice, or I'll have Celia wave a magnet on you."

CHAPTER
EIGHT

WE WENT INTO CEDARTOWN THAT SATURDAY. DADDY'S mood was fine. He mangled the words to songs in his very nice baritone, and most of his jokes made me laugh except for the one about how a dog walks twice as fast as a child because he has twice the number of legs. That joke put me in mind of Leo walking slowly, and my stomach went tight.

We went directly to the Opera House. Every other time I'd seen it, the two-story brick building had been shut up tight, but today we'd go inside. On a broadside pasted to the door, I read that BARLOW & COMPANY'S MAMMOTH MINSTRELS, were coming next week. J. BRAUNSTEIN, ESQ., "PROPRIETOR" rolled across the bottom of the page. Just like the newspaper, where J. BRAUNSTEIN, ESQUIRE, "THEATER MANAGER," was always written as the last line of the advertisements for the Cedartown Opera House.

Daddy breezed past the broadside as if a name in print right in your face and big as life meant nothing. A fancy-dressed boy barely old enough to drive a plow peeked out at my father's knock. The boy smelled like floral cologne. I resisted the urge to check my boot heels for dung.

"Help you?" he asked, leaning against the door frame.

"I'm here to see Mr. Braunstein," Daddy said. "I left my calling card last week."

Had he?

"Sure thing," the boy said, not caring. Daddy let me enter first. The theater lobby was a cave, dark and cool. The boy shut the door shut behind us. It barely made a sound.

"I'll tell Mr. Braunstein you've arrived. Take a seat."

The boy tilted his chin toward a set of velvet benches before disappearing behind another door. The theater was deathly silent, except for Daddy jingling the loose change in his pockets. A horse clopped past outside, followed immediately by squeaking wheels in need of oil.

The theater manager had fountains of money and prowled a lavish office in which he entertained actors he'd brought down here from New York and Chicago. I had never spoken to him. I'd heard that Jews baked their bread with baby's blood. He dressed elegantly, considering. His four-story linen collar and top hat all but screamed, *I'm just passing time in a small town.*

Daddy sat, unfazed. He wasn't going to look at the posters, but I certainly was. Oakley's Minstrels sang and danced in a line. On another, delicate actress Lily Langtry posed in profile. Sandrine Dupree appeared three nights with the Parisian Gardens Orchestra. Iola McBride, the Sweetest Voice on Earth, had her mouth open to sing.

Miss Lulu Hurst, The Magnetic Girl. I could see my name in tall letters, and all that I would do—the "Programme," as these other broadsides had it—listed below.

Part One: Knocks a fellow over by wrestling with a walking stick.

Part Two: Extends her Magnetic Power as she lifts YOU in a chair—men faint from the electric shock!

Part Three. We'd need a part three.

What would Mrs. Wolf tell me if I could open her book this minute? I'd committed her words to memory, but my mind had turned to mud. Slowly, she bubbled up in the thick sludge in my head.

I believe myself tranquil and firm of character.

Tranquil, I told myself. Firm.

When Mr. Braunstein strode into the room, he welcomed Daddy and me by name, and bowed extravagantly, first to Daddy, then me. No one had ever bowed to me, and I was agape. His accent was jumbled, with harsh consonants and long vowels. I'd never been this close to a foreigner before. I'd only read about them in novels and serials. Mr. Braunstein waved us toward his office, and we shuffled in ahead of him, sinking into leather armchairs after he took his seat behind his ornate desk.

"How can I be of assistance?" Mr. Braunstein began.

I wondered again if Daddy had left his card, and why he hadn't told me.

To Mr. Braunstein, who looked too pleasant to eat babies, Daddy spun the tale of a young girl in Cedartown, as kind and obedient as she could be. The ideal daughter. His own. He turned to me as if I were a wrapped gift. I nodded and smiled, proud that we were so finely tuned that we hadn't needed a plan. Daddy's smile lit me up. He asked Mr. Braunstein did he recall the lightning storm last month that split old oaks in two? Mr. Braunstein nodded, saying nothing.

That storm, Daddy said, revealed something remarkable about me. The push and pull of the copper and iron beneath our feet had leapt wholly into my veins. I could move furniture with the slightest touch of my fingertips. I could send a chair flying just by brushing my magnetized palm along its back. Walking canes darted across the ceiling like a flock of sparrows when my gentle, electrified touch connected with another's hands across that ordinary stick of wood. Works with an andiron, too, he added casually.

I had a hard time keeping my expression blank when he said what he did about the furniture. I could certainly captivate a person across an andiron, or a shovel, or a cart, if I chose, but the picture fell on the piano because a man fell against it. We'd have to practice if someone wanted to see that on command.

"And you are here to tell me this because you would like to see her on my stage?"

Mr. Braunstein was a successful businessman and didn't mind being so honest. Even so, his abruptness made me shift in my seat.

Daddy tugged a stray hair in his beard. Seeing my nervous habit in him made me want to hold his hand. Mr. Braunstein busied himself with the documents strewn across his desk. When he spoke, he addressed me directly.

"I've heard about your attractions, Miss Hurst. You are truly a blessing to your family, and I agree with your father. Your unique gifts must not be hidden away on what I imagine is your lovely homestead."

The way he said "lovely" made clear that he didn't mean it, but I was in no position to argue. Mr. Braunstein made a show of pawing through the papers on his desk, although it seemed likely that he knew where everything was down to the last pen nib. Extracting a calendar from a nest of papers by his elbow, he dragged his index finger along a row of dates.

"I can book her two weeks from now. November sixteen, a Friday night, the first act, before Fyodor Dubrovsky, a refined instrumentalist from Europe, and Europa and Pearl, the songbird twins. We had someone else, but they flew the coop."

And just like that, we had a date. He hadn't asked me to perform a test, or to speak, or do anything but sit. Easy as pie. I turned to my father, sure he'd be getting to his feet and shaking Mr. Braunstein's hand.

Daddy hadn't moved. In fact, he had let himself slide a little in the armchair until he was nearly slouching. He looked like an imitation of a bad-mannered child. I moved to touch his shoulder, but the fury that radiated from his jaw and shoulders pushed me away. I glanced at Mr. Braunstein, but he hadn't appeared to notice.

Daddy spoke.

"You haven't understood me, Mr. Braunstein. The Magnetic Girl is your top billing. *After* the foreign musician and the singing twins."

Mr. Braunstein wiped a fountain pen with a white cloth, bleeding black into the weave. He glanced up once, clearing his throat.

This conversation—this argument—was about me, but I hadn't said a word. My eyelids lowered as I prepared myself to captivate him, but what would I do with him? Captivation would only suspend this disagreement, not solve it.

"I understand your devotion, Colonel, truly I do. But this is business, no? Your daughter is a novice, as powerful as she must be. I have obligations, commitments, to what you call a foreign musician, to those lovely sisters. Let us allow The Magnetic Girl the comfort of demonstrating her power to an audience soothed by music. The savage beast, you know."

Thirty-two people had confronted Momma on our lawn, asking to see me. That should count for something. *Our lawn,* I thought, lowering my lids at my father. My words bounced back to me, raindrops pinging off tin.

"One night only," Daddy said, still slouching. This was an act. He was pretending he didn't care if we walked out without an Opera House show.

I counted a dozen of my own breaths before Mr. Braunstein spoke.

"We will draw up a letter of agreement," he said, "and send it you. In the interim, a handshake will suffice, I am sure?"

The boy from the front door appeared as if on wheels.

"Of course," Daddy said, accepting the handshake like an afterthought. I wondered if he would clap the theater manager on the back like I'd seen him do with fellows at church. This man was a foreigner, though. A Jew. Perhaps they didn't do that.

"Tickets will be twenty-five cents, fifty for the box seats," Mr. Braunstein said. "The house share is sixty per cent of the box office receipts, the remaining forty allocated among the *artistes*. With the other performers on the bill, that would amount to an overall ten percent for you, representing Miss Hurst."

The boy held the door open.

As soon as we were on the street, I grabbed Daddy's arm and almost shouted from joy. All that money for less than ten minutes of work, and hardly work like wash or weeding the vegetable garden. Daddy shook me off his arm. "Ten percent of the house, Lulu." He sounded tired. "You fill that Opera House—which you will—and all we'll see of what's due us is next to nothing."

Like a child, or worse, a fool, I hadn't thought the arithmetic all the way through. I worked on the idea as we walked, Daddy taking the street side and me on the inside, customary for a man and woman walking together in town. People pushed past us on their own errands, their thoughts barely penetrating my thinking. One show would lead to another. Mr. Braunstein didn't want to take a risk on me, although had he asked I'd have done a bang-up cane test for him. I should have offered, even if he thought I was deaf and dumb, a regular Laura Bridgman. All the more interesting. We could earn more if I were magnetic *and* impaired.

"We're going to the *Appeal*," Daddy said. "We'll need to take out an announcement. We'll fill that theater and get every fraction of a penny there is. Next time around, we'll have a sold-out show for a bargaining chip. No ten percent for you after this."

The *Appeal*. My atlas of the world. I didn't care if anyone was watching: I ran ahead to the end of the block.

The newspaper office smelled of machine oil and pencil shavings, with a dash of horse manure. Assiduous boot scraping on the sidewalk did little to eradicate the source of the odor. Skirts collected mud, and animal waste and tobacco spit clung to boot heels. The sudden, indecent image of hundreds of hind ends and limbs wearing down the jewel-green sofa under the windows made my cheeks hot.

When I read the paper at home, I liked to think of the reporters walking across the road to the train station to catch up on news from the telegraph out of Atlanta or Rome. The telegraph was quicker than the Central Georgia rail line. The men would don their hats and jackets before they strolled into a workaday building that they barely noticed. That train station was my doorway to the unknown.

"Help you, Colonel?" asked the man at the desk.

Daddy removed his hat and held it behind his back, ducking his head toward the man before straightening again. I always wanted to laugh at strangers' expressions the first time they had to step back to take in his height.

"I'm here to place an announcement."

The desk man fished a pencil from a drawer. Using it as a pointer, he directed us to the counter.

"Write it out there on a sheet, bring it back to me and we'll tote it up."

I took a slip of paper from a pigeonhole and handed it ceremoniously to my father. He played as if he was Mr. Braunstein, bowing with a flourish, and we laughed.

> *Cedartown's own Miss Lulu Hurst, The Magnetic Girl.*
> *The sensation of the day! One night only at the Opera House.*
> *November 16.*
> *Defies science! Baffles the brilliant!*
> *Admission 25¢, 50¢ box seats. Call at the box office.*

Two nights before I took the stage at the Opera House, Daddy said we were done with after-supper practice for the time being. My rest was primary. At the table cleared by hands other than mine, he opened a new People's Regulator. He had made a list.

> *Intr'dc The Magnetic Girl; rec. audience applause.*
> *Test #1 cane.*

His finger on the page drew the shape of my future.

> *Test #2 chair*
> *Test #3 cane*
> *Test #4 chair*

He had written nothing after number four. Four tests went by too quickly. We couldn't allow anyone's attention to wane with every pair of eyes on me.

"I'm sure if someone we knew asked me a question I could—" I offered.

"—you won't," he answered. "No Spiritualist questions, no diversions from this outline. This here is all you do, Magnetic Girl. The chair-sitting fellows won't be willy-nilly," he said. "The volunteers will be gentlemen I know. They won't be fine specimens like me, but they won't be bulls, either."

He winked, and I grabbed my bangs, anxious.

"But what if someone insists?"

"I will inform them that we've run out of time."

He handed me a contract. Across the top were the words J.B BRAUNSTEIN, ESQUIRE, PROPRIETOR & MANAGER, GRAND OPERA HOUSE, CEDARTOWN, GEORGIA. Words like "box office" and "revenue" danced across the page until the last paragraph.

Failure in the performance of any of these conditions shall operate to render this contract null and void at the option of the party aggrieved. The destruction of the [Grand Opera House] by fire; the illness of the principal performer[s], or the occurrence of any event beyond the control of the manager shall release both parties from all obligations growing out of this contract. This contract to be null and void in case of fire, railroad delays, or illness.

Mr. Braunstein, who had bowed to me as if I mattered, presumed that I would fail. Daddy's signature was solid proof that he agreed.

Thanking Daddy for signing the contract, for arranging this next step in the life of The Magnetic Girl, I wished my parents good night and excused myself to bed. There was nowhere else to go.

I couldn't quit thinking about failure. Everywhere I looked, something failed, each one my fault. While I tore the husks off corn at the back steps, I longed for what Mrs. Wolf called *that place of tranquility. A restful luminosity.* She wasn't specific about if the tranquil, luminous state belonged to the Mesmerist or the person receiving the benefit, but my belief was that the sensation was shared. *Mesmerize daily for half an hour, for more than a month,* Mrs. Wolf prescribed. I couldn't captivate anyone for that long.

After Sarah Hines spoke up for me in school, we began cautiously to eat our dinners together, she no better at friendship than I. Her pal Jenny Wynne joined us because she went wherever Sarah did. One afternoon Sarah rolled a hard-cooked egg across her lap, leaving brown flecks of shell on her glove. What I saw wasn't an egg, but an object that wanted my safeguarding.

"Lulu," Jenny said, talking around the potato in her mouth. Taking my time, I removed my winter gloves and stuffed them in my coat pocket before picking at my cold biscuit.

"Listen, Lulu." Jenny tried again, food swallowed. "My mama read in the *Appeal* how you're going to be on stage at the Opera House."

Staying quiet might get Jenny to keep talking, a diversion for Sarah while I took her egg. Not to eat. Just to hold and then give back, time stopped.

"You're the sensation of the day," Jenny said.

Sarah quit rolling her egg to ask what I would wear on stage.

Time to speak up.

"Y'all know I've only played at being The Magnetic Girl in our house so far. The stage is my father's idea. You heard," I whispered, sorry that I was playing them, manufacturing a confidence to share with two girls who could be my friends, "you heard how I have electricity in my fingers. You saw how Ada tried to get me to show her. It started with that storm. I have a power."

I was pleased with myself, even if I'd just buffaloed the only people who liked me.

"I heard," Jenny said, unscrewing the lid from a jar of tea. "People were talking. You told that fellow Mr. Rogers his age, and you threw another fellow like he was a cat, and all he was doing was trying to take some chair out of your hands. Hey, ain't Mr. Rogers related to you, Sarah?"

Proximity to my power made Sarah blush. I reached for my bangs but caught myself and licked jam and biscuit from my fingers instead. Jenny, still talking, began inspecting a hole in her boot. With her looking away, I was free to stare directly into Sarah's eyes. Holding her gaze, I counted silently to three, feeling a heaviness in my arms and legs. My center of gravity sunk like a bucket into a well. I bit my lip to steady myself as the blue sky pinwheeled into a tunnel. And then I plucked the boiled egg from Sarah's hand, feeling its perfect shape and the odd weight of it, strong and delicate both.

From the corner of my eye I saw Jenny accept that she couldn't fix her boot. My time was nearly done. Gently, as if the egg were hatching, I placed it in Sarah's lap and drew my hand back to my biscuit.

"I need to fix this boot," Jenny said.

Sarah looked at her lunch like she didn't recognize it.

I wanted to shout with joy and relief. Captivating hadn't left me.

CHAPTER NINE

ON THE DAY OF THE PROGRAMME, DADDY DROVE THE wagon, Momma, and me into Cedartown. The street was brittle with frost. The five syllables of "The Mag Net Ick Girl" pounded in Jack's step. Over and over, Daddy hummed the same eighteen notes that he said came from an opera by Mozart, a sure sign that he was feeling sentimental. A few shoppers and tradesmen hurried along the plank sidewalks. These same people had been in our parlor and in our yard, but as we passed them, not one acknowledged us. When I went to wave at folks, Momma pulled my hand into my lap.

The glass case beside the Opera House door shone in the last rays of sunlight. Before Daddy could tie Jack to the post or help Momma down from her seat, I jumped from the wagon. The broadside read, in large letters, FYODOR DUBROVSKY, DIRECT FROM THE CONCERT HALLS OF EUROPE. EUROPA AND PEARL, THE SONGBIRD TWINS paraded over a litho of two plump ladies with bustles big as watermelons.

Like an afterthought across the bottom of the page were the words RENOWNED! CEDARTOWN'S OWN LULU HURST, THE MAGNETIC GIRL! SCIENCE CAN'T EXPLAIN! ONE NIGHT ONLY.

From behind my shoulder, Daddy spoke.

"One night only means you're scarce. People always want more of what they can't get easily."

I was nothing more than a postscript in a letter. P.S., the neighbors dug a new well. P.S., the cat had kittens. P.S. you will fail when this many people watch you.

Daddy's hand on my shoulder turned me to the front door and into the theater lobby. The room was transformed. Potted ferns framed the ticket window. Ornate carpets ran from corner to corner. From somewhere down a hallway, two women screamed at each other in a language that sounded like barking. A balding man wearing only a nightdress and boots wandered past us, engrossed in tuning the fiddle he held to his chin. The notes his bow drew from the strings stacked atop each other like layers in a cake. Engrossed in his tune, he seemed unaware of how the silver and red flocked wallpaper glowed from the lamps, or the velvet tassels on the draperies. Momma pressed her hand to my cheek to make me look away, but I didn't.

The boy from Mr. Braunstein's office appeared as if conjured. His hair stank from whatever he'd used to make it slick. He'd been solicitous the day we met, but he was irritated now.

Leaning away didn't get me clear of his odor.

"Acts don't come in the main door," he said.

I wished I could have spanked his rear and sent him running, but he knew the answer to the question of where we were supposed to go next. Daddy wasn't going to be knocked around by a pipsqueak. He asked where we could unload our chair and walking sticks from the wagon. The boy shrugged and pointed to a door almost hidden by one of the potted trees.

"Ask Hamlin. He's the stage manager."

"Oh, for heaven's sake," Momma sighed. "You don't have anyone to help?"

The boy waved us away. I tried the stage-smile from my mirror at him, but he rolled his eyes. Momma and Daddy went in the general direction of Mr. Hamlin, apparently located behind the nearly-hidden door. I followed, not wanting to waste captivation on a lesser person.

In a narrow room away from the lush carpets and drapes, the cold leaked through lathe and plaster. The bare walls were striped black from soot. No one had trimmed the lamp wicks or banked the stove. Piles of rope coiled here and there, some thrown into the rafters or scrolled across the floor. A dressing gown lay across a settee. Someone's s luggage looked blown open, clothing exploded over the sides. At a mirror, the two women from the poster fixed each other's hair. If theirs were the arguing voices, they had come to a stalemate. They didn't speak to each other, or to us. Daddy excused himself to the wagon for our chair and canes. Before the door shut behind him, the fiddle-man came in. He hadn't changed out of his nightdress.

He kissed Momma's hand and then mine. Mr. Dubrovsky from the poster.

"Is your first time on grand stage, no?"

He spoke like he was gargling. He was kind, but I wouldn't admit I was green. My hand tickled where he'd brushed his lips against my skin.

"She's very popular," Momma said, inching closer to me. "Miss Hurst has performed before crowds of admirers, and a newspaper story has been written about her. Very tasteful," she added, eyeing his nightclothes.

Speaking about me in third person was elegant, I had to admit, and I preened despite myself.

"Sing!" Mr. Dubrovsky said. "Play! You're given gift to perform."

Instinctively I stepped backward, away from his exuberant blasts. He took my hand again and held tightly.

"Enjoy your youth and beauty." He said *yoos*, but I understood.

I wasn't beautiful, but I thanked him sincerely.

Beyond the wall, someone at a piano lurched into the first notes of a waltz, and the sound triggered the chilly room into action. One of the arguing ladies made *O*'s with her mouth, stretching her face and saying oh, auw, oh, auw. Face powder flaked from her cheeks onto her ruffled collar, and the other woman—likely her mother, now that I saw them closely—adjusted the padding of her bustle.

I hung my coat on a peg and went to warm my hands with the little heat I could coax from the weak stove.

THE CURTAIN ROSE ON stage lights hissing at full strength, releasing the stupefying odor of a good dose of gas at close range. With my hand in the crook of my father's elbow, I focused on center stage: a single wooden chair from home and an umbrella stand holding an assortment of walking canes. I clung to Daddy's arm and tried not to hear the rustling seats in the theater.

Afraid we looked like rubes trying to steady one another, I slid my arm away, and just as quickly tried to inch it back. The distance between us had grown huge in those seconds, and I felt alone. A few faces stared up expectantly. I shouldn't have looked. Look over their heads, Daddy had said, and I lifted my chin until my gaze went to the very back wall, a field of black. But eye to eye was how to captivate, so I fixed on one pair of eyes, then another. The theater was hot and stuffy. I clasped my hands at my waist, motionless as our chair beside me. I felt a little sick.

"My good friends and neighbors, ladies and gentlemen."

As Daddy spoke, he took three steps to the front of the stage, each one booming under my feet. Footlights in their little iron cages raised a golden light around his boots.

"You are about to witness a Power and Force never before seen in our own Polk County, and never seen in a Southern lady in all of history. You have paid your hard-earned money and secured seats here tonight in order to witness feats inexplicable to the most educated of men."

He waited out weak applause before speaking again. A few dark silhouettes stood to leave. Others roamed in the blackness, dark on darker. Rooted in place, I was too scared to leave and too nervous to move forward. When did he write those words? Inexplicable. All of history. Each word pushed me farther out of my own skin.

"Tonight, we will test the power of Magnetism. Ever since this Wonderful Force made its presence known around this little girl, everyday men and women, scientists and scholars, have tried their hand at understanding the Force. None have been harmed, but all have come away puzzled. This is your night to test The Magnetic Girl. This power will not harm! Come to the stage and test The Magnetic Girl's Force."

He swept his arm out and bowed so deeply his nose nearly touched his knees.

The audience shifted their weight like stabled horses. I heard a few murmurs of "you go first" and "not me." Daddy straightened up and pointed to a burly, neatly dressed older gentleman in the front row. Colonel Furman, pretending he was a stranger. Lightheaded from relief and shame, I giggled.

Daddy addressed him. "You sir, look like you've seen a few wonders in your day. Will you join me and the young lady here?"

There was no turning back now.

"Show them how it's done, Granddad," someone hollered. Someone else let out a Rebel Yell.

My legs didn't feel connected to the rest of me. Colonel Furman walked up the steps to the stage. I didn't look away from the back wall until, as we had practiced, I walked up to the urn and pulled up a cane. The hissing gas from the lights, whoops and calls from the audience, the murmur of my father's voice explaining to Colonel Furman what he already knew from our parlor wrapped me in a deafening blur. And then, silence. All I heard was my heartbeat. To that rhythm—*I am, I am*—I stretched my arms forward with the cane parallel to the floor.

The Colonel winked. I scowled, trying to concentrate. Too loudly, I explained to him what he'd heard me say to others at my house: where and how to place his hands on the horizontal cane. Colonel Furman placed his palms over the stick. I moved my hands between his and clasped the cane from below. And then I looked into his eyes.

"Push toward the floor," I instructed. I felt adult, a mother or a teacher telling someone what to do. He pushed, too gently, and I pressed upward equally. He was more than twice my weight, but if I caught his eyes, if I *formed a union*, as Mrs. Wolf described, that wouldn't matter.

I pressed harder and he responded intuitively, pressing downward with more force. I lowered my eyelids as I had with the fox, with Mr. Campbell, with Sarah and her egg. Digging my heels into the splintered floor, I concentrated on the cane. Every beat of Colonel Furman's pulse fed directly through my hands and up my arms into my shoulders and across my upper back. Like Newton's law, we were equal and opposite. A high-pitched vibration trembled in my ears, fine as violin strings made of spider webs. This was so easy. A giggle erupted before I could recognize the sound, girlish and provocative, new to me. The Colonel pushed down more, and as he did, I lessened my push. The cane's handle flew up toward his left temple, the foot swinging toward his right ankle. He stumbled, saved from falling only by Daddy's steadying hand at his elbow.

The audience leapt to their feet, and the roar of "me next," hit me like a runaway train. Dizzy, I busted out laughing. Men in the front row cheered and applauded, and like Mr. Dubrovsky and Daddy had done, I bowed. I didn't need to look at the back wall when I came up: I could look them all in the eye.

I began the subtle work of humbugging the city's finest. Turn to the umbrella stand and remove an elegant cane. Hold it horizontal to the carpet, arm's length from my chest. Invite the fellow to place his hands on the cane, toward the middle. Hold the cane as he did and let him press down before I pressed upward against his intentions, no different than I'd done in practice. Face to face, girl and man, cane immobile until, when the tension was just right, my left hand flew up, the fellow's right hand flew down, the cane seemed to buck him off his feet, and the exalted guest stumbled backward. I managed the speed so he'd lose his balance just enough to laugh at himself, but never enough to fall.

"Like a divining rod," Daddy gasped, as if the fellow had escaped with his life.

I was a wonder for sure. The cane turned itself like a paddlewheel.

Daddy peered into the audience for the first chair-test "volunteer." He chose a toothpick of a fellow, barely older than me, and raw with pimples. I'd never seen him before, but Daddy knew plenty of fellows.

"Take a seat," I said, patting the cane bottom of the chair. "I'm not going to hurt you." His eyelids were pink-rimmed, like a rabbit's. I wondered if he'd been crying. He winced. He was a real volunteer, a stranger.

"This will be fun, and you can brag to your friends," I whispered, a little sorry that I was about to frighten the wits out of a fellow already short of them.

I patted the seat again, and the man sat. Someone in the audience crumpled paper, and someone else scolded, "Hush." Behind the chair, I lay my hands against the splats by the man's shoulders. Inside my skirt, I touched my knees to the back of the seat. I had proven myself with this test before. Tilting the chair backward less than an inch would make the fellow lift his feet from the floor without thinking, same as if he were arranging himself at the supper table. Pulling back on the chair would confuse him before I rocked man and chair forward. For that crackle of an instant, his disorientation would assure him that he'd risen, chair and all, from the ground. He'd tell anyone that was true because he believed the same. What we hadn't figured until now was how people seated past the front row would have their view blocked by the seats in front of them. They wouldn't see the chair legs on stage. This rabbit-eyed man would need to shout when he went up.

Daddy was watching me, and I pulled. The fellow in the chair shifted back, and his legs went straight out as I tilted the chair against my middle. As I rocked the fellow forward, Daddy walked center stage, and I set the chair and the fellow in it right. Before I had worked the curl out of my fingers, he leapt up and grabbed my hand. Letting me go, he galloped from the stage. He looked as if he would have preferred to kiss me, but he hadn't hollered like I'd wanted. I needed to try again.

"She's done it, ladies and gentlemen, and I pity you if a neighbor crowded your lookout." Daddy paced the stage, clapping and shouting like he'd turned into a revival preacher. Good thing Momma was backstage with her needlepoint. She'd be furious. Me, though, I beamed at him. He knew what would excite an audience.

"The Magnetic Girl's power can lift a fellow straight off his feet, seat included," Daddy shouted. "No need to miss it, just move on up."

A man with the girth of a winter bear lumbered to the stage. I cut my eyes at Daddy, but he didn't acknowledge me. He was smiling and nodding at the big man. The bear clambered onto to the stage and pumped Daddy's hand with his paw. He was so tall that had we embraced, my head would have rested on his chest. The bear made eyes at me. If we hadn't been on a stage, I would have given him a hard look. The reality of what I was doing caught up with me, and my knees went weak. I couldn't lift him in a chair. I gave him what felt like a smile, but instead of taking my spot behind the chair, I went again to the urn.

I chose the polished walking stick with the silver handle. The bear stood before me, his hands on each end of the cane. I had to drop my head back to see into his eyes, and the position strained my shoulders and closed my throat. His green eyes mocked me. He was either ignorant or mean, but either way he would make me fail. *Look here, bear man*, I thought. *I can captivate a fox, and you're no different.* His gaze twitched away from mine, then back to me, and as I caught him, I pushed the cane upward, not caring if I broke the middle. I'd blame that on him. Five more seconds passed, me pushing, him resisting, our eyes locked, my breathing turning coarse before the cane flew up and away. The man tumbled backward. The bear became a monstrous cockroach.

Perspiration soaked my collar. My neck was sore and sweat tickled my back. I went to wipe my brow with my sleeve, but if the audience saw that, they'd know that I'd struggled. With my hand already halfway to my head, I waved, and the audience erupted in cheers. Three men rushed to the stage and helped the fallen colossus to his feet. Once righted, he gleefully waved his hat above his head. Before Daddy could speak, the big man embraced him and turned to the audience.

"The power in that girl is true," the man shouted. Like me, he was winded. His voice was tenor, surprising for a man so barrel-chested.

"I've been bested by the force of an electrical current, and it's come from that little girl yonder."

He pointed at me, and all eyes in the room pinned me in place. I fixed my smile and breathed not enough air through gritted teeth, praying that holding my hands to my chest would return my heart-beat to normal. I ducked my head to get a good suck of air with-out the crowd seeing. I'd thrown the biggest man I'd ever seen. The crowd began to stomp and chant.

"Magnetic Girl," they shouted. "Magnetic Girl."

Refreshed, I lifted my head and waved again.

Daddy held his hands skyward, encouraging their joy. Despite my sweat and soreness, I wanted to stay in that spot all night.

In the wings, Mr. Hamlin pointed to his pocket watch.

Daddy shouted into the audience. "As powerful as she is, our Magnetic Girl is also a *young* girl, and surely no one in this house would deprive a child of her rest."

I didn't care for rest, or that Mr. Dubrovsky was peering at me from behind Mr. Hamlin, or that a button at the back of my skirt had popped. I didn't care that this test would show up as a beauti-fully straight line in Daddy's notebook. I'd mesmerized people, all but one of them strangers. Each of them, in a way, had been cured of what ailed them; complacency, meekness, and self-importance.

As soon as I was off the stage I broke into a run, dodging fabric palm fronds rolled into corners and a garland of faded paper flowers strewn over a hump of sandbags. Behind me, Mr. Dubrovsky's violin sang again. I burned like a candle. I shoved open the dressing room door and came face to face with Momma. I grabbed a newspaper and fanned my neck.

"Nobody wanted it to end," I told her. "Momma, did you come out and see Daddy not minding the stage manager pointing at his watch?" I switched to fanning her. "That big fellow was a stranger, but I was glad the first one was— "

As if he'd been waylaid somewhere, Daddy strolled in, water to my fire. He cleared his throat, a warning.

"Sal, they were like children with their hands out for candy."

As he whistled his admiration for them or me or both, he stepped out of the doorway to let in a well-dressed fellow.

"This is Mr. Getty," he said. "He saw those people go all to pieces over Lulu. He has something to say."

Mr. Getty set his hat on a stuffed owl lying on a box.

"Mrs. Hurst, Miss Hurst, my name's Franklin Getty, and I manage the Nevin Opera House up in Rome, Georgia. Our charming theater has been the local home to refined entertainments like the Jolly Pathfinders and Professor Boncher's Marionette Family. Other than Atlanta, we're the only Georgia stop for grand shows like *The Pirates of Penzance*."

I leapt from the chair, but Momma grabbed me by the newspaper fan and pulled me back down. Mr. Getty waited for me to sit.

"I would like to extend to Miss Hurst a multiple night engagement to present her powers on the stage of Rome's Nevin Opera House."

Daddy shook his hand.

"Mister Getty, we would be honored—no, immensely moved, sir—to bring our little girl up to Rome, where do I business on occasion. I have seen your Opera House, of course, but never would I dream that my own child would engage patrons of such a place."

Mr. Getty extended his hand to me, and I shook it. I wish I hadn't noticed that he wiped it against his trouser leg.

The giant man from the stage wobbled in my mind, knocked around by a sea of laughter and applause. That contract was wrong. I hadn't failed. We were going to do this again, for a bigger audience in a bigger town. The money would roll in, making the mule a horse, the wagon a buggy, the possum a beefsteak. This was fine. And Leo wouldn't need all the medicine I could buy him, because in every circumstance, every city, every kind of person, I would put Mrs. Wolf's words into practice until I could lift the *afflicted person from the depths of their malady*.

WINTER

CHAPTER
TEN

Rome, Georgia:
January 1884

IF THE NEVIN OPERA HOUSE COULD SPEAK, IT WOULD have said that Cedartown's Opera House was nothing more than a shed. In Rome, workmen tugged a moveable wall with a painting of a Parisian park, complete with a bench and ladies in parasols, onto a massive stage. A woodland forest on a board came next, and then a nighttime avenue with gas lamps getting smaller as they appeared to go down a lane. Watching the workmen, I bounced on my toes and gnawed a loose strand of hair. I didn't care that they smelled of drink.

Pierre the monkey held my finger before his act, his tiny hand like Leo's when he was newly born. Pierre's trick was riding the hat of a man on a wheel. The bicyclist's name was a usual one like Smith, although he was swarthy, but Pierre was the most enchanting thing I'd ever seen. His doll-sized sailor outfit had a hole for his tail. While the audience applauded for the bicyclist and his monkey, I asked Momma if she could make those outfits. She stood behind me, brushing my hair with a new stiff brush.

"How much need in the world you think there is for monkey sailor outfits?" she said, yanking my head around. "One or two would probably cover it, and then we'd be stuck with a pile of little clothes with a back door. Anyway, they've got fleas."

Pierre stank worse than a privy, but I could ignore that if I had a pet monkey in an outfit. He would be so useful: braid my hair or ride my shoulder at school so all the girls would come talk with me. Their pets were kittens or canaries. I could surely teach a pet monkey to communicate by pointing to things. In fact, a monkey could help Leo. Cut up his dinner or make his bed. And together we could wash the smell off the monkey.

A boy banged out an enthusiastic tune on a piano at the corner of the stage. The crowd's shouts sent sparks through me: they'd been doing it the whole night. If there wasn't one thing to look at there was another. A rowdy had called out, "yum, yum" during Miss Marie's dance, a saucy waggle of her curvy leg, her flouncy skirt lifted up like a curtain nearly to her knee. She drove the crowd to distraction by leaning over and waving goodbye with her backside. As she did, Pierre the monkey rode atop the man with the forgettable name as they bicycled in figure eights onto the stage.

When the piano thundered to a stop, Pierre and the man rode off the stage. Momma put the hairbrush away, and I made myself quit thinking about teaching Pierre to sew. I straightened my skirt and blouse, no longer stiff and new, and peeked around the edge of the curtain. The house—the knowledgeable way to say "theater"—was dense with shapes that could have been paper cut-outs had they not coughed and talked. From across the stage, Mr. Getty stepped over stray confetti and a greasy yellow smudge that I realized with a start was a monkey dropping. He held up his hands for silence.

Someone yelled, "Shut the hell up." The girls at school would have been appalled, but for me, the foul language ignited an illicit thrill.

"Ladies and gentlemen, we'll close out our night with a debut performance"—he drew out "day-bee-you," sounding so elegant that I spit out the hair in my mouth, "from a wondrous young lady from our own glorious Southern state."

He waited out the surge of patriotic applause.

This was me, Lulu Hurst. I danced a step in place and wished Leo were here to watch.

"This Georgia girl is indeed a wonder, a scientific miracle discovered in the tiniest hamlet not a day's ride from here, a source of magnetism, a conductor of electricity—"

A stagehand pushed past me, my wooden chair on his shoulder. He put the chair on stage as if nothing momentous was about to happen.

"The esteemed Colonel William Hurst, an expert in matters of science as well as the greater mysteries of the universe, will explain."

Mr. Getty knew that Daddy had selected Colonel Furman for the stage back in Cedartown. This afternoon he told him not to select fellows in advance. That kind of thing gets around too fast, he said. There was no telling who'd decide to come up now, but I had practiced well and hard, concentrating on how everyone out there in the dark—those cut-outs—would see that I was magnetized.

Mr. Getty's bow seemed like a signal, so I stepped from behind the curtain onto my right foot for luck. Daddy swept past me and nearly knocked me off balance. Alone on stage, he shook Mr. Getty's hand and addressed the audience with the exact same words he said to the folks in Cedartown. I'd assumed he'd say something new for a different audience. Momma shoved me forward, just a little. The piano player started a waltz with dull keys. With Momma's shove and Daddy's going out ahead of me and the music sounding thumpy and me missing my first cue, I stumbled. Daddy paced the stage as if he were deep in thought before he stopped short and spoke.

"I know you all would like to see the true force of the magnetic power that resides in this young lady."

Some affirmations came up from the darkness, but mostly, the audience was still.

We needed to put my bad start behind us. Waiting, I rocked the chair back and forth with my hand. When Daddy asked the men of Rome to line up and get ready to "fly into the air in a simple kitchen chair," one, two…five men clambered into the aisle. Daddy asked each man's name and introduced him loudly to the audience and to me, but because I was supposed to be in the throes of Magnetism, I could only nod. True Mesmerists knew the tastes inside their subjects' mouths. Was this man's throat dry and sour as mine? That fellow, did his lips burn and taste like iron, like blood?

Fizzing with energy, I swung my arms in the air. The audience laughed. Aloft on their current, I laughed, too. The few rows I could see were tinted gold from the gaslight, and those open mouths gaped wet when they laughed.

Daddy brought me Doctor This. Judge That. Mr. Someone Else, each more dignified than the last. I wanted each of them to feel knocked loose, uncertain, desperate to know something solid. My fingers curled against the chair, seeking the pleasure of puncturing a thick mattress. The flesh on my arms crawled, that delicious, savage feeling like an itch begging for a scratch or a taut surface begging to be torn.

The cane tests and the umbrella tests we'd devised, where I shook an umbrella open and let it fly like it had caught a gust of wind, came and went. Pretty soon the umbrellas we'd brought littered the stage like dead crows. Roman men returned to their seats, some skulking after being outdone by a girl with an umbrella, others red-faced and sweating, beaten but basking in attention.

We got paid that night, money for my natural skills. The silver dollar coins looked like full moons reflected on water as Daddy counted them out across the top of the chipped bureau at our rooming house. Our contract was new, and an honest deal. Seventy percent for us, thirty percent for the Opera House.

In the rooming house, I learned that a few dollar coins weighed enough to rip my pocket open in my everyday dress. They clattered from the hole they'd torn and rolled like wheels into the grooves in the floor. I ran to retrieve them.

"Not all of that's ours," Daddy said. "Some goes to our landlady here for this nice hospitality."

He pulled a face and I laughed, glad that my discomfort with the make-do curtain dividing our room in two and the curled-edge mattresses wasn't wrong.

"We don't need to expect elegant," Momma said, "and Mr. Getty was thoughtful to find us a place. Riding all night in a wagon in the cold isn't healthy."

Daddy took the rescued coins from me. My hands floated when I let the metal go, and I made fists to bring them down to my sides.

"He took his percentage before he handed this over," Daddy said, "and likely he slipped something to the stage manager, the piano player, and that fellow with the miniature ape."

I pulled the curtain and lay on my bed gingerly. I was spent, but I wouldn't undress, not with my parents so near and strangers I could hear on the other side of the walls. I left my boots at the foot of the bed and spread my coat across the lumpy pillow, refusing to think too much of strangers' noses and spit and hairs that were surely on the fabric even if the widow who ran the place did her wash every day.

I wouldn't have thought Mr. Getty would give our money to other people in the theater.

Griping was disgraceful. I'd dreamed of this moment every time I thought of a train station. A person changed their scenery like a train would, here in a rooming house with their meals prepared and an alien view through their window.

Sleep wouldn't come. My muscles seized and twitched as they remembered their motions: bend here, lift there, wait, push. Count one, two, three. My shoulders ached deep into my back. I was tired enough to split in two. *The Truth of Mesmeric Influence* was at home, packed away in my keepsake box. To lull myself into something that resembled normal, I wrote a letter in my head to Leo, even though we'd be home before supper the next day.

Little brother, the audience tonight laughed at me, but I wanted them to, like when I tickle you to make you laugh. This isn't like you've ever seen before. Momma told Daddy when she thought I wasn't listening that she didn't like how I swung my arm. She said I looked like a brute. Daddy told her to never mind. He says that he and I are a "well-oiled machine." I am learning all this for you.

WE DRANK OUR HOT coffee and ate our runny eggs with silent strangers before sunrise. The world had gone about its business without caring what I thought. The widow who ran the rooming house scurried around so much that I barely glimpsed her skinny back. Her shoulder blades pointed at me like accusations. Mr. Getty came around while Daddy loaded the wagon. Like fellows in Cedartown, he slapped Daddy on the back, and all but jumped up the three wide porch steps to embrace Momma and me.

"You'll be heading to Atlanta soon," he said, breath steaming in the cold. Because of the hour and my having slept poorly, I thought he meant right then.

"No, sir, we can't," I said, sorry to have to correct him. He was a nice man, although excitable, and there was the question about him giving our money to folks in the Opera House.

Daddy joined us on the porch. Had anyone driven by and seen us, we'd have looked like a portrait: a mother, father, and young lady tucked into their coats and hats, reacting in their own ways to a young man alight with certainty.

"I've arranged a booking at DeGive's Opera House. Atlanta audiences will fall all over themselves to get a turn on stage with The Magnetic Girl."

Had he done this last night? While we counted coins in our room, was he at the telegraph office, sending a message about me, receiving one back? My ears whistled as if wind whipped hard around us, but the air was brittle and still. Look at me, I thought, trying to catch his eye. Look straight at me and I'll captivate you and when I do we can all take a breath and revel in this.

Here was the *reward in my work*. Silently, I thanked Mrs. Wolf for teaching me how to name it.

"She's overcome," Momma said, giving me a little squeeze.

"We'll want to go to Cedartown first," Daddy said. "Our youngest has been with the neighbors for the night, and we have family obligations to arrange, and—"

Mr. Getty held up his hand.

"Not right away. They've got bookings to run out, but the folks at DeGive's know me. They've made a spot for her—for *you*, Miss Hurst—ten days from now."

And one night would certainly lead to a return engagement. After all, he said, smiling, hadn't just one night in Cedartown led him to me?

A return engagement.

We went home, the wagon clacking out not "The Mag Net Ick Girl," but "look what you have done, look what you have done," rolling toward exactly what I'd said I wanted. What I wanted and what was right weren't always the same. All I'd wanted from Daddy's shelves were illustrations for my dreams and a guide to the world beyond our hills. I'd wanted to leave. And now it looked like we would. All of us.

Momma gave me a chicken croquette from a pail. Tasting other people's food, seeing their manners and their kindnesses up close were the benefits of getting what I'd wanted. I picked flecks of chicken bone from my tongue and flicked them over the side while I considered the boarding house. Too much work. All that cooking and spending your day at the beck and call of strangers. What we did—what I did—was a better life than that.

I tricked people into believing that I could lift a man and the chair he's sitting on or throw him by applying electrical force to a cane. These were merely distractions for the audience. What I could do without any tests or audience is Mesmerize. I could do it before I read Mrs. Wolf's book. Leo saw me do it, when I called it captivating, before I knew another person had a name for it.

"You can do it well," the wagon wheels admitted.

Mr. Getty was right. One show in Atlanta could lead to two, and then who knew where we'd go after that. At least Leo would be with us. I could watch him in the day. In the evenings he would have a front row seat. Put some cushions around him, and maybe lean the chair back. Did Opera House chairs lean back? I would wink at him when Daddy brought up this or that fellow to get thrown by a walking stick or lifted in a chair.

"Momma," I said.

She turned, smiling full on.

"Momma, Leo will love going to Atlanta." I smiled back. We'd be almost like we were before, the four of us.

Momma's face changed.

"I don't see how, Lulu."

The wagon tilted and jerked, and we kept rolling. *You can watch him, Momma. You're the mother, not me.* The sudden thought was shameful, and I went hot. Even though I hadn't birthed him, I acted in a way like his mother. Leo was the way he was now because of me. We couldn't go without him.

Daddy clicked his tongue at Jack, and the mule quickened.

"You told me yourself that you're doing this for Leo," Daddy said. "A person makes sacrifices for what he, or in your case, she, believes is right."

"Leo can come with us," I said, my fingers moving toward pulling my bangs. "You know I can help him, and he'll only fall behind in what he's learned if we leave him." The last words drifted away like smoke.

"I'm going to pretend that you didn't hear me," Momma said. "Travel to Atlanta, and more if that's how the Lord guides us, isn't healthy for Leo. He needs to be in one place, with someone watching him all the time. Can you imagine how dangerous it would be for him, bumping around on a train?

Momma knew I'd never been on a train and therefore couldn't imagine Leo or anyone else bumping around on one. My brother was too far from me already. I'd made a terrible mistake agreeing to go up to Rome and do my tests. Yes, I'd seen a monkey up close and watched a lady scandalize an audience and enjoy herself doing it. This was my one glimpse of the world. There was more out there, I knew it. But I'd never intended to go before Leo was ready for me to leave.

"You can't go back on your word, Missy," Daddy said. "Hypocrites are the lowest of the low."

"I wasn't," I said. How could I even begin to undo what I'd put in motion?

"Listen to your Momma," Daddy said. "You're the strong one. Those people, I'll tell you, they'll bleed the life out of you if you're not careful. That's why you always move like an ocean's tide—"

Daddy stopped. I leaned between Momma and Daddy.

"How do you know?"

"Never you mind, Missy," Daddy said. Regret shuddered in his chest. I felt it in my own.

"The matter's settled," Momma said. "If the Lord sees fit to send us hither and yon to display your gifts, the Lord will see fit for Leo to stay safe at home."

My next test would be to tell Leo I was leaving him, and to promise that I was coming back.

I know you remember that time with the fox, I'd say. *And the oath we took with our blood, the same blood that people who come see me want to believe is magnetic fluid.*

Did he remember his fall? Did he blame me?

Daddy thought we were driving our wagon home, but he was wrong. We were rolling over a cliff. Look what you have done, said the wheels.

I TOLD LEO ON the afternoon before we left, while I took *The Truth of Mesmeric Influence* from its safe home in my keepsake box. The book, not my brother, would be my traveling companion.

"Hold the wall," I reminded Leo. "One foot out but don't let go."

He sat, a ploy for my attention rather than physical weakness.

I scooped him onto my lap. His eight-year old limbs were getting long. He pressed his brow to mine.

Something big's on your mind.

He squirmed, expectant.

"You'll not sleep here tomorrow night," I told him. His elbow jabbed my rib as he tried to slide down from my lap.

"Me and Momma and Daddy, we're going to Atlanta. On a train. We'll be gone for two days." Talking fast wouldn't make this easier.

What about me?

"Mr. and Mrs. Hartnett are going to keep you like before. They know to help you walk and cut your food and they will make sure you're happy. Momma told them. I heard her. She told them right."

Leo smiled. I couldn't make a promise yet, and so I told him nothing more.

"Are you ready to play the game?" I asked.

Leo pressed his forehead to mine and squeezed his eyes shut.

I closed mine, too, and counted aloud. "One, two...!"

At three, he opened his eyes wide, and together we hooted, "Hooo!" At a fraction of an inch from my face, my brother's eyes were my entire world.

"*Owl!*" Leo shouted, throwing his arms around my neck.

"You're a wise old owl," I agreed. I hugged him hard.

"I know what you'll do when me and Momma and Daddy are gone."

I hated the forced cheer in my voice, but without it, I would cry.

Leo's wet fingers found his mouth. I could understand his loose, squishy words. Without me, his talk might meet empty stares. If this happened enough he might quit speaking altogether.

I pried his fingers free and kissed them, slimy as they were.

"You're going to *be good*. The time's come for you to be a big boy and do your share."

Why you crine? Leo leaned away to examine me.

"Silly. I'm not crying. See the dried-up wasp's nest out there?" With his wet finger in my grip, I pointed out the window to the eaves. "I'm just worried one might crawl out and bite you."

I stood Leo on the rug and poked his rear lightly with my boot toe. "Start for the door and I'll be right behind you. We'll get supper going."

I was going to leave my baby brother. Watching Leo gingerly tackle the few feet to the door, I almost told him to mind he didn't fall, but he was so careful. Tears pooled at the corners of my eyes no matter what I did.

Early the next day, as our cow and mule waited to be tended by Mr. Hartnett, I waited with my parents in the train station. A few people milled around, unaware that my life was changing. Below us, the earth churned in reaction to the force of the oncoming train.

"Do you feel the train?" I asked Momma. "The ground—it's moving."

"The train's not due for half an hour," she said. "You can't even hear the whistle yet."

It was a hard thing, living without awareness. I felt badly for her. She was missing so much. I wound my scarf around my throat and went out to the empty platform.

The train's whistle was far away, but it was piercing enough to twinge my back teeth. I'd heard that whistle a thousand times, but never from the platform coming for us, for me. Eight o'clock in the morning in Cedartown would the same in Atlanta. Hours would pass before we arrived, but right now it was five o'clock in the morning in a place far away as California, where people were only now starting to wake. Miners were probably digging for gold. Time was as hard to hold as a string of fish. If the train could go fast enough that we'd meet ourselves coming around again, three members of the Hurst family plunging south toward Atlanta, passing four members of the Hurst family, happy at home, how perfect that would be. Why couldn't such a feat be a *fact of natural philosophy*?

When the train pulled into the station, the wheels and rods and steam and noise were restless as me. My parents and I climbed the steps and sat together in a tight row. Even the wooden ceiling gleamed with varnish. Mud and soot streaked the windows, but no matter. The train lurched and belched while more and more passengers loaded their valises and lunch pails and whatnot under their seats. Daddy had done the same with ours. He'd traveled by train before, and Momma too. Through the window's grime, I watched passengers hurrying out of the station. There on my little wicker bench, above and away from a regular morning, warmed by the train's steam and my own exhilaration, I watched the busy world and wanted to sing.

A steam blast and a series of shudders startled me. Outside my dirty window, trees began to blur into a gray-green river. Queasy from the awful speed, I clutched the windowsill, unable to tear myself away from the very picture of motion.

When the whistle blew again, the blast came from in front and above and behind all at once, and I jumped as if bitten. Turning away from my laughing parents, I considered the curve in the rails ahead, so deep it seemed we'd tumble into the woods. Only when Daddy poked my arm, unable to control his laughter, did I realize that I'd been leaning away from the curve with all my might, countering the train's imbalance.

In Dallas, Georgia, we boarded a train that had left New York several days before. We'd get off in Atlanta before the train went farther south. Around me, sophisticates read their books or chatted quietly among themselves. Mrs. Wolf tugged at me from where I'd stowed her in my reticule. I released her and settled in with my paper companion.

"Put that up," Daddy said. I pretended I didn't hear him. Mrs. Wolf was explaining how *nature explains all wisdom*.

"We can't have people thinking you're studying up on hoodoo." Daddy reached over and closed the book, interrupting Mrs. Wolf's statement about kind-hearted people. *The Truth of Mesmeric Influence* returned to my bag at our feet. Like Dale to her hats, I whispered an apology to the pages.

CHAPTER
ELEVEN

Atlanta, Georgia:
February 1884

WE ALL BUT FELL OFF THE TRAIN AT ATLANTA, knocked about by a carnival of humanity. A fellow reached for our bags, and Daddy followed him outside, hesitating when the man extended his hand, palm up. I hadn't thought we'd need to pay someone to haul our clothes, and I supposed he hadn't either. Momma was more worldly by half.

"Pay him," she whispered.

"Get us a carriage and you'll get your money," Daddy snapped at the greedy man.

The fellow shrugged and pointed his thumb toward a few buck-boards clustered across Alabama Street. Daddy glared at him until the man dragged our dusty bags, one with a buckle about to come loose, to a mule-driven wagon uglier than ours at home. He tossed the bags in the back, raising a cloud of straw. I'd swaddled *The Truth of Mesmeric Influence* in my clothes, but even so, I flinched as the bag took a knock on the buckboard's floor.

In the wagon, we rattled past houses and people crammed together tight as kernels on an ear of corn. A nightmare of horse dung, smoke, and people-stink swam around us. A knot of colored boys brawled on a corner, oblivious to the swarming life around them. A water tower stood in the middle of the street, and when I craned my neck get a better look, a top-hatted fellow on a jittery horse nearly sideswiped us. The cart driver swore and spat before he hollered back to my mother and me, "Sorry, Misses." He didn't bother to hold his tongue when a goat blocked our path, or at the sorry clutch of beggars outside a cigar store.

By the time the driver dumped us and our bags outside our hotel, nausea and a blinding headache had curled me into Momma's lap, praying I wouldn't spew into the wagon or on the street. Momma held me close, her gloveless, cool hand across my eyes, and walked me carefully into the hotel. I collapsed into an armchair while the train ticket desk, telegraph office, a man selling newspapers and candy, and doors leading this way and that lurched in my peripheral vision. Daddy dealt with a clerk behind a desk and another fellow about the bags. Finally, we climbed a steep staircase past a busy dining room and several parlors. We ascended another stair, and Daddy led us past door after door along a carpeted hallway until he came to one door like all the others. He turned the key to the door of our room.

I had an urgent desire to scrub my hands and face and neck thoroughly once, then twice. I'd done little more than sit the entire day, but I was drained. No tests would come easily. But the minute I rested my hands along the back of a wooden chair (had Daddy asked that one be set aside for us?) my power came to me straight away.

Relief allowed me to surrender and weep.

FROM THE WINGS AT DeGive's Opera House, our umbrella stand and wooden chair looked like distant lumps. The stage was vast, and it was dark. The idea of Atlanta had thrilled Momma so much that she put aside the child-like get-up I'd suffered. In a black silk skirt that brushed the tops of my boots and matching blouse with sleeves wide at the shoulder, I looked ready for a city audience. I felt regal, every bit the match for the ornate iron columns that held up the Opera House verandas.

After the harmonica band, but before Julia Graydon's rendition of *Hamlet*, the house manager turned a key and dimmed the gas lamps, descending us into a brief midnight. The moneyed patrons had seats in private balconies, one over the other for three levels, with arched tops and artful scenes on the walls. Deep, dark galleries filled with seats stretched below. On the parquet floor in front of the stage plush seats made orderly rows. When the house manager rotated his gas key again, every seat glared under an artificial summer sun.

The stage manager pointed at us and I took Daddy's elbow. Polite applause came from above, but catcalls and whistles shrilled from the lesser seats. The walk from the wings to the center of the stage took a lifetime and went by too quickly to grasp. My silk rustled as I moved. At center stage, Daddy let my arm go. He brushed his hands against his trousers and began to speak.

"You have read about her in the *Atlanta Constitution*," he began. "Not one person can explain the Force. The greatest scientific minds of this city have seen The Magnetic Girl perform her feats. Is it science? Is it mystery? You are here tonight to see the power of electricity manifest itself through the touch of a young girl!"

His big voice sounded small in the huge theater. No scientific minds had seen me perform anything.

"Don't hesitate," he said. "Who will be the first in Atlanta to know the Force for himself?"

Slowly, a string of men gathered and moved toward the stage. Selecting from those assembling around him, Daddy tapped heads if he could get close enough, calling out "you in the felt hat," or "the gentleman with the spectacles," if he couldn't. There were so many of them. I greeted man after man with a smile, let him select a cane, instructed him how to hold the object, and gravely set my hands upon it. One after the other, I won every time. As each fellow left, he believed he'd fought a cane and lost the battle.

At the five-minute mark, a slender gentleman approached us at center stage. The fellow waiting behind him was small, too, and ancient. I gestured for the second man to come along with the first. The first man, carried away by the moment, squeaked, "Come on, my friend, it's nothing personal!" The audience roared. With no advance plan, I walked around the two men as if inspecting them. The idea came to me to instruct the smaller man to sit side-saddle across the knees of the larger. Two men in the chair was easy—there was only one pair of feet on the floor.

The fellows did as I asked, and the two men pet each other's hair and pretended to be sweethearts. The audience was in convulsions.

In position behind them, I breathed deeply and counted to myself. With my shins to the chair and my hands against the rails, I waited for the tunnel in my mind to pull me in. And then Daddy's voice swam past me, declaring that I'd lifted nearly four hundred pounds of Southern Gentlemen. Setting them down with a bang, I stepped back and began to clap, expelling the spinning feeling in my forearms and shoulders. The flustered men stood, bowed, and then applauded along with me. They returned to their seats to shouts of "hurrah" and "good going, soldier."

A man in a checkered jacket approached the stage. He didn't acknowledge Daddy or me but helped himself to a seat in my wooden chair. *Well, be that way,* I thought. *You won't be civil, so up you go without nary a word from me.* I placed my hands on the chair and instructed the man to place his feet square on the floor and his hands along the rails. Instead, he crossed his legs and leaned back.

The audience roared.

"Sir, the Force is unpredictable," I warned, without any idea what to do. "Your safety is paramount."

Daddy thundered at him.

"Sir, please seat yourself as The Magnetic Girl asks. We don't want to see you injured when the Force comes at you full strength."

The man leapt from the chair, knocking me backward.

"This is a sham!" he shouted to the audience. He shoved Daddy in the chest. "Your child is a crime against nature! No man should take instruction from a girl."

Row after row of paying customers held their breath, waiting to see what we would do. Pairs of eyes peered at me from the wings. No one moved. And then Daddy swung at the man. The fellow danced a step away from the blow, snatching up the wooden chair and brandishing it like a shield. Women in the audience screamed. Fellows rushed to join the free-for-all. I ran to Daddy's aid, but he swung his arm out like a gate, keeping me at bay. The stage manager bolted past me into the fight, grabbing the chair from the naysayer, who was shouting about charlatans and whores.

A woman called out, "Leave the girl alone." A man hollered, "God works in mysterious ways."

When Daddy yanked the chair from the stage manager's grip, I saw what would happen. I sprung forward to stop him, but he side-armed the chair across the fellow's back. The audience was on its feet, booing. Our assailant swaggered off-stage in the stage manager's clutches, his arms above his head like he'd won a prize. His checkered jacket was ripped across the shoulders. Hats, playbills, and bags of peanuts collected at my feet. These weren't my flying hickory nuts from back home. These were real, a confirmation of my failure.

Daddy grabbed my wrist and pulled me with him off-stage. Laughter and taunts trailed us as we left the spotlight. Mortified, I kept my head down. A tall man in an old-fashioned velvet cape strode past, carefully pronouncing, "Now is the winter of our discontent." Yes, it was. We would go home ruined. I wailed. Daddy dropped my wrist and stormed down a flight of stairs, leaving me behind. I wanted to smash something and feel it break, and I wanted to cling to someone who loved me. Momma hurried to me in the half-darkness, cooing my name. She'd bought herself a new dress when she purchased my stage outfit. She'd looked so stylish in the green velvet at the hotel, but now she was a guest at the wrong party. She held me against her chest, emitting a blast of floral, sticky steam that left me struggling against the need to vomit.

"Lulu, that terrible man. Daddy had no idea that rabble was out there."

That didn't matter. Unable to speak, I shook my head.

"Some people just can't enjoy themselves at all," she said.

I didn't know if she meant the man on stage or me. I craved fresh air, and the sting of cold down my collar, on my face, in my hair. I bolted for the door. Behind me, Momma peeped like a bird.

I burst into the alley. Alone in the open space, I sucked icy air into my nose. Across broken crates and piles of garbage-clotted snow, two familiar shapes stood beneath the gas lamp on the Broad Street corner. The stage manager was counting out money to the fellow in the checkered jacket.

I jerked forward in time to miss the granite steps, spewing tea and toast onto a drift of white snow.

CHAPTER TWELVE

DADDY COLLECTED OUR PAY AFTER LISTENING TO rousing congratulations from Mr. Getty that left him shaking his head in wonder. I watched him count the dollars before he went, at the stage manager's cheerful encouragement, for a second round of handshakes. What good would it have done to speak up at that moment, forcing my awful vision of back-alley conspirators into my father's joy? He would see me as a girl who thought she knew more than her father. Daddy had never raised his fist to me—no man hits a woman, I'd heard him say—but his words could bruise hard as any touch.

When I was eight years old, he hauled me in from the yard after he'd discovered Dale locked in a wardrobe. "You put her in," Daddy said, "so you'll let her out."

When she scurried free, hiccupping with tears, the hem of her dress wet and reeking, he shut me in the same dark space where I'd imprisoned my cousin. After the key clicked twice and he shook the handle once to test that it was fastened, he spoke through the key-hole. Now you'll know what suffering feels like, Missy.

Aunt Beth gave me the evil eye the whole rest of their visit. I didn't think I deserved it. I was the only person who couldn't excuse Dale's saying Leo might be better eating in the barn since he chewed like an animal.

In the hotel that night, as if I were again confessing a terrible act, I told Daddy what I'd seen outside DeGive's. The stage manager paid the heckler in the alley and they had laughed together before the heckler, hunched in his torn jacket against the snow, had walked off into the night.

Daddy threw back his head and howled with delight as if I'd told a wonderful joke.

"I'll be damned," he said, full of admiration. "You can't fault a fellow for making hay. We have a good show, but Getty went and figured he'd play it safe and go one over us. No wonder he was so happy."

How any heckler made our show better was beyond me and I said so. Momma turned down my blankets and plumped the pillow, her signal for me to leave well enough alone. Fatigue rose in me like water, but I kept my eyes on Daddy.

"How does a stranger provoking us make it better?" I asked. "All he did was start a fight and spoil the test."

"That's where you're wrong, Missy," Daddy said. "You got to credit that fellow. Getty had him do right by us, and damned if I didn't fall for it. Audiences are going to hear about that ruckus and want to come see us next time and the time after that. We're not getting a heckler unless I say so—I'll make sure a stage manager knows we're onto that trick—but in the end, it's Getty giving out that pocket money, not us."

Needle, finger, silver, pink, filled my vision. Hard metal, yielding flesh, watching for the metal to break the skin. Pushing, watching, I could feel my heart beating and hear my breathing as if someone else's mouth were against my ear. Sleep sidled in next to me, and I yielded to the hotel's delicious feather bed.

THE LETTER CAME FROM Max Berlin, Esq., "Southeastern Regional Scout for an Array of Theatrical Concerns" in Chattanooga, Birmingham, Savannah, Charleston, Baltimore, and New York. He had read about The Magnetic Girl and wrote that he could promise engagements in the finest opera houses in those cities and more. The letter had been at the post office for weeks when Daddy collected it. Something about him was lying low.

But here, on thick paper the color of curdled cream, with Mr. Berlin's name engraved across the top, was a proposal that The Magnetic Girl appear on stages in more than five states. He would pay six hundred dollars for each performance. When Daddy read that figure aloud, my knees buckled. The name of the acts Mr. Berlin managed danced across the page: Bill Willis and the Dollar Brights, Freda Robert, and Charles la Pay's French equestrian act. I'd never heard of any of them. They were all wonderful.

I am prepared to begin with a two-night engagement in Savannah commencing January 25, he wrote.

We would pay for the train tickets and lodging, but six hundred dollars for every performance would make that insignificant. We would be, *on tour in his employ*, he wrote, until the end of April.

If we said yes, and of course we would say yes, life would change forever. The escape I'd searched for arrived in a letter from an unknown entity, not in a book on my father's shelves. But I'd made this with my own two hands nonetheless. Momma was right: I was a gift to my family. Daddy left for town to send two telegraphs: one to Mr. Berlin, and another to Mr. Getty. Hello and goodbye.

By the second week of January, every curtain in the house was drawn shut and tied together at the hem. Every piece of furniture was covered in sheets. The carpets were rolled up and stood on end in the corners of the parlor. Mr. and Mrs. Hartnett took the live-stock and the dog to their place.

Mrs. Wallace from church would care for Leo. Her sons were grown, and she missed them so much, Momma said. Mrs. Wallace had the time for Leo. The "time" for Leo, as if he were a creature who required the patience of a saint or the lonely hours of an elderly woman. Leo would have to do without. I was the one to speak for him, to do for him. I was the one who'd stolen those abilities from him.

Four months was a canyon too deep and wide to see across. By the time I got home, Leo could forget that I understood his talk and knew how to cut his food just right. His games would have dissolved into memories: me pretending to saddle the dog before trying to ride him as if he were a pony so Leo would laugh, Leo squealing with terror and delight when I extracted his wooden soldier from my mouth to say that the toy man had been mining for gold. The dog shook off being ridden, the toy soldier fell apart. Mrs. Wolf had written of *months unto years* of treatments. An ill person might meet two or three Mesmerists before finding the one with whom they felt that *fierce bond of sympathy*. Leo and I had that bond. I was the only Mesmerist for him.

That much money was a strong argument against sentimentality. People believed that I could conduct electricity with my fingers, that magnetism in my blood mirrored the copper and iron that had risen into me from the earth below my home. A lightning storm had changed me, and before any of us could do a thing about it, I could give life to a cane, or make a fellow and a chair rise from the floor. If I believed this, too, the idea would tick and tap into my mind and the minds of my volunteers as if I were sending a telegraph.

My hands would make a boy's speech clear and his legs strong.

My power would quell the high-pitched whine that rose when I stood too near Momma, the sound that wasn't a sound, a noise I felt but didn't hear. When I cured Leo, that whine between Momma and me would fade into a quiet place where we could talk and listen. When money became plentiful as stones, Daddy would smile in a way I couldn't fully remember, his hands under my arms as he swung me just above the ground like a low-flying kite, the two of us laughing. In my mind's eye, he swung me above the rutted street in front of the hardware store, wagons and buggies sparkling by.

In this way, what was wrong would become right.

"I will write you from every city," I told Leo as I washed his face on Sunday morning. "I can buy pretty postcards and send gifts from places we can't even imagine."

I cannot write you back.

"I will tell you everything that I am practicing so I can make you well," I told him on Monday as I ran the wet clothes through a wringer.

You cannot make me well. Leo smoothed the folded dry clothes, appreciating their sweet smell.

"Oh, but I can," I told him.

I'd become a real go-ahead type, creating this luxury of time. Sitting on trains with nothing to do but read was an inconceivable extravagance, and I'd keep *The Truth of Mesmeric Influence* close at hand. Mrs. Wolf would accompany me everywhere, one sharp, clean sewing needle tucked into the spine.

On a cold morning, Daddy and Leo drove to Mrs. Wallace's house, halfway to Cedartown. From the doorway, I watched my brother lean the slightest bit away, as if he were grown and all this arranging and rearranging was merely a household concern from which he could distance himself. I watched that spot in the road until I was sure that the distant bursts of sound I heard were crows, and not my brother's voice.

Dear Leo:

You could line up the people in train stations in Cedartown, Atlanta, and Savannah from the Post Office to the warehouses in Cedartown and you'd not have room to sit.
We have been on one train and another for two days, and I like to look out the windows. I hate to say so, but one town looks a lot like another when you go that fast. I do like watching the fields and trees rush by and picturing them as the ones on the wheels.
Be good to Mrs. Wallace. Can you show her how to play "owl?"

Love, your sister Lulu

CHAPTER THIRTEEN

From Savannah to Saratoga, 1884

THE MORNING AFTER MY SHOW IN SAVANNAH, A negro sweeping the steps of the tobacco shop on the corner outside the Pulaski House Hotel stared at my feet. When I crossed to Bull Street, the three Negro men attending the horses at the livery stable stared, too. Every block I walked, Negroes eyed my feet.

I sat on a bench to examine my boot soles for a stray piece of paper or worse. Nothing. Leaving Warren Square, I held my skirt down and wished I could crouch while I walked.

Seagulls dipped overhead, and the sunlight sparkled on the water. Moss hung in witchy curls from the oak trees, begging me to pull at them the same as I tugged at my hair. The gray-green strands were dry and springy to the touch. I put one against my lips. The salty tang made my mouth water. Two women strolled past me, deep in conversation. They nodded politely in my direction. I spit the moss out and hid the strings in my palm before I nodded in return.

At dinner in the hotel, a Negro waiter cleared our plates. He had to know the men at the stable and the ones on the corner. I interrogated him.

"Why do those men outside watch my feet when I walk?"

Momma's teacup met her saucer with a loud clang.

The waiter looked quickly to see that nothing was broken and resumed brushing crumbs from the tablecloth with a whisk.

"Yes, ma'am," he said. "People say sparks fly out of your feet when you set them down, so likely the men were looking to catch it for themselves."

"Can you see it?" I asked, tucking my feet under my chair.

"No, ma'am," the waiter said, looking straight at me. "There's carpet between your feet and the ground."

People say. Negroes and certainly others were talking about me. If they were watching me so closely in my daily events, then every one of them believed. *The Mesmerist's highest duty is the transference of belief,* Mrs. Wolf had written. And look what I had done.

No dinner had ever tasted better.

In Birmingham, three acts were ahead of me on the bill. From the wings, I watched a boy switch the easel-card from HUEY AND MABEL FENTON IN "THE VILLAGE DOCTOR" to SCHWARTZ & MENDEL, HEBREW COMEDIANS. The acrobat couple skipped offstage, making a bridge of their hands above my head as they passed me at the curtain.

The piano player struck up a vivacious, slightly Oriental number, and two men with false beards and fake noses stumbled center stage. They insulted each other in accents that ended every sentence with a question. Soon enough, they began shoving each other in a mock fight. The audience shouted and booed, but I laughed when an egg pelted either Schwartz or Mendel's back and broke in a teardrop of slime. When a barrage of rotten vegetables came at them, I wanted to turn the projectiles back to their foe in the audience. Mendel and Schwartz shielded their faces with their caps and made for the wings.

No one wiped up the garbage left in their wake. The boy went out again to change the placard to the one Mr. Berlin had sent with us. On it, the words LULU HURST, THE MAGNETIC GIRL, streamed from jagged lightning bolts emanating from a woman's skirt. She juggled nine men over her head in an arc. I never lifted a fellow with my bare hands, and I certainly never juggled one. When Daddy and I waited for Mr. Braunstein back in Cedartown, posters like this were the stuff of dreams. Did those artists doubt the image on their posters the way I did now? This sketch was any woman, her skirt bigger than mine, her hair in an outdated style. This was me, the girl with sparks flickering from her boot soles.

The pianist started a polka, and I became a lightning bolt ready to strike. Too many empty seats in the back at this show meant that anyone who wanted to get up in front had already said a few "Excuse me's," and "Sorry's," to slide past knees and over feet.

"Entice a man for silver and steal his strength," came from somewhere in the back. A woman stood. I could see her shape in the last row. As she shouted "Sinner," her neighbors shouted back at her, calling "Go away" and "Run home to your husband."

Daddy strode across the broken eggs and browning lettuce. At center stage, he held his arm out to me. I measured each step as I went to meet him, although I wanted to gallop. As I walked, I smiled and waved into the darkness beyond the footlights. Mesmerism was not anathema to God. Mrs. Wolf didn't need to remind me that God made all of us, and the iron and copper in a magnet, too. Every one of my tests meant perfecting my ability to heal my brother, and that was no sin.

Skidding on the garbage-slick boards, I turned the blunder into a curtsy. The audience stamped their feet and chanted "Magnetic Girl."

My steps onto the stage became a kind of dance toward the wooden kitchen chair and the urn filled with umbrellas and canes. As Daddy chose volunteers, I made a show of arranging the chair in profile to the audience. Clamoring men eddied into the aisle, and Daddy pointed at one after the other like Michelangelo's painting of the hand of God.

The chanting continued, peppered with catcalls and shouts. *Calm is the method of exchange,* wrote Mrs. Wolf.

The first fellow took the stage but hesitated when he faced me.

"It's just a routine accessory, bought right here in town," I said, offering him the cane.

He blushed, but he took the cane. I figured he wanted to check for buckshot secreted in the handle or the foot to shift the balance around. An illusionist had used that trick in Savannah. There was no charade in my material: a cane was a cane, a chair a chair. I instructed the fellow on the grasp, and then I gazed into his eyes, captivating him. He was Mr. Campbell, Sarah Hines, a woodland animal. His eyelids drooped, and his lips pursed. As he pressed downward on the wood, I pressed forward and up. The seconds passed.

"Our new friend can't beat The Magnetic Girl's force," Daddy called out, encouraging the audience to cheer louder. I could hear them, far outside my tunnel.

"The electrical, magnetic force emanates naturally from her hands. When will he succumb?" Daddy was underwater.

The cane dug into my palms, the fellow's unconscious signal that he was about to let go. A man never knew that about himself. Increased pressure was his natural effort before his muscles gave out. Relief made me giggle, and with a grunt, the man stumbled as the cane jumped from our four hands. The audience saw me catch it easily before it hit the ground, but it never left my hand. The theater shook with applause. Daddy straightened the red-faced, sweating man's collar while I made a flourish of placing the cane back into the urn. My hands burned.

As Daddy talked and a fellow prepared himself to best me, I shifted my weight just the slightest. A regular person, if he noticed it, might chalk the movement up to nerves, but inside the privacy of my skirt, my center of gravity changed as I slid one foot ahead of the other. The epic battle of perspiring man and giggling girl in the gaslights transfixed the audience, until, like a jet of steam, the cane popped up, the man stumbled, and I helped my father steady him as if he had aged a hundred years.

Dear Leo.

When you are grown, you will take a train wherever you like. Think of the whistle that we hear at home when the train comes into Cedartown. Now, imagine the sound of that whistle close above your head and around your whole body while you fly forward inside a snug and fancy parlor with strangers sitting in rows behind you. Outside your window, trees and farms and warehouses go past faster than you can dream of, so fast you could hurt your neck and make yourself dizzy trying to keep up with them. The train rocks like a baby's cradle, and so you fall asleep, even though you don't want to miss a thing. When you wake up, you're in Birmingham, Alabama, or Charleston, South Carolina. When you're grown, you will give coins to the man who fetches your valise while you walk down the metal steps to the train platform.

Love, your sister Lulu

IN NEW ORLEANS, MOMMA bought the sheet music for a song called "Tarantelle" by a composer with a French name. We asked the pianist at the Varieties Theater to play the music through so we could hear it, and we all agreed Momma's choice was better than fine. I'd have my own music now, fast as a gallop and mysterious-sounding, too, a song that would excite every audience. Daddy sent Momma to the music store for several copies in case we lost the one booklet.

Backstage, I wasn't a girl with hovering parents. I was a performer, the same as Miss Marie or Fyodor Dubrovsky. The stage was called the "boards." A disinterested crowd was "cold." I polished these words like stones, collected them like treasures.

When Aerialist Angela Feathers fed her trained cats on butcher's scraps, I pet their knobby backs while they wound around my feet, growling at each other to show off for me, but purring to their food. A juggler in tights winked at me. I couldn't help but blush, but I looked at his revealing tights. In the dressing room, I dipped my fingers into someone's open pot of rouge and patted what I'd heard girls call the "apples" of my cheeks. The mirror made clear that while my hands could grip a chair or a cane hard enough to fool an audience, Momma was right about me not having a delicate touch. I looked scalded. Scrubbing the red away, I vowed to observe the other performers' face routines at the mirror.

We three never ate supper with other artists on a bill. Daddy's rule. Momma followed his orders, although I saw her look longingly into the slender windows of Commander's Palace and the little shops. We ate in the hotel. A hotel was as good as our home, Daddy said, private and peaceful. After the vivid noise of any opera house in full swing, the silence in our room was dense and woolly as a tomb.

"You're too good for those people," Momma said, passing the bread basket.

"They're a bad influence," Daddy added, buttering his bread. I wondered if he'd seen me looking twice at the actor's tights.

To change the subject, I told a story I'd heard about a strongman named Bruno who was all washed up because of his brush with John Law. I loved "all washed up," same as I loved how picture-perfect it was to call a cowboy actor a "roper."

Before I could make clear that I hadn't heard what the strongman had gotten into with Mr. Law, Daddy slammed his fist into the table. I jumped, splattering my soup on my sleeve. While I wiped up the mess, Momma said, "I told you so," to my father. I looked up from my spilled bowl. My parents sat rigid.

"I will not hear that language from you," Daddy said, angry enough to spit.

"Don't listen to any talk about a Mr. John Law," Momma said, trying to get in front of Daddy's agitation. Daddy patted her shoulder.

"Your momma's right," he said, handing me a clean napkin. "No one named John Law needs to be a part of our day."

"I was presenting a cautionary tale," I said, hating how the words came out in a mumble.

"We want you to be a young woman to be proud of. The more

you associate with these types"—Momma gestured absently at the window, as if the types were out there in the streets, surging against the hotel's walls—"and disregard your responsibility to the family, the more you'll be like summer meat."

I shrugged, uncomprehending. Momma sighed.

"In hot weather, you can try to keep meat cool with straw and ice. You can cook it or salt it or pickle it, but once good meat starts to turn, there's no stopping it."

"Momma, I'm not meat," I said.

Daddy had resumed eating, pushing his beef aside in favor of his rice.

"I taught you because you have talent," he said, picking a string of celery from his teeth. "Your talent is God-given and real, unlike that of people who populate the cracks and crevices of the theater world."

Dale's crack in the earth opened then. My parents didn't see it. The deuce spots and the patter-acts were more like me than any Ada Shoals, or Colonel Furman, or even Mr. Braunstein and his little opera house in Cedartown. If I *was* meat, raised and slaughtered to keep a family alive, what would it matter if I spoke up?

"You read to us once about that lady in Ohio—" I said.

"—who started a fire with her fingertips," Daddy answered, bored. "I read that to you because I wanted you to see how this kind of thing, done poorly, can be taken as a joke. Consider *her* your cautionary tale."

I looked at my meal. Mrs. Wolf wrote, *In a skeptic's secret heart he hides his ardent craving for the Mesmerist's grace.*

"Yes, sir," I said.

I had landed on one side of an invisible chasm, my parents on the other.

Dear Leo:

I imagine you want to know how I keep up my practicing. Before every show, I do an exercise Momma thought up to make my hands flexible. I run my fingertips in the air like practicing piano scales.

I can't eat but tea and toast before we "go on" to keep my figure and because Momma fears that too much food will make me sluggish. Too little food makes me peckish, but I feel okay because there is so much to see. Leo, I wish you were here with us. You know I tried to take your side, but Momma and Daddy would have none of it. All the men who come to our tests say they are magnificent. One fellow called them "peculiarly affecting."

Love, your sister Lulu

MOMMA BEGAN LETTING ME change into my stage outfit and do my warm ups on my own. Daddy went into town before a show. Momma went to window shop or gab in the hotel restaurant.

"A person never knows who I can interest in coming to a matinée," she'd say before swanning off. She always came back to the dressing room an uncanny few minutes before Daddy.

I took my clothing from the trunk: black silk skirt, black top with the buttons down the back re sewn to give me a little more room to move. Fashion dictated big puffs of fabric at the shoulders, a lucky turn of fate that hid my muscles. If no one was around, I'd read my way through *The Truth of Mesmeric Influence*. I'd finished it in one dressing room and started it again in another. While I read, I soaked one hand, then the other, in a bowl of milk to keep my skin soft and white. While I read, I listened to whatever fat was getting chewed by the other artists in the dressing room. More words to collect and love; chalk-talk. In one. Olio.

Leaving a stage drained me. I was weak as a kitten after our fifteen minutes. Stairs from the wings to the dressing room swayed like a rope bridge. Clutching the banister with both hands, I made my way into the incline. With each step, I saw Leo's hands pressed to a wall. When tears made me sightless, I traveled by touch.

In Louisville, a pretty woman in a corset and stockings ran a lit candle quickly along the end of a hank of her hair. People walked around backstage in all states of dress, but Momma wouldn't have stood for me being slovenly or singeing my bangs. I told the lady good evening while I looked for a place to hang up the sheet I dressed behind.

"What's your act?" she asked, turning to take me in.

Daddy had drilled the word "tests" into me so thoroughly that she caught me up short. Seconds passed.

"Do you speak?" she asked. She was laughing now.

"Of course I speak," I told her. Nobody laughed at me and got away with it.

"Oooh," she said. "Listen to you. Straight up from where? The hills? The Con-Fed-Racy?"

"I'm The Magnetic Girl," I said, extending my hand, dignified. "Pleased to meet you."

"Dorcas Edwards," she said. "My better half is coming later. We're a double act. You know, a Mister and Missus with jokes? When we get going we wake snakes."

I hadn't read the poster. Guilty, I shook my head.

"I'm sorry. My father and I, we magnetize—*I* magnetize—fellows and perform scientific tests on them when they're captivated by my power."

Dorcas Edwards didn't seem impressed. She arranged her bosoms inside her corset, pushing them up like so much rising dough. That looked like a thing to try, but she had more to work with.

"You pick them in advance, the marks?" Dorcas Edwards had moved on to her chin, from which she plucked a stray dark hair.

"We never did that," I lied, taken aback that she seemed to know we'd done it once. Twice, counting the parlor. "If you mean the fellows who come to the stage."

"Oh, honey, we call them 'marks.'" Dorcas Edwards turned from the mirror. "Like a target. You know, hit your mark?"

The word was the answer to a question I didn't know I'd asked. Sarah had been a target, and Mr. Campbell. The fox, too. Every fellow who came to the stage was my target. My mark.

"A mark," I said, the word perfect to say. I dug my finger into the pot of rouge she held out to me. Watching the mirror, I rubbed careful circles onto my cheeks.

"Yep," she said. "Now you sound like you've being doing this your whole life."

"Doing what?" The color was too bright. I wiped my finger on the table. "Hornswoggling!" Dorcas squeaked. She squeezed my face between her hands and nodded my head for me. My brains sloshed, and I pulled away from her grip. The look on my face must have been awful because her glee turned sour.

"What," she said. "You think you're too good? You and your father out there picking fellows and you acting like you're doing science on them or whatever all you're doing with that furniture?"

"We're not lying," I said, shaking my head. "I really can lift them."

"Maybe yes, maybe no," she said, getting back to work on her hair. "You can't take *me* for a mark, though. If you're backstage like you are now, you've got a game going."

Dear Leo:

We have our own sheet music for the pianist to play at every show. The sensation is one of emerging from a living music box. I have seen more people than I thought possible on this earth, and while such a great number of faces could make a person feel insignificant, I'm delighted to be among them. On the stage, I'm above the crowd.

Please let everyone know that I say hello. As for you, look in the mirror and give yourself a kiss from me.

Love, your sister, Lulu

CHAPTER
FOURTEEN

SALLY SNACKED FROM THE HORN-OF-PLENTY GIFT BASKET
the theater manager had sent to their hotel.

"You could round up fellows from the taverns," she said, extracting a chocolate from decimated straw. "They probably read the paper. Maybe they just haven't got around to buying a ticket yet."

Will had seen more than few empty seats in the last few towns, and he hadn't been winning at dice like he'd expected. A good game could double what Lulu brought in of a night, but the touch he'd had back home had gone missing. She earned, and he spent. Not every dollar—he had never been careless—but his errands to the telegraph office were becoming an exercise in self-mockery. His mother had gambled with hearts. He merely speculated with money.

He reached across his wife to take the last item from the basket. An apple. Sally moved toward him for an embrace. Polishing the apple against the back of her dress as he held her, he watched the morning's drizzle. Poor weather was a good sign. Any fellow up in a logging camp would be more than happy to come into town, take in a show. Too many empty seats last night and two more shows before The Magnetic Girl left this tired bug hill.

Deciding against an umbrella—not rough-and-tumble enough—Will rented a horse and cart from the livery. He had a few hours' ride ahead before he could talk up the camp manager and find some fellows ready to cut loose. He could carry them back in the cart as a courtesy. How they'd get back wasn't his problem. The risk perked him up. Sally could have her hotel and her basket of treats, and he'd take the thrill of speculation every time. With the muddy road falling behind him, and the damp green mountains ahead, Will whistled a snatch of opera he'd heard somewhere a long time before.

He drove into camp around one o'clock and tied the horse to the post outside a shack. A hand-painted sign reading *Mabry Co., Logging* dripped rainwater onto a single slick, mossy step. A few barracks clung weakly to the picked-over ridge. The place was a sea of mud in the bright scent of freshly cut timber. He knocked on the shack's door. The sign overhead and a battered spittoon were the only signs that the structure was the office.

"In!" shouted a reedy voice from inside. Will let himself in. A fellow who appeared no older than his early twenties sat at a desk strewn with maps. A stove burned in the corner, but the heat didn't dissipate the dampness.

"They're all pulling logs today," the desk fellow announced. He was defensive. "Got every chain out, every mule and every man out but three in sick bay. If you need to ask Doc, go and check."

Will looked back over his shoulder. Perhaps someone had come in after him, but there were only the two of them in the office.

"You're mistaking me, I believe."

Startled, the young man stood. He was knobby as a baby bird, and his Adam's apple protruded like a stone.

"You're not a Mabry man? Damn. I'd heard in town they'd be sending an inspector out. I've been working my fellows like one-legged men in an ass kicker's contest, expecting someone to come bawl me out."

"Then allow me to cheer your day, seeing as how I'm not the dark cloud you expected." Will extended his hand. What with the ripe blemishes on the fellow's face and the uneven whiskers, he made the boy closer to eighteen.

"I'm Colonel William Hurst, and I'm here to invite you and your men to a show. Seems like since your Mabry fellow didn't make himself known—"Will raised an eyebrow.

"Arden Mabry," the boy answered. "Pleased to make your acquaintance."

The kid was an heir. Will fanned a dozen programs advertising The Magnetic Girl across Arden's desk. Pick a card, any card.

"You've heard about The Magnetic Girl, no doubt," Will began. Before Arden could respond, he put a program in the boy's hand. "Feats of strength and mysterious power you'd not believe if you hadn't read the papers or heard the talk. This young lady will lift a grown man, bigger'n you, pardon me, with the tips of two fingers, and set him down again like a feather."

Will watched Arden study Lulu's image on the page; a curvaceous girl his age or thereabouts, properly dressed and demure, but her smile—Will knew how the boy would read it. Above her head a U-shaped magnet floated like a halo, emitting zigzags of what was intended to represent electric current.

"Girl looks regular to me," Arden said, without tearing himself away from her picture.

"She's looking for new fellows to come to the theater tonight, ones who don't mind her lifting them in the air, or her power to invest their daily tools—by this I mean their walking canes and umbrellas—with her splendid power. Your night's tonight, Mr. Mabry. I can bring you to town easy if we leave out now, but you'll be on your own getting back. Got any fellows here honorable enough to join you? Your boss ain't coming up tonight in this weather, that's clear enough." Will pointed to the steady rain outside.

Arden jutted his chin toward the window.

"If I leave, someone's still got to stay here."

The kid was dedicated. Will had to give him that. And scared of his family. All the more fun to turn.

"Tell me this," he asked. "Who on your crew has a girl back home and misses her? Who's in the infirmary and might need a little incentive to get back on his feet?"

Arden said nothing. Will tried again. "Who needs to owe you?"

All the boy needed was that one push. Telling Will to "wait here," he jammed on a wide brimmed hat and walked out into the rain. Will waited until the boy was out of sight before he eased behind the desk. The top drawer held three folders. Will flipped through them, one eye on the door. Fussy records of payroll and work hours, nothing of value to him. The center drawer held a pile of railroad timetables, a pouch of tobacco, and a Meerschaum pipe with no tooth marks on the stem. He bypassed the pipe: the kid used it as a prop, and he'd check for it the first minute he got. Farther back in the recesses of the drawer Will found what he was looking for. An inch-thick stack of money. Without counting it, he slid the money into his boot. Will was seated and reading Arden's newspaper by the time he heard footsteps splatting in the mud.

Arden came in followed by two men: one brawny and red-faced, the other thinner and a head taller. Will stood to greet them and saw instantly that the brawny man's right hand was a rag-wrapped stump. Will shook the fellow's left hand instead.

"I'm a veteran. Nothing that befalls a man turns my stomach," he offered, exhaling to block the foul odor of necrotic flesh.

"This is Simon, and over here is Emil," Arden said.

Emil hacked up what sounded like gravel and leaned out the door to hawk into the spittoon. Returning to an upright position, he wheezed, "Pleased to meet you."

"Mabry here's giving us a night on the town to get our blood boiling." Simon extended his stump. "You think I can saw one-handed?" He guffawed, signaling that he'd made a joke.

Will made a show of checking his pocket watch, although he had been there less than an hour. "Show's at seven, men. We'll want to be on our way. Hate for you to miss it."

Arden banked the stove and took his coat from a peg, stopping to slide open his desk drawer. He took his Meerschaum pipe and pocketed the key.

The four men drove out of camp in Will's rented cart, rain pelting like stones.

"Witness the Force of Will, Momma," Will said under his breath. Three easy marks and a pinch of dollars beside. Too bad she couldn't see it. Easy as pie.

"What's that about pie?" Arden called over the wheels' rattle. "I could use some homemade pie. Hadn't had any of that in far too long."

Will smiled paternally at the boy. "Did I say pie?"

"Just that one word. Pie."

Arden looked at him hopefully. Home cooking meant more to this boy than a shake-leg show or Lulu's hands, but he was good for three tickets and a turn on the stage.

"You're wondering what I'm doing up there, I know it," Arden began. Will turned his attention to the reins.

"My father took me out of Princeton. 'Get your hands dirty,' he told me."

Arden spit, the glob missing the road and landing white and foamy on his sleeve. "So here I am, six months on a sorry excuse for a logging outfit that he's running into the ground. He's Mabry, I'm the same. I can read between the lines, Mr. Hurst. This one's failing, the crew is drunk half the time, the equipment's in sadder shape than the fellows, and he's hanging it on me."

"Why's that?" Will was curious.

Arden was glum. "Show me failure, teach me about money the hard way, some high-minded idea."

Simon bayed like a hound and tossed an empty bottle off the side.

Arden and Will watched the bottle roll into the brush.

"Liquor masks the smell of his arm, anyhow. He's going to lose the whole thing. I couldn't get a Doc to sew it up."

"You told me to go ask the Doc when you thought I worked for your Daddy," Will said.

"And I was praying you'd choose not to," Arden laughed.

The young man was a natural bluffer. A man had to admire that.

"You'll have a fine time tonight, son," Will promised. "The Magnetic Girl's just up your alley."

WILL SAW HIS MISTAKE when he dropped Arden at the Opera House with Simon and Emil. The two roughnecks would get along fine together: Simon was already ogling a scar-faced woman who appeared to be crossing the street to get away from him. Arden, though, was entirely out of place.

Will beckoned to him.

"You aren't of the class to spend your leisure time with these fellows."

Arden looked relieved. Will upped the ante.

"Buy the tickets, and then come on with me. I'll put you right up front. When I ask for volunteers, how about you take the challenge? I'd hate to have a new friend miss out."

Arden attempted to punch Will in the shoulder, man to man, but underestimated the height difference between wagon and street. He grazed Will's rib and excused himself to the box office.

A LITTLE AFTER SEVEN that night Will stood in the wings and watched the stage manager pinch Irish Meredith's bottom. He admired Europa's composure as she ran out onto the stage, smiling into the audience if she hadn't just slapped Pearl. The mother and daughter act didn't give him the time of day and didn't appear to remember him or Lulu from the Cedartown bill.

When Will took the stage after Europa and Pearl, he fixed his sights on Arden in the front row. The boy's eyes followed him as the crowd pounded the floor and chanted "Lulu Hurst, Lulu Hurst." Arden stomped his feet and chanted alongside them.

Lulu swept center stage in her black silk, glowing like a star. Will reached for his daughter's hand, and they bowed to the audience before separating, father and daughter, two planets in orbit. She selected from a clutch of walking canes, and Will made his call for volunteers, aiming his voice directly at the logging camp boy. In a frenzy, Arden leapt for the stage.

Will welcomed him up the steps, shaking his hand as if they had just met, turning him to face the audience, then swiveling him like a puppet to face Lulu. The boy could barely catch his breath.

"Thank you for coming on up," she said, shaking his hand just once. She pushed her Georgia accent, making "on" into "own." Good girl.

"Put your hands on the middle, right here," she said. The boy complied.

"Now I'm going to hold it like this." She placed her hands beneath the cane as if cupping water from a spring. "You're going to push *down* hard as you can." She was practically whispering, and Will thought briefly of lovers sharing pillow talk. "Soon enough, you'll feel the Magnetic Force rise up and carry you away."

She's better at this than you, Momma, thought Will. *No one's going to bring her to ruin.*

The boy couldn't look away from her.

When the floor smacked the kid hard on the knees, the cane flew into the air before it clattered to the ground behind him. Lulu never let the thing go until the mark fell. When he did, she released the cane timed to the sounds of the mark's collapse.

Will helped him up and made a show of brushing him off. Lulu led the wave of applause that surged in the audience. In the eye of that applause, the boy returned to his seat, but not before Will clutched him briefly in a fatherly hug.

WILL SAT ON A three-legged stool outside the dressing room, counting the night's take. His private allotment before he banked the money amounted to two hundred dollars. Add to that the ten dollars he'd picked up in the game at the livery before he'd set out in the morning, and things weren't looking too terrible.

Footsteps in the hallway made him look up. That owner's son from the logging camp stood there grinning at him like an idiot.

"Hello there, son," Hurst called out. He pocketed the cash.

The boy—Arden, that was it—pumped Will's hand.

" —life-changing evening," Arden was saying. The boy glowed with the fire of the converted.

Will congratulated him for taking the stage. Not an easy thing to do, be the first man in a crowd to tangle with The Magnetic Girl.

"Looks like you did pretty well," Arden said. "I saw that pile of cash you were counting."

Will narrowed his eyes at the boy. Arden held up his hands and backed away. "I'm only making an observation. This work of yours beats being holed up with the weakest of men, trying to wrest a living from a useless stretch of earth."

A person had to admire the boy's drive.

"Son," he said, "you don't know the half of it."

SPRING

CHAPTER
FIFTEEN
Knoxville, Tennessee:
March 1884

I DIDN'T MEET ANOTHER LIVE MESMERIST UNTIL WE were leaving Knoxville. On my way to breakfast on our last morning in town, I found Daddy chatting outside the hotel dining room with a knock-kneed man in a yellow cravat. I wasn't of a mind to visit with an admirer. Words were slow in my mouth, and I'd woken with a headache that banged like a dinner bell. I turned away so the fellow wouldn't see me, although not so many girls stood six feet tall in a hotel lobby in Knoxville.

Daddy saw me and called me over. Without a choice, I smiled sweetly when the fellow took my hand and gaped. Only Daddy's repeated throat clearing kept me from yanking my hand back. They were my instruments, after all, and this yokel was cramping them. After too long, the man spoke up, shifting his eyes to somewhere above my hairline. He was so nervous I expected him to faint.

"I am Randolph Luckie," he said. He talked fast, like he was trying to get the whole interaction done in one sentence.

"I'm wondering, seeing as how Miss Hurst is visiting the area, if the Power might cure my widowed sister. She suffers day and night from fierce shooting pains in her face and limbs. She don't sleep, don't eat solid food. She is beleaguered."

Spent, he backed into the wall.

Daddy stroked his beard and acted like he thought about it for a minute. He gazed over my shoulder as if my Magnetic Power might reside on the stairs. He cracked his knuckles. Even if his audience was only Mr. Luckie bumpkin in a hotel, Daddy was theatrical. If I hadn't enjoyed watching him, I would have felt badly for Mr. Luckie.

We were leaving on the noon train, Daddy said.

This was true. Our trunks were already at the station.

He was sorry, but he couldn't guarantee that the Power could cure a lady in what he regretted was surely dire distress. Daddy turned to me.

Mrs. Wolf wrote, *My heart seemed to stand still. I had ringing in my ears. My hair seemed to rise upon my scalp. The noise in my ears crackled like a mighty fire. I felt as though every muscle in my body was fixed and rigid. The roar in my ears grew louder still, and I heard, above the roar* *noises indeed sounded like artillery and musketry. Then above the din of the noise, a musical chord. I seemed to be absorbed in this chord. I knew nothing else.*

We wouldn't be on any noon train.

I could just see Mr. Luckie's sister, festering with sores and coughing up blood. Neuralgia might be only the first of a long list of ailments. Any attempt I made on Mr. Luckie's sister would require days at the very least. Mrs. Wolf said so. *A Mesmerist and a seeker of healing should repose together in knowledge and power. Weeks, perhaps a month of daily contact strengthens that bridge between the seeker and the one sought.* A Mesmerist required time with an ailing person. A newspaper had recently printed that The Magnetic Girl cured tooth-ache by laying a hand on the sufferer's jaw. That was just ink-slingers making things up. But what if proximity, more than time, would at least lighten pain?

Daddy was hoping I would give my regrets, and he'd be right about there being no guarantee of aid. And no good money would come from an audience of one. But what an opportunity this Mr. Luckie presented. Mesmerizing his poor sister in a single visit, not to tilt her in a chair or test my strength across a cane, but to truly ease her pain would allow me to improve on Mrs. Wolf's rules.

My heart raced. Afraid to seem eager, I avoided Mr. Luckie's hound dog eyes.

"Daddy, I don't know that the Power will come to this poor woman's aid, but I'm honored to try." *Honored* practically stuck to the wall from my sweetness. Mr. Luckie looked ready to weep with relief.

"There's a good girl!" Daddy said, patting my shoulder. His touch was too firm.

Mr. Luckie wrote directions to his home on the back of his calling card. When Daddy showed him out, I excused myself to the dining room, where Momma was about ready to climb the walls wondering where we'd gone to.

Momma used a piece of toast to wipe butter and soft-cooked eggs from her plate. I nibbled on a piece of bacon and flipped the lid to the metal teapot up and down. The pot would have made a good diversion for Leo. Maybe a porter could send it to him.

When Daddy came to the table, he told Momma our change of plans.

"Lulu has made a heedless decision," he said, directly to me. "But I have rectified the inconvenience. Mr. Luckie will compensate us appropriately for missing our train."

Daddy lifted an empty juice tumbler and grinned.

"A toast to The Magnetic Girl," he said.

Momma lifted her cup, and I had to raise mine.

I wouldn't try to lift this lady, in a chair or otherwise. She might slip from my hands and hit that floor with a thud like a pumpkin falling off a porch. I'd jump back, stunned, before I reached for her, turning her this way and that looking for bruises or trickles of blood. She'd scream all the while, and I'd rock her and tell her hush, baby, hush, baby, wondering if I should cover her mouth with my sleeve so Momma wouldn't come running and see how I'd broken my doll, my Leo.

Uneasy, I took more bacon from the serving dish.

"Daddy," I said, "don't make me think about money right now. Mrs. Wolf writes that a Mesmerist has to have a benevolent and tender feeling toward their wounded."

"Mrs. Wolf is not a theatrical type, is she?" Momma glared, assuming I'd been socializing.

Daddy answered, annoyed. "That's from the book Lulu stole," he said, baiting me with "stole." "I never read past the first few pages of that thing. Your Mrs. Wolf's personal feelings are pure bull crap."

Momma threw her napkin on the table and stood. Language. His swear called me up short, too.

"This lady's not going to have a cane or want me to raise her up in a chair," I pointed out. "All she wants is to feel better."

"And all I want from you," Daddy said, "is to make it so we can collect a fee before I send a wire home to the *Appeal* saying Cedartown's own Magnetic Girl has cured a lonely woman of what ailed her. And that is all you want, too."

Momma sat since neither Daddy nor I had made a move to leave the dining room.

Leo, Leo, Leo thrummed in my head. One two, one two, one two. Mrs. Wolf would say that what I intended to do with only a brief visit to this woman was sham Mesmerism. An embarrassment. The cane test, the chair test, even lifting a boiled egg—these were parlor tricks with captivation on the side. Not one of them applied to actual illness.

But *our magnetic fluids are conducted by our nerves, electrical pole to pole in our bodies.* My blood was alive with copper and iron and magnetic elements. My father said so. Mrs. Wolf said so. There was no reason that I couldn't *return a suffering entity to its inborn state of balance.*

Leo, I will get this done and we'll be gone on the train to the next city, another day closer to home. And I will have practiced my healing touch on this poor woman so that when I see you, *benevolent and tender healing* will be assured, and come as easily as lifting any fellow in a wooden chair.

On the way to Mr. Luckie's house, I imagined a theatrical performance of The Magnetic Girl's introduction to a sickly old woman.
The widow would be bedridden in a darkened room, *hostage to her
innate weakness.* Her curtains would be drawn, her illness inconspic-
uous in the dim light. A hired girl would hover and straighten the
bedclothes in a room that stank of camphor and something vaguely
rotten.

My mind wouldn't stay on the image. I had dropped the cane last
night instead of pulling it away from the first mark. That man, a boy
really, never smiled, never moved away throughout the test, but his
eyes danced the entire time as if captivation were nothing at all.

Picturing him in front of me, his eyes alight, I looked up from
counting my steps on the stone sidewalk. My parents would know
my thoughts if I weren't careful. I looked down again, determined to
shut the fellow out of my mind.

He smelled good. Soap and something I couldn't name.

My own odor released in unpleasantly warm gusts with every
step. Sour and awful, the thick smell of a closed, unventilated space. I
made my stride longer, hoping cold air would swirl upward between
my thighs. I needed to wash.

"You won't get the right kind of paramour," Dale had said. She
scorned me, but did she have a suitor? She likely had dozens, pomp-
ous and scrawny fellows who brayed like donkeys when they laughed
and kissed her cheek.

How would they kiss her cheek?

Paramours rested their arms around their sweetheart's shoulders,
leaving them there for minutes sometimes after helping the girl with
her winter coat or introducing her to his friends. I'd seen couples in
opera house lobbies and hotel restaurants. An arm around me would
be a comfort, a place to rest. No, an arm across my shoulders would
pin me in place. I rolled my shoulders to release the yoked feeling. I
dug my fingernails into my arm to let out the pressure in my chest. I
wouldn't be able to plan anything if my insides were in a knot.

I changed my focus to a genteel vision of illness from a ladies'
novel. Slivers of sunlight would pierce the room's darkness from the

gaps where the curtains didn't meet. If I held my hands over the sick woman, would she expect them to conduct heat or light? If she had a tumor, would she want it removed? Would she expect an open sore sealed? I could do none of these things. Not yet. Add together one sick woman, her fidgety brother, and me. The answer? *The phenomena are various.*

Mr. Luckie opened the door at Daddy's first knock. A scrawny child appeared behind him, sucking her thumb. Pale and in need of a wash, she stared at us so blankly I wondered if she were sleepwalking. The front hall smelled of candle wax and boiled cabbage. An ornate grandfather clock loomed from the top of the stairs.

"Colonel Hurst and oh, my, Miss Hurst, and Mrs. Hurst, we are so happy to welcome you." Mr. Luckie clapped his hands as if he were a performer summoning dancing dogs. I tried smiling at the little girl, but she hung her head.

"Mrs. Voorhees's hired girl's child," Mr. Luckie explained, bringing us into the hall. "My sister is teaching her to read."

"Who's Mrs. Voorhees?" I asked too quickly, anxious for information. All the things I couldn't ask fought for space in my thinking: what's wrong with her, is she malformed, is she contagious, will there be spit-rags or a foul bucket to avoid?

Mr. Luckie patted my arm. "My sister. I must not have explained well. Our family name is Luckie; she married a Mr. Voorhees. He passed to the Lord only a few months ago."

Mr. Luckie opened the drapes, setting dust motes whirling. Two goats with bells around their necks wandered the lawn. "She has a grown son in the maritime trade." He made a *tsk-tsk* noise and hung his head. "She went ill after Frank—that's my nephew—left."

My new arithmetic problem involved a widow, a grown son gone, and a house with the look of money in the family. Daddy had already sussed out that last part. With her husband gone, maybe she wanted me to hold a séance. I had no desire to get near that idea. *False mysteries,* Mrs. Wolf called them.

Mr. Luckie handed a lamp to the somnambulant little girl. Together, they led us up the stairs. At a closed door, he turned to us.

"You'll wait here," he said to my father. "You understand, of course. A lady's chamber?"

Daddy nodded and stepped back. Momma came forward and took my hand. We followed Mr. Luckie into the room.

Mrs. Voorhees lay on a sapphire divan. Her skin was the soft white of a gardenia, and her gray hair swept across her cheek like a dove's wing. I hadn't figured that she'd be beautiful. Smiling sleepily, she arranged her cushions and propped herself upright. She was so lovely that the state of the room came to me late. The place smelled of camphor and rot, just as I'd anticipated, but the drapes were open to a view of the shady street. My makeshift theater would not be dark. Something had to be done fast in order to make her sickroom my stage.

"Ma'am, thank you for inviting me," I said, before Mr. Luckie announced us.

Mrs. Voorhees didn't break her smile. She kept her hands folded atop her lap robe.

"I hear that you're suffering, and I've been asked by Mr. Luckie here"—I gestured, and he beamed—"to try and bring my Power to your assistance. May I rest my hands upon your face?"

Mrs. Voorhees nodded gingerly, as if her head were mounted on a wire. I could feel Mr. Luckie and Momma watching. I was alert and nervous, but when I got close, the sudden urge to curl up at her side like a sun-warmed cat overcame me. I tugged hard at my hair to snap myself out of it, and then held my fingertips to her temples.

Mrs. Voorhees's skin was creased. She'd spent some hard time in the sun without a bonnet. I heard Momma shift from foot to foot, then silence. Very quickly, the room held only Mrs. Voorhees and me. Someone began to hum a steady drone, nearly an identifiable tune but not quite. Summoning my power, I drifted my hands close and far from Mrs. Voorhees's forehead, touching the bony planes above her eyes in a rhythm of light, firm, light, firm. I moved in time to the cyclical hum, a new sensation that pleased me. This felt more true than captivating on a stage. Like the fox in the field, what was happening under my fingers right then was pure. Our *rapport*. Could she taste the salty bits of bacon in my back teeth? Could she feel the stray thread from my dress itching my back? My eyelids drooped to their halfway point and I caught Mrs. Voorhees's pale blue gaze in mine. My heart fluttered.

As I moved my hands around her head, something tugged at my wrists, holding and releasing in time to the humming sound. Mrs. Voorhees's hands lay inert in her lap.

My head swam as if I'd developed a sudden fever. Golden spots floated in the periphery of my vision. Odic orbs, Momma said that first night. My concentration wavered. The stuffy, foul air in the room didn't help.

Mrs. Voorhees's hands flew to her face. Cut loose, I rocked back on my heels, but my feet had gone numb and I fell to the floor. Mr. Luckie sprinted to his sister. Her eyes were closed, her chest rising and falling like a wounded bird's. This was a disaster. I had caused some kind of a fit. I was too afraid to get up, and too afraid to look at Momma.

After an eternity, Mrs. Voorhees spoke.

"My gracious." She said this several times, finally opening her eyes. "I feel so lightheaded!"

She fanned at her face and tried to sit, bones creaking as she moved. Relieved, I collected myself from the floor. Mrs. Voorhees took my hands with a grip too strong for a woman so sick. I tried to pull away, but she tightened her hold. Her quiet voice whispered on, and her pale blue eyes looked directly into mine.

"My brother saw your performance yesterday, and he brought me an idea. I feel so sorry for him, me lying here needing care since my husband passed. I haven't got the energy to teach little Ouida like I had been doing, and my son's gone. I told my brother 'go on, bring me The Magnetic Girl.' I certainly want to meet the young lady who's been in all the papers. Perhaps she can be my savior."

When she withdrew her hands, I tumbled through space without moving an inch. Her eyes did the real work. How had I not seen this coming, the sleepy eyes, the humming, the push and pull on my wrists? She had captivated me with an expertise that took my breath away, and she had taken her time releasing me.

At my back, Momma was moving out of the room. The show was

over as far as she knew, and she'd want to return us both to Daddy's side. Her leaving was my cue to follow, but Mrs. Voorhees clasped my hands and smiled the way Miss Marie or Angela Feathers did on stage: genuine and false all in one. This show had just begun. *Lightness as if I were sleepwalking*, Mrs. Wolf wrote of being the recipient of Mesmerism. Mesmerists and somnambules in the throes of their behaviors were no different, according to her. Ouida sleepwalked, or looked like it. When I'd intended Mrs. Voorhees to be in my thrall, I had sleepwalked, too. She was the Mesmerist, not me.

Mrs. Voorhees spoke to Momma without looking away from me. "May I have a moment alone with our young lady? I suffer greatly from female troubles, and it seems likely that she can help me in that matter."

Her daring astounded me. No woman I had ever met would say "female troubles" with a man in the room. Mr. Luckie began to make himself scarce, but Momma hesitated at the door.

"Dear Mrs. Hurst, I know you'll trust me with your wonderful daughter. She's nearly grown, and, well, you understand?"

Momma mumbled something in reply and shut the door behind her.

Mrs. Voorhees and I were alone, captivator and captivated. She inched closer to the window, patting the space she'd made beside her on the cushions. I hung back. Now that I understood I had never been in control in this room, choosing whether or not to sit was at least something.

"I don't have female troubles." Mrs. Voorhees said, no longer weak. "I'm too old. And even if I did, you won't catch them by sitting with me."

If I told her I already knew about female troubles I might sound rude, which could lead her to not pay us. I perched on the edge of the cushions. Mrs. Voorhees turned my face to hers. Her hand on my chin was warm and light.

"You're making a lot of money at this?"

I swallowed hard.

"Oh, don't fret," she said, letting go of my chin. "Your daddy will get paid for your time today. I know how hard you work, believe me."

"This isn't work. It's my gift." My voice rose, even though showing my nerves by sniping at an old woman proved how weak I was. Mrs. Voorhees took a sip from a glass on the table beside her, then held the drink out to me. The reddish-brown liquid smelled of something sharp. Mrs. Voorhees lay back on her pillows and sighed.

"You and I are the strong ones, really." Her smile bared yellowed teeth, putting me in mind of our dog, Tom Thumb.

"Why did you ask me to cure you?" I said the first bald thing that came to me.

Mrs. Voorhees struggled to sit comfortably. I helped her with her pillows and she settled again.

"You can't cure me, dear. I wanted to see if *you* knew that. But you don't. Not yet."

I wondered if my parents were listening at her door, but Mr. Luckie had to be jawing at them in the parlor. He'd want to get as far from female troubles as he could.

Mrs. Voorhees's eyes drifted shut. I'd lost my train of thought for a few seconds, and here she was fading. I nearly shook her. The pull I'd felt between my moving hands and her tranquil face had been every bit as real as the moment when water overflows a bowl.

"Have you read Mrs. Wolf?" I blurted. With her being so skilled, I needed her to agree with me about how reassuring I found the *consoling comfort for the diseased*, to imagine with me the *phosphoric radiance* illuminating a Mesmerist's surroundings.

Ouida, barefoot and dirty as she had been at the door, appeared beside the table with a brown glass bottle and a filigreed silver spoon. Ouida's eyes shone. She whispered, "Excuse me," as she approached the side table. Mrs. Voorhees shook her head. Ouida put the bottle on the table, confused. She evidently had one task, and anything other than preparing the medicine was outside her comprehension. I thought of the treatments Momma had given Leo when he was at his worst, and I shaded my eyes against the list of dark words glowering from the label. Mrs. Voorhees asked Ouida to fetch her jewelry box. In the corner of my vision, the girl drifted away.

"I told my brother to invite you here because I can't go out," Mrs. Voorhees said, eyes now hard and bright as a fox's. "I asked myself, 'how much does this child know,' and it was clear that the only way to determine that was to go eye to eye with you." She smiled an actress's smile.

"I know a lot," I said. "I read Mrs. Wolf. Before I knew about her I captivated—" I stopped. I'd given something away, but I couldn't tell what.

"So you have your own word for this thing we do," Mrs. Voorhees said. "A childish word, because you're a child."

Mrs. Voorhees might be truly ill in her mind. I should feel sorry for her. She had no family nearby. Her son was a cad who had turned his back on his widowed mother. Instead of pity, I felt dread.

"You probably started by Mesmerizing your dollies, before you knew what you were doing," she said, and I stopped myself from telling her about the morning I'd wanted to hear the sunrise. "But a doll is inanimate unless you're moving it yourself, so what good is it for practicing what we do?"

We. She said the word so casually.

I ventured again. "Do you sometimes feel that you can't breathe for all the smells and sounds, and how worn out you feel?"

Mrs. Voorhees waved as if she were shooing a fly. Even though she'd said "we," there was no one like me. The sounds and smells of daily life and the bone-shattering weariness after a test made me feeble.

"Corporeal burdens are no matter," she said after a while. "And yes I read Mrs. Wolf. Everyone on the circuit did."

"I admire Mrs. Wolf," I said. "I've read *The Truth of Mesmeric Influence* front to back."

"You thought she was writing just for you, but you and I have a lineage. Your Mrs. Wolf is part of it, certainly, and Leah, Maggie, and Catherine Fox up in New York State forty years ago. You're here in my house today because now that I know what you can and cannot do, I will not have you flouncing from stage to stage without understanding *deeply* that you are lesser than your forerunners."

"I am making lives better," I said, defending myself and my plans for Leo.

"You love your family," Mrs. Voorhees said. "I understand. You've got someone at home, I'm sure. Your parents wouldn't throw everything away on this—" she paused, reaching in the air for a missing word. "What you're doing are simply parlor tricks with the weakest hint of magnetism on the side, little girl. You're not talented enough to make me well."

"And that's what you wanted to see for yourself?" This is what rage felt like, the crawling skin, the drumbeat of blood at my eardrums. Watch me captivate you and end this moment, I thought as I lowered my eyelids. She returned my gaze twice as hard, shaming me.

"Parlor tricks like yours are an easy way to make money, if you have the skill," she said. "My husband had the skill. My little boy and I rode with him half the year to the saddest places, living in our wagon like old-time pioneers. We sold geegaws."

"What kind?" I asked. She wasn't spinning a tale to entertain me. She'd sent Ouida away for privacy.

"Imitation birds made of magnets and chicken feathers dyed yellow. We fashioned them to look like canaries. My husband, like me, and like Mrs. Wolf before us, followed the beliefs of Anton Mesmer. More than a hundred years before we did our work, Mesmer floated people in wooden tubs, studying how fluids and magnetism would render his medicine more perfect. His theory of the way celestial planets act on our physical bodies—"

Bodies. My blush went all the way to my ears until I remembered the kinds of things she'd already said.

"—they act the same as they do ocean tides." I completed her sentence, but she didn't bother to compliment me.

"He discovered animal magnetism and named it after himself, so we made *Mesmerica Canaria* and named them after him. Latin for Mesmer's Canaries. We sold those things in every little crossroads from Virginia to Georgia for several years. People lined up to buy them. Mesmer's fame grew when he convinced people he could cure them of their ills by magnetically controlling the fluids in their bodies."

Knowing I'd been right about her having done hard work in the sun felt only a little good.

"But Mesmer did cure them," I said. "Mrs. Wolf said as much, and I've studied *The Truth of Mesmeric Influence* more than a schoolbook. It matters more."

Ouida appeared at Mrs. Voorhees's table again, holding a polished wooden box heavy enough to require both hands. Her soundless comings and goings weren't as unnerving as they had been. She was a physical manifestation of her mistress's intentions, a filing drawn to a magnet.

Ouida placed the jewelry box on Mrs. Voorhees' lap. If she gave me a ring or a necklace, Daddy would be furious. Momma would want to wear the jewelry, and he would want to sell it.

"Miss Hurst." Mrs. Voorhees snapped her fingers in my face. I flinched, but she laughed. "I'm not giving you my jewelry, young lady, as much you would like me to."

I looked to Ouida, but she was impassive. Mrs. Voorhees took from the box a length of fabric and unwound it until she held an object the size of an egg. She balanced it on her palm as it could fly away.

"What we have here is the very last *Mesmerica Canaria,*" she said, proud of her handiwork.

The thing was sorrowful. Old chicken feathers stuck to the wicker sides in faded yellow patches, and inside, like a black heart, was a disc. Mrs. Voorhees shook the bird slightly, and the insides rattled and slid. She was showing off a piece of junk.

"It's a magnet from a compass," she said. "People believed." She'd read my mind, or more likely, my expression. "With the magnet inside, the little bird would cling to a cook stove or a harness-tack or something else unremarkable in a mark's daily routine."

I recoiled at "mark," and she patted my shoulder.

"This was over and done with long before your time," she said, "Although I see you're familiar with the terminology. My husband ultimately went into more legitimate businesses."

I reached out to touch her keepsake, extending my finger as if I were petting a newborn chick. Mrs. Voorhees pulled the canary away.

"My husband's name was Charles, but for a while he called himself Harmony, for a group of Mesmerists who called themselves the Harmony Society."

Mrs. Voorhees held the canary to her eye and peered at me through the gaps in the straw.

"It's said that Anton Mesmer had a pet canary that became so overcome with grief when he died that it stopped singing. Charles decided that he could sell replicas of the canary and tell folks that the principles of bodily fluids and health that Mesmer promoted would manifest for them through the bird keepsake. He didn't tell them about the bird dying."

She set the bird down. Handling the decaying toy had sapped her strength, and she sank back into her pillows. I wished I could cover my soul with a blanket.

"I envy you, Miss Hurst."

The conversation had switched so quickly I thought I'd misheard her. She was the one with the grand house, the servant, a brother who might as well have been her servant. But then again, she was bedridden, and I was strong and young. I traveled in train cars, not in a medicine-show wagon. Handling a toy bird didn't wear me out.

A feather floated from the toy canary, and I threaded it back into place, smoothing two feathers together. Mrs. Voorhees, half-asleep, let her lap robe fall to the ground.

"I envy your naïveté," she said. "You're as big and strong as a man, and yet you think like a little girl. You still believe they're lining up for you, parting with their cash for you."

That was precisely what they were doing. She hadn't seen the crowds of people at our home. She hadn't heard the way a theater's walls and floors shook when audiences shouted my name. I didn't say so, I only handed the throw to Ouida. She took it, and then spooned drops from the brown bottle into the drinking glass and lifted it to her employer's mouth.

Mrs. Voorhees pushed the glass away.

"Miss Hurst," she said.

I didn't move.

"Girl, every audience is like the next: a wall of people who radiate need. My husband opened his arms to that need, as do you. But fame is like a fire. At first, you're grateful, warm and glowing in its light, but soon enough, if you're not careful, you bear an ugly scar or worse. Think of Icarus."

Ouida spoke for the first time, addressing me. Her voice was surprisingly firm.

"You can go now."

Mrs. Voorhees pursed her lips for her medicine. I watched, frozen. When she had swallowed, she rolled her head in my direction. She was fading like water soaking into a cloth.

"You need to remember who should really be out there," she murmured. "A person who understands the responsibility in magnetism."

The skin on my back crawled. I wished for a pin or a needle to work into my flesh.

"Miss Hurst?" Mrs. Voorhees tried to rise, but Ouida's hand pressed against her shoulder, holding her down. "That bottomless need burns hot. Watch your wings."

No one was going to show me out. "Thank you," I said, to say something before I escaped the room.

Mrs. Voorhees and her words made my head want to crack open. Comparing me to Icarus blamed me for my own death if I remembered the myth correctly. We didn't peddle geegaws from a wagon, humbugging poor folks into spending their last cent for a toy. Audiences at The Magnetic Girl tests asked to be captivated, to have my hands together with theirs on a shared object so that they could permit themselves to succumb to their secret weaknesses. A toy bird was purely deceptive. The Magnetic Girl didn't need a magnet inside a chicken-feather trinket to convince a person that his fluids were in her control. The Magnetic Girl was powerful, special. A gift.

Walking back to the hotel, I worked the problem over in my mind. If Mrs. Voorhees had been such an influential conduit of magnetism, why hadn't she cured herself? If she was right about forerunners other than Mrs. Wolf, I'd never heard of them. The three women named Fox made me smile. I imagined them crouched in my field, red-tailed, black-footed, and stilled by my captivation.

Momma and Daddy walked ahead of me, arm in arm. Momma said something, and Daddy threw his head back and laughed. I dropped back a few steps. Watching them, I slid my hand between the buttons of my blouse and drew my sewing needle from the cotton lace of my chemise. Then I eased the tip across the soft flesh of my palm.

Dear Leo.

Your gift from Knoxville, Tennessee is a rowboat made from a pecan shell, small enough to float in a cup of tea. Your gift from the wild swamplands of New Orleans, Louisiana is part elephant and part Chinaman. The salesman said it was once a button from an Oriental's padded jacket, and sure enough, if you look closely, you can see the hole in the back for the thread.

Love, your sister Lulu.

CHAPTER SIXTEEN

Baltimore, Maryland:
April 1884

A REPORTER WROTE ABOUT HOW I PASSED MY HANDS over my eyes to create a trance. He'd also written that I'd lifted a table with twenty-five little children seated around it, and made a good team plow twice as fast as usual. The story made us laugh, even Momma. Lately, for fun in a test, I drew my hands slowly over my eyes. The audience in the front rows always gasped. I did it so often that Daddy finally hissed, "What on God's green earth are you doing, missy?" as he rearranged the walking sticks in their urn.

At our last show in Baltimore, the pianist rumbled through the first bars of the next performer's tune. I took my bow, Daddy bowed, and we ran together to the wings. We passed the send-off act on their way out, a group of fellows with banjos and a harp who emulated the tones of the human voice with their strings. In the backstage catacombs of debris and sawdust, Daddy paused to get a cup of water from the bucket. I kept going, untying my hair. Out of the lights, a person could act like they were alone. While I shook my hair loose, a boy I hadn't seen before came up the stairwell that linked the Opera House to a tavern.

"It's for you," he whispered, slipping an envelope into my hand.

Someone must have instructed him to whisper, because no one was in earshot. This was like playing with Leo.

"Okay," I whispered back. "Who's it from?"

The paper wasn't blue, so it wasn't a warning from the house management. "Blue material" write-ups would have gone directly to Daddy, and The Magnetic Girl wasn't salacious. I barely spoke enough that anyone beyond a mark could hear me, and my skirts stayed down.

The boy whispered again. "House manager said to give it to you and not to take no money. He gave me some instead."

I slit the envelope with my thumbnail.

"Where's my mother, do you know?"

"Yes, ma'am," the boy answered. "He gave me money to tell her that Mr. Field in the front office wanted to see her." He snorted. "Mr. Field ain't even in today."

I wish I'd thought of that, and I told him so. After a pause, the boy said, "I like your act. It's funny," before skipping downstairs to the bar. A burst of men's voices and clinking glass escaped with the opened door, leaving cigar smoke in his wake.

Daddy was nowhere to be seen, and Momma hadn't returned from her phony errand. I ducked into the ladies' toilet and locked the door. Then I read the note.

Dear Miss Hurst,

You surely do not remember me, but I cannot forget you. You have, in fact, been on my mind since those very few moments you allowed me to join you on your stage.
We held a walking stick together, and your eyes held mine. It was a certainty that you would take that object from me, for that's the goal of the performance, but I did not expect the very real struggle

*in maintaining my temporary ownership not of the object, but of
my self-assurance.*

*I am enthralled by your secrets and hope someday to meet you and
discuss our shared interests. If that becomes a possibility, I hope you
will write me care of the Mabry Lumber Concern, Washington,
D.C.*

*I hope, too, that this correspondence as well as any future exchanges
remain our own, rather than including your father and mother,
for I am sure that you travel in their loving care.*

*My very best wishes,
Arden Mabry*

I read the letter twice. He'd been thinking of me. I'd been thinking
of him, and of course he had a name. I smoothed the paper, wrin-
kled from the boy's poor treatment, and folded it carefully back into
the envelope. We would be in Washington soon enough, although
I wished we would be there tomorrow. I would write to Mr. Mabry
and tell him, *yes, let's please meet.* Writing I would be delighted to
make your acquaintance would mask my excitement, make me a girl
who responded to an admirer with aplomb. Corresponding with an
individual who had attended a performance was certainly an artist's
responsibility. Mrs. Wolf had gone beyond letters and written an
entire book for her followers.

I tucked the envelope into my blouse. No one but me would
know about it. My parents and I were, after all, on opposite sides of
a chasm, and Mr. Mabry had sent his words directly to me.

Not until later did I realize I'd placed the paper against my heart.

WE WERE EARNING MORE money than I could get my mind
around. I lay awake at night figuring calculations in my head. With
bricks of money I built a wall. In a hayloft of money Leo had strong
arms. He chopped with a hoe at the stacks of paper and piles of
coins. Three nights in a city with a mid-sized theater brought in as

much as twelve hundred dollars after Mr. Berlin's percentage and the cost of hotels and trains were deducted. I was easily making enough to care for Leo the rest of his life, although of course he wouldn't need it.

Money never kept still. Those coins rolling on the floor in the boarding house in Rome, Georgia were no longer objects to hold in my hands. Electricity moved numbers from one place to the next in telegraph messages. When we finally got home, numbers would be tangible once again, stacked and rolled for us in a bank office just a few strides from the newspaper where we'd written out that first advertisement. I could hold time still for longer periods now, and soon, I would be able to hold money in my hand as well.

Daddy paid buggy drivers with a coin. Coins sang from his pocket, their high voices shrilling metal to metal. He signed for hotel rooms, writing his name for desk clerks and paying with paper money when we left. He gave me no money of my own, and I had no real need for it other than to *have* money and feel it in my hands—the hands that did the work, after all. I wanted to touch the solid weight of our reward.

On an afternoon without a matinée, I helped myself to a newspaper. Swells never failed to leave their papers by their armchairs in hotel lobbies when they left. We saved on expenses by taking them for ourselves. We wiped tobacco from corners and read through grease stains. No need, Daddy said, to be profligate.

The advertisement for Richman's Grand Depot showed "one hundred different styles of bicycle skirts for ladies, in a department for 'dresses, Paris-made.'" With so much money waiting in the bank at home, I should have the clout to choose a new dress and a hat for myself. My black dress stage outfit was like mourning garb. A young lady with the spark and pull of a magnet should wear colors.

The top left corner of the page confirmed my idea.

This store is Equipped with Edison Electric Light.

When I'd told Dale I'd never seen an electric light, I was telling the truth.

The use of Electricity for Lighting is in NO WAY harmful to your health, the advertisement read. *We sell Electric Corsets,* shimmied across the page in smaller letters. *Curative and revitalizing power for frailty peculiar to ladies. Men's electric boot insoles!*

I needed to see electricity. I needed that as much as air to breathe and food to eat.

"Daddy," I said, showing him the newspaper. "Electric lights."

He looked up from his notebook.

"Pardon?"

A version of me who had never crept into his study looking for books about travel and finding *The Truth of Mesmeric Influence* instead would have put the paper away and said never mind. But the me I was now had left that place. I *was* electricity.

"They have electric lights, Daddy. We have to go see them right now. I was going to show Momma that they have bicycle skirts from Paris—" I looked at Momma, enlisting her allegiance, "—and I saw this."

"Give me that," Momma said, reaching for the paper.

"Dresses from Paris," I said, frantic. I tugged at my hair until Momma reached out a hand to still me. My mind was halfway to Richman's.

Daddy read the advertisement over Momma's shoulder.

"They're hawking a piece of ladies' clothing to cure backache and rheumatism," he commented.

"Men, too," I said. "Inside their shoes." Anything so he wouldn't say "corset." Mrs. Voorhees's comments about female complaints had unnerved me enough for a lifetime.

"Thank you for bringing this to my attention, Lulu," Daddy said.

"Three dollars for a garment," Momma said. "People won't go for something that costly."

RICHMAN'S WAS BETTER THAN the store I dreamed of back in Cedartown, lulling myself to sleep inventing the freedom to buy dresses and hats to match my jewelry. Even with daylight flooding the store's tall windows, electric lights blazed from the ceiling, hanging in green metal cones far out of my reach. Dale's warning about the lights in Paris had been factual. Light this bright stung my eyes without my looking directly at the brilliant glass bulbs. My ears rang. Electricity made an incessant din that no one but me seemed to notice. Somewhere deep in the store, a hand slammed a brass bell, jangling my teeth. I couldn't stay by the doors forever, hands on my ears, eyes squinting against the relentless light from above. Shoppers brushed past as I wondered at the painful brightness Dale had called God's power on earth.

But Daddy vibrated like a plucked string. He ignored the oceans of linens, laces, dresses, sewing machines, shoes, and boots, and walked right into the fray. With my eyes half-covered to protect them from the glare, I watched him move like a boat riding a wave past countertops and shelving radiating from the center of the store.

Momma fell in love with the bright light, calling it a blessing for matching colors. My hands came down from my ears. Wondering where I could purchase a pair of dark glasses, I forced myself not to squint and followed Momma's trajectory toward a sign reading LADIES' GOODS. Men and women in fine clothes clogged the aisles, chatting, stooping to collect a wayward child, pausing to fondle a square of clothing or casually examine a framed portrait. I felt like a trespasser. The music department's shiny black grand piano tops stood open like wings. The Industrial Machinery department sent up a tang of oil and metal shavings that floated overhead in a cloud I could nearly touch.

Pets, pianos, books, candy, hardware rushed at me. Stimulation this great could render me too ill to perform. Missing a performance would be failure. The contract said so, in black and white.

At Ladies' Goods, I ran like a three-year-old to Momma. She took my hand. With our hands joined, she pointed to the ceiling. I thought of Leo and our blood oath, fingertip to fingertip.

"Any flaw will show right up," she said.

For a moment, I believed she meant me. Momma dropped my hand to inspect a dress form next to a stack of velvet. She was talking about flaws in a dress.

"Do you like the rose pink or the moss green?" she asked, fabric in each hand. "The rose is more mature, but there's no reason we can't have one for day and another for evening."

"Ma'am?" The ringing in my ears.

Taking a measuring tape from the glass countertop, she calculated the length of my arm as if she hadn't looked at me in years. A clerk fluttered toward us like a moth.

"Both please," Momma said, still measuring. "And I think we like the wool in that deep midnight blue, and in the bright blue as well."

My ordeal with the electric lights mixed with Momma's accumulating rainbows of fabric, the turmoil in Mrs. Voorhees's sickroom, and the letter from an unflappable man with light in his eyes. Dizzy, I pulled Momma away from the counter.

"Can I wear those on stage?" I asked. "They're colors!"

"They're for entertaining," she said, decisive. "In the Opera houses, you have a certain class of people, Lulu. Black intimidates them. It's supposed to."

No one had ever said that was the goal of the black outfit.

"When we're done here, we'll take a look at ribbons." Momma prattled like she did when she was anxious about Leo. "I would so like for you to have a fan, but you need your hands free, so we'll see what we can do with your hair instead."

She was arranging my hair when Daddy emerged from an aisle. I waved, glad for the distraction.

"There's a scientific reason for the circular pathways," Daddy said, pointing around us. A fellow walking by nearly got his hat knocked off, and Daddy apologized. After the man passed, Daddy continued. "Electricity naturally moves in circles, as does magnetism. They flow through a body in repeating loops."

The sales clerk busied herself arranging the fabrics nearest to the three of us. Fine with me. She could learn something. Daddy wasn't as formally schooled as some, maybe even this clerk, but what he knew, he taught himself. He didn't read Mrs. Wolf, but he'd read Shakespeare, and mythology, and *Modern Marvels of Alchemy*.

"'Magnetic fields imitate the motions of the planets,'" I said. My

father patted my shoulder. I was quoting Mrs. Wolf. As if I were
brushing off a stray hair, I wiped his touch away.

"This is a wonderful place, Lulu, a real example of the forefront
of science and commerce," he said. "Thank you for bringing us here."

Momma set her hand on the stack of fabrics she'd chosen. The
sales clerk appeared at her side, a bouquet from a magician's sleeve.

"I went to see those insoles," Daddy said, "and yes, I examined the
advertised women's garments in the interest of science."

Sunday school, I thought, to rid myself of the flush in my neck
and cheeks. Hen house. Frying pan.

"The insoles, the garment, any item of that sort is merely a token,"
Daddy said.

"A geegaw," I said.

"But we're above all that," my father said. "Three dollars for a—
what did you call it, Lulu, a geegaw—is a great deal of money, even
for these swells." He gestured again, this time more lightly so as not
to knock over another swell's hat. "What we give them is an *experi-
ence*, a moment with the Magnetic Girl in which they truly feel that
power as it turns in repeating loops through *her*."

Her. Was I invisible? The chasm between us stretched.

"Daddy, that 'her' is me," I said.

"I know that, Missy. You have a gift. Your Momma knows it, I
know it, and Leo knows it, too."

Leo was theirs, too. Their son, my brother. They had barely mentioned Leo since we'd left home, and now here was his name on
Daddy's lips. I kissed Momma on the cheek. I came away scented
and gritty. She had lately discovered face powder.

Momma and I went upstairs to see a seamstress. Daddy excused
himself. The bank. The telegraph office. The stage manager. The
pianist.

"Have fun," he said.

In a narrow room up three flights of stairs, a girl not much older
than Ouida draped the blue velvet over my arm. She held the claret
against my back, and turned me right and left, not under electric
light but the usual daylight from tall windows. This was a light I

knew, the same as Momma used at home when she sewed, the same I used when I added a new row of hooks to my too-tight dresses. From a plush bench, Momma watched the girl's hands on the velvet. What a joy it would be for her to handle this heavy fabric. I was sorry that a seamstress took that tactile pleasure from her. The tall mirror's face was clean and true as any glass I'd ever seen. My reflection wasn't a nearly six-foot-tall girl, humped at the shoulders from her attempts to shrink, but a woman elegant as a Greek statue. Head up, back straight, a seamstress winding the measuring tape around her so very feminine corseted waist.

The body being measured was mine. The costumes would be beautiful armor protecting the kind heart of the young lady inside them. I could call it a miracle that we had come so far, and only because of what I could do with my eyes, my arms, my shoulders. A miracle was a shiny, beautiful thing. With this back and these arms, with my skills of observation, I was building a bridge between the past and the future for Leo, my parents, and me. And if that laughing-eyed fellow, that Mr. Mabry, saw me now, what would he see? A girl with a genuine smile, worthy of his courting, a paramour in velvet and beneath that, a corset he would someday find. As a paramour, a sweetheart, I would be loved entirely.

Who would he love, though? In his eyes, I was The Magnetic Girl, not Lulu Hurst. A pin from a marble tabletop, long and thin, its head a real pearl, found its way to the hotel in my boot.

Dear Leo.

Do you remember all those people in the parlor at our house when you thought I'd done something bad? Momma and Daddy and I went to a store last week bigger than you can imagine. Five stories of brick and iron, on a street with more people than you saw in our parlor that night times one hundred, all going about their business with hardly a nod to one another. Leo, the store was lit up with shiny white light that didn't need a match to start. Brighter than stars if you could get close to them. Bright enough so I had to squint, which was exciting because it was so new.

Momma doesn't need to sew the dresses we bought. A dozen seamstresses and their sewing machines do nothing but wait for appointments with people who need their clothes made.

I have black dresses for the stage, with a high collar and ruffle. They are merino wool and gabardine. I have bright party dresses for when we do private "tests" for a Mayor or a Scientist. I know you don't care about ladies' clothes, but someday you'll take notice of how a woman should dress, so learn from your sister! I have new boots, too. Momma went crazy for the idea of a colorful silk corsage for my shoulder, and now that I have some, she picks them from my traveling trunk like eggs from the basket.

Love, your sister, Lulu

P.S. I was going to buy you insoles for your boots, but they were for grown men's big feet. I should have got you some for fun, though. They had electricity in them, the advertisement for the store said, that healed aches and pains. The store sold other electric things too, but I can't say other than they're garments for ladies.

Daddy says the insoles and the lady attire are humbug, although he liked the electric light just fine. I tend to agree about the humbug. Electricity runs not through shoes, but through the human form as magnetism. I will show you when I am home.

Love, your sister, Lulu Hurst

CHAPTER SEVENTEEN

Washington, DC: 1884

WHAT IS BEAUTY? ON THE BROWN-EDGED, BRITTLE pages lying open in my lap, Mrs. Wolf and a physician friend debated this question. If I'd been in that room with them years ago, sipping tea or fanning myself with lace or crenelated paper, I would have asked the same question. Beauty wasn't in the rolling landscape outside a train window, although in my first two or three or five train journeys I would have insisted otherwise. Beauty was an Opera House with every seat filled, my father would have said, or the rare return on a crop that paid for his labor and our well-being. A robust son, my mother would have said, and a charming daughter. A life that lent itself to wearing the few pieces of jewelry she had brought into her marriage, a pearl ring, an enameled brooch, a gold necklace that I knew lay tucked away in a square of quilt in her bedroom.

I'd seen myself in enough mirrors to know that my eyes were too close-set and my nose too long to be anyone's ideal. Momma had brushed and pinned my thick hair all my life, *tsk*ing and clucking so much that I'd come to think my hair was a wild animal's pelt, a heavy layer to shelter beneath while traveling in the wagon in winter. My mouth, if I admitted it, wasn't terrible, my lips naturally curling into the slightest smile, their color not too vivid, my teeth hidden, not peeking through a gap in my lips like the hideous mask I'd seen in a chaser act last month.

Principles that through their very existence radiate innate beauty, Mrs. Wolf told her companion, who agreed. *Simply acknowledging the loveliness of a moral being expressing those morals in the quotidian existence is a form of beauty,* the companion added.

Before we left our hotel for a performance, in the few minutes I carved out for myself, my relief with the pin was sloppy. I rushed through my ritual, impatient for liberation, but unable to focus. When I raised blood with the pin, I stuck myself harder, digging in.

Can we say, then, that beauty emanates from the devotion to, indeed the labor involved, in the effort expended toward others in keeping the body's fluids in a state of balance? Mrs. Wolf suggested. As the dark red collected in a line across the crease at the base of my left little finger, I fumed. I was so careless I drew blood. I couldn't right even the smallest wrong.

Blood ran into my palm, and I put my tongue to it. The bright taste evoked the scent of a plow blade or a wash pot. Iron and copper, the minerals that pulsed in the ground below my feet. Common elements that made me the Magnetic Girl. Smearing a drop of blood between my fingers, I tapped them together as it thickened. Not so different from my woman's blood.

I prodded the open place on my finger again, making another red dome rise. I stared at my tiny reflection shining in the blood until I went to the wash basin and rinsed away the traces of my escape. Closing my eyes, I saw Mr. Mabry, his hands uncapping a pen, dipping it in ink, and pressing the silver nib to a clean white sheet of paper.

I hope, someday, to meet you. In a way, I was beautiful. His hand working its way across a page obscured the image of two faceless women chatting over their teacups in a world gone the way of ghosts.

During the matinée, Mrs. Voorhees appeared in my mind. She knew Mrs. Wolf's book, and she was laid up in that coffin of a house. Why had no one Mesmerized her? Perhaps she was teaching Ouida, but the girl hadn't seemed to have much innate light or educable qualities. Perhaps Mrs. Voorhees could walk. But if she were able, wouldn't she have come downstairs to greet me, rather than having her brother bring us to her like disciples?

On stage, I smiled into the darkness. Daddy brought the first fellow up for a chair test, promising "more fight in that furniture than in Buffalo Bill's Wild West." I took extra time to bend my knees gracefully and slide my feet apart the fewest inches I could. A woman should be demure.

When the mark departed, he winked and thanked me "for a great ride." I didn't know what he meant, but I thanked him, which made him laugh. Unsure what to do, I laughed with him.

For a week, my body performed while my mind and soul sought the reassurance of Mrs. Wolf's words. When I read, my habit with my pin relieved the twists in my stomach. I examined my hands. There were no red marks or welts where the cane had pressed. There never were. My forearms were sometimes sore, but that was nothing a person could see. What salvation was there in being, as Momma admonished, gentle?

I performed physical labor, same as plunging a butter churn half the day. But in every city, men of power acted as if my successes were their doing. If they believed that my power emerged because of their presence, then that was how we'd play it. No one cared that my power was ordinary physical strength aided by that one extraordinary thing, captivating. Every test I did, I felt Mrs. Voorhees watching me, her hand turning my face to hers, her worn-out toy canary cradled in her palm. She insisted I was less than her, that I was minor. But Mesmerizing—captivating—the creation and transmittal of the breathtaking feeling that Mrs. Wolf called the *cool comfort of distress oozing away from my anguished bones*—made me a greater version of myself. Greater than Mrs. Voorhees, too, in her bed, or once upon a time with her contrived birds. I had no geegaws, no vacant-eyed child feeding me a tonic for my nerves. Captivating came easily for me, and with it I erased whatever might go wrong. I *eased the anguish from my own bones.* This made me not insignificant at all.

Daddy performed alongside me, disappearing in the mornings from the hotel, appearing in Opera House wings moments before the curtain rose on the first act on the bill. After the shows, Momma consoled me, sensing distress, but I shook her off, preferring solace in Mrs. Wolf and in my letters to Leo.

Dear Leo.

Be glad you're a little boy. Children have such easy dreams and small pleasures. Mrs. Wolf, who wrote the book I read everyday, calls children "cursory thinkers." Do I sound old or weary to you? That's because I am, a little, but I will tell only you. The newspapers write such foolish stories about me. Did you know that I lifted a table with twenty-five little children sitting around its edge, and made a good team plow twice as fast as usual? Of course I didn't but that story gave us all a good laugh. Even Momma.
I will send you a toy bird next time I am able to send a package. It reminds me of one that a lady I met showed me, but the one for you is nicer. It's made of tin and jumps when you wind a key.

Love, your sister Lulu

BACKSTAGE, I SETTLED in to read. Mrs. Wolf's soothing voice came alive in my mind, musical, soft, and confident. A don't-you-tell-me-what-do-Mister voice in the most agreeable manner. The stub of a train ticket marked my place, a favorite passage in which she wrote *medical science's exhaustion does not foretell all curative means.*

Alone, I settled into a less than filthy armchair, slinging my legs over the side and leaning against the other arm. *Disputational types,* Mrs. Wolf was saying, *should be left to their poor views.*

Behind me, the door opened and shut. Deep in my reading, I heard someone yank at a stuck drawer.

"That garbage won't do a thing but give a girl the morbs." A man's voice.

I was as good as naked, barefoot and only partly fixed up. I screamed once, more like a bleat, and snatched up someone's pink dressing gown to throw over myself.

"Sorry," the man said, although he clearly wasn't. "I was looking for rouge."

Dumbly, I pointed to a pot of rouge on another table. He dabbed his finger in it and applied the counterfeit color to his cheeks in expert strokes.

"I mean it," he continued, nodding toward *The Truth of Mesmeric Influence.*

I clutched the book harder.

"You can believe that foolishness if you want, but science proved Mrs. Wolf and her ilk wrong a long time ago. Honestly, that mess about the ocean tides?"

He turned to the mirror, checking his teeth. "I had that book when I was a lad."

He twinkled his fingers at my book as if it were an old pal, and I held it closer to my chest, away from him. I must have looked like a coot, huddled to cover myself under an upside-down pink robe, clutching a book to my heart like it was a bawling infant.

"You look awful," the man said. "Sorry, but you do."

My blood had drained away, and I was trembling.

"The body has its poles, oppositional. Fluid goes back and forth evenly if a man's in balance," he intoned, then laughed.

"You read the book," I said, dumbly.

"I did, and too bad, because I read some years later that a person died at the hands of that lady."

He beckoned, and I gave him *The Truth of Mesmeric Influence.* He was careful as he turned it front and back before returning it to my open hands. Then he lay his hand, soft and warm, on my wrist.

"Melancholic, that thing. That Mrs. Wolf made her money and all I got was confused. Poor little me had to figure out on my own how to cure my troubles."

He didn't look sick at all. He looked like a delicate man with rouge on his cheeks and a fur-trimmed ladies' coat over his arm. His grey hair formed a half-circle around his fly-rink bald head.

"Nothing's wrong with you," I said, angry.

"No, ma'am. Not one thing." He inspected the pockets in the coat and stood.

"You're who they call the Magnetic Girl," he said, bowing. "I'm pleased to make your acquaintance."

I couldn't get up and greet him properly. The dressing gown wouldn't cover me, and my feet were bare. Instead, I nodded, not at all pleased that he'd made my acquaintance. I didn't know what else to say but, "And you," before I asked his name.

"I like to be called Nancy," he said, and left. A beat passed before I realized he'd stolen someone's coat.

Time was short. Thumbing through the book, I looked again for an illustration that I knew wasn't there. I wanted to see the face of the woman who I knew in my heart would never cause a death.

Every point gained has been steadily held. That was her answer when I did what I loved best, opening her book without looking and letting my finger fall blindly onto the page for an answer in her words. Through the book's leather binding, I pressed my fingertip against the shank of the needle, the stubborn metal grounding me to my body. *Stay calm, stand firm. Peace is close at hand.*

That night when I was supposed to be asleep, I planned how to get away on my own to meet Arden Mabry. He'd signed his note with his given name, his permission to use it. Calling a man to whom I'd never been formally introduced by his name was something Miss Marie with her short skirt would do, or the girls who slunk away with one fellow or another after a show. I knew what they were going to do, but I couldn't imagine how they would do it. The fellow might rear up like a horse or a dog, but I got lost trying to feature the woman's part.

"I'm going for a walk, Momma," I mouthed, making the words casual. If I presented the walk as an afterthought, she might feel I could go alone. I'd been free more often to stroll a few blocks on my own during the day. The fresh air cleared my head.

But if she got a whim to go with me? I had to dress the part and sweep into the place in a hat, gloves, a fine dress. Alone. I would be a lady out for the day, surprised to meet briefly with an acquaintance who also happened to be a gentleman.

Daddy would observe that I was dressed up. That would stop the whole operation in its tracks. He would have already gone for the day, though. He left most mornings after breakfast, to the theater, to the bank, to the telegraph office, to somewhere. Momma would hand me what she decreed as school work before disappearing for the morning into a ladies' magazine.

Daddy's out, Momma's reading or doing needlework, and I would have a mood.

I got up and went to the mirror, congratulating the serious-faced girl there. I'll pretend I haven't slept, am having a day when I'm hearing and smelling and tasting too strongly. The only way to right myself for the tests would be to walk off my troubles. Poor girl, misses Leo and home. She feels pent up. I whispered my line.

"Momma, if I'm going to be worth anything with the tests today, I'd like to just go clear my head for a while. I promise I'll stay close by."

And the fancy clothes?

"They're so pretty, they'll cheer me up."

No one would deny me that.

BEFORE A LADIES' SHOW on a blustery afternoon in Washington, DC, one of the Merrymount Elocutionists pronounced at me that "a lady left a letter for Lulu." She rolled every "L," practicing her elocution while we warmed up, me in my drawers and stays, making piano scales in the air, swinging my arms and bending my knees because Momma had read in a magazine about calisthenics. I marched in place while the elocutionist made peculiar shapes with her tongue. In a day, I would share a table with Arden. Twenty-four hours. I marched down the numbers, twenty-four to one, and back up to twenty-four again. From the only chair in the dressing room, the elocutionist pointed to a nest of paper tacked to the wall. Letters addressed to The Magnetic Girl often came to me in packets by way of hotel desk clerks, but lately more and more got left for me at theater box offices. Daddy had read parts of those letters aloud to me until Momma made him stop, saying he should know better than to expose me to unsuitable correspondents. I'd picked a letter out of the trash only once. I saw a crude drawing that was so disgusting I scooped dirt over the paper to cover it. I never looked at the thrown-away mail again.

The note was from Dale. I knew before I saw the handwriting. The paper reeked of her toilet water. The card read:

> *I will be at your ladies' performance with several of my best girl-friends. We are in Washington DC on a cultural tour of the Capitol of the Nation and have been blessed with a few free hours that must, of course, go toward visiting you and your exhibition. And to think that this power was revealed in your own little home, and that I was there to witness its birth! May we call on you backstage at the conclusion of your presentation?*
>
> *Yours, Cousin Dale.*

There was no telling what Dale would dream up if she came backstage to visit and tripped over an uneven carpet in the half-darkness or trailed her skirt in a spittoon. From the note, I couldn't determine if she'd gotten wise about the pin and the mattress that night at home. My apology letter lay dormant in two halves inside a book on Daddy's shelf, our secret.

"Anything good?" the elocutionist asked. She didn't enunciate this time. I'd forgotten her name. Naomi? Paula? Maida? She recited poetry while juggling ninepins.

"Oh, just a letter from an admirer," I said, pushing the word "admirer" so it flew from my mouth like a bird.

Dale or her friends weren't likely to volunteer, and under no circumstances did I want her as a mark. My cane tests for ladies required thinner, more delicate canes and less pressure from my hands. This left a woman merely tottering on her heels like a child pretending she was a spinning top. A vision of Dale hurtling head-first from a chair made me cringe. But she was on her way.

Note in hand, I left the dressing room to find Daddy. He had gone in search of the piano player to make sure she had my sheet music. He'd been gone a long time, but he could be checking the delicate canes in our urn or wiping down the chair before a stage-hand brought it out. For this show, we switched out our standard wooden chair for an upholstered parlor chair. More attractive to ladies. Even if we hadn't replaced the cushion's wool stuffing with cotton and taken out the wooden stretchers and half the nail heads, the whole piece would end up weighing the same or less as any other parlor chair, since ladies tended to have less bulk than men.

Daddy emerged from the back staircase, under the "NO SWEAR-ING, NO TAKING THE LORD'S NAME IN VAIN, NO INDEL-ICACIES. YOU WILL BE FINED!" notice. I handed him the note. He waved Dale's card away from his face. The scent burned his nostrils the same as it did mine.

"You're the headliner," he said, not bothering to read the note. "That will impress the daylights out of them," as if that was all they'd need. I hadn't been anything but the headliner for weeks, but those extra minutes on stage and my name at the top of the bill wouldn't mean a thing to Dale.

Daddy arranged box seats for them, courtesy of The Magnetic Girl. As if their visiting me afterward was a good idea, he directed me to welcome them backstage. Before I could ask where he'd gone to all day, he was out the door again. We thought alike, though. A bang-up show would distract Dale from any questions she might have about all that he and I had made of that stormy night at home.

After all, she was the one who'd said there'd been sparks.

During the first numbers, I couldn't stop watching Dale and her girlfriends from my spot at a gap in the curtain. They had fallen in love with the trained cats walking their balance beam. All the ladies in the audience who pursed their lips and cooed at the line of tabbies and calicos would never know how the cat's territorial markings made their cart shimmer from that night-soil stink. They'd never know to cut a wide berth around the cats' cages to protect their skirts from getting snagged by a playful claw, or how to step high to keep their heels and hems clear of ropes and buckets and sometimes, a wad of workingmen's snot.

The dumb act's fabric horse's head and tail shambled past me to the stage, the two fellows under the costume tugging the strings and buckles to hold the body together. Dale and her friends would never have the kind of knowledge that I had. They were naïve as calves.

When the minstrel act came on, Dale and her friends clapped for his songs. She would have been repelled to know that behind his corked-on blackface, Mr. Rice was a lame and ancient cowboy. We'd shared a bill in Paterson, New Jersey for two nights, and now we greeted each other backstage like old friends. When Mr. Rice began his last number, and Mr. Holbrook, the enormously fat man who yodeled while he beat enthusiastically on a cello, got ready to go on, I scurried to the dressing room for a last smooth over my hair and a few more hand stretches and deep knee bends. Ladies' shows were easy as pie.

My "Tarantelle" thundered through the walls, played more musically today but with a convulsive rhythm I'd have to waste energy ignoring. Nearly late, I ran upstairs, arranged my stage smile, and walked brightly to the wings.

Daddy was already on stage talking our way in. When he said, "The Magnetic Girl," while turning stage left, I stepped out to meet him. Dale and her girlfriends were an invisible presence beyond the footlights. Daddy's voice was too loud. The creak of the floorboards when he paced set me on edge. Finding that tunnel in my mind to calm my breathing was taking too long. What *The Truth of Mesmeric Influence* said about my *stronger nature* hovered around me. The thought floated by that this was how Mrs. Voorhees felt drinking her droplets from a glass. Life inside the theater tipped out and away, Mrs. Voorhees with it, and I watched my disembodied hand shake that of a woman in a striped dress. She took the walking cane I offered. The rainstorm washed out the sounds of my instructions: hold the stick to make the middle of the letter "H." The music started up again, the sound pulsing through the wooden floor and into my boots, rising through the soles of my feet. The woman became a watercolor stroke, and together we worked the cane, the woman pressing down, me pressing forward and up. Our eyes locked and the rain evaporated as it always did, becoming a glowing blue light. As soon as I felt the need to pull back, the blue vanished, and the lady faltered backward on her boot heels, nearly collapsing into Daddy's waiting arms. She was someone's mother, someone's wife, not so much older than me, and I brimmed with kindness for her. Applause and laughter rose from every seat in the theater. She laughed like a child.

Another lady, and another. A girl Leo's age, then a grandmother. No Dale. The pianist rumbled through the closing bars, signaling the end of the act. I took my bow, Daddy bowed, and we ran together to the wings.

While the chaser act was on upstairs, that same Irish tenor who'd been on the bill in Savannah, Dale called "Yoo-hoo," at the dressing room door. She didn't have the courtesy to give me time to freshen up and take a few minutes' rest, but that could mean that I hadn't appeared to need it. I set my washrag by the basin and gave her a peck on each cheek. Foreign performers did this as casually as Americans shook hands, and I'd wanted a chance to greet a visitor this way. Dale pecked me back. Her friends crowded the doorway behind her. She introduced them and their chaperone, and I smiled and nodded as if I'd remember them. The one in yellow clutched my hand like she was about to faint. The girl in blue tried to take in every aspect of the dressing room, swiveling her head, eyeing a territory she didn't understand. The worn floor with drifts of face powder in the corners, the mounds of yellowing scripts, newspapers, and playbills crowding the tabletops belonged to me more than any cow I'd milked or chicken I'd plucked and dropped into a pot. The girl didn't have the sense not to let me know she was memorizing. I could have told her look around without moving your head like a goose, and then test yourself. Where is that drift of face powder? Which table has one shoe forgotten beneath it? I did no such thing. Memorizing led to knowledge. No one knew that better than me.

"You!" Dale squealed. "You've come so far from that terrible night in Cedartown! Who'd have thought a girl like you would be so gifted?"

I scowled at the ogling girl before turning to Dale. "A girl like you" was a slap in the face.

"Silly me thinking it was bugs making that sound," Dale burbled. "If I hadn't called for your parents, who knows what that Magnetic Force of yours would have done!"

"I'm so thankful you were there," I lied. "Without you, I might not have seen this miracle for what it truly was."

My debt was paid. She pretended she hadn't acted like a silly little girl back at home, and I pretended to have forgotten. Dale swayed me side to side in a hug until the chaperone stepped up. She was sure, she said, that Dale and her *so very interesting* cousin would like time together, and of course, Miss Hurst would want to change from her theatrical get-up. I liked my "get-up," but I wanted to wash the sweat from my creases, and I said so.

The girls and the chaperone stood, unsure what to do.

"All that perspiration," I said, with the same confidence Mrs. Voorhees had when she'd said "female troubles."

In a heartbeat, Dale and I were alone. She pushed someone's flowered bonnet off a bench and sat.

"You're getting so famous," she said. "When you meet Lily Langtry or that Japanese wrestler, will you introduce me?"

I took a corset from my trunk, using the time to think. She wasn't here for cash money, and she wasn't going to torment me outright. She'd want something more rewarding and more public, although that didn't exclude the other things in private. I slid into the corset and turned to her, making sure I looked sad.

"I read all about you in the papers," Dale said.

"I can't help what those scribblers write," I sighed. Safest to presume that Dale was a genuine believer. "They love to spin tales and compare me to whatever idea strikes their fancy."

Dale came over to help me lace up.

"Wouldn't it be nice if some of them knew I'd been there when we discovered your power? What an exciting thing that would be, my name in a newspaper. And you never know who might read it and want to meet me: mayors, industrialists, maybe even a governor!"

A spider crept up a wall pipe. I couldn't guarantee a thing. I never knew who would come to a show. Anyone could buy a ticket. I took a red dress from the trunk. To make her jealous, I held it out as if I were considering another, better, choice.

"This new you—" Dale swept her arm around the room, "—is the cousin Lulu I'd always knew you could be. A refined and fascinating woman of the big city. You were never going to make anything of yourself before. Marry a farmer, be a farmer's wife."

I had a vision of myself squatting on a milking stool, wearing a faded, stitched-up black stage dress. Lulu Hurst, the Miss Havisham of Georgia.

"Daddy's a farmer and he's doing just fine," I said. I meant to sound calm, but the milking stool vision scared me. We weren't fine, and she'd said as much right in our house. We weren't fine not because we had so little money, but because we weren't whole. So much needed fixing because of me and what I'd done.

Dale chirped at my reflection in the mirror.

"I think you should thank the Lord every time you're on a stage. You know who's behind the miracle that led you to places like this one."

I did know. Me.

I smiled at her in the glass. Captivating her at this angle would be a frolic. I could catch her eye in the mirror, hold her still, make her lose time. Narrowing my eyes and dropping my lids, I let my breathing go low and deep. The room spun around us. Dale and I stayed upright and still, she over my shoulder, me holding her gaze in our shared mirror, two people, one surface. I could cure me of her, but what malady would I relieve in her? Venality? Arrogance?

Suddenly numb with exhaustion, I let Dale go. *Calm, translucent intellect*, Mrs. Wolf had written about our skill. *Bissful radiance.* What if captivating were a talent that could be depleted? If that were true, one day I'd go to lay my hands upon Leo and I'd be empty as a dry lamp.

Dale's hand was on my shoulder. Without realizing, I'd shut my eyes.

"You know it's nonsense," Dale said. She leaned in toward my ear, so closely I thought she might kiss me. I jerked my head away.

"An antique fashion," she whispered. "Mesmerism is for old ladies trying to conjure up their war dead and silly people with nothing better on their minds than ghosts."

"So why did you fall for it?" I said to her face in the mirror.

"In your house? You weren't doing it then. You like to believe you're more clever than anyone else. You've always been that way."

"Your girlfriends believe I did it. You saw the ladies on the stage go into a trance, follow my guidance, and then lose their balance."

I had nearly called the ladies "marks," but I caught myself before I gifted Dale with learning. I went to my trunk. Dresses for every day, and clean black dresses for each performance. Hundreds of dollars going into the bank every week. I was quick and clever with chairs and the canes on stage. Dale didn't recall that I'd captivated her at the supper table. She didn't know that I'd started to just now in the mirror until I'd thought better of it.

My Sunday school teacher lost his place because I Mesmerized him, formed in my mouth. *I saved Leo from a fox,* I started to say. Captivating, hypnotism, Mesmerism was mine, and Mrs. Wolf's, and Mrs. Voorhees's, and someday soon I would put the talent to use for Leo.

"All you did at your house was frighten me," Dale said. "That one time, interrupting my slumber like you did."

"Believe what you like," I told Dale, while I straightened the collar on my bright red dress. "Next time a newspaper man asks about my power, I'll be sure to tell him how you were there at the beginning," I lied. "No one reads them anyway," I added.

That wasn't true. Why would anyone come to a show if they hadn't read about me in their papers?

CHAPTER
EIGHTEEN

AT PRECISELY NOON THE NEXT DAY, IN A LAVENDER dress with lace cuffs and a violet bow at the neck, I swished through the doors of the McGill Dining Room and didn't stop walking. I concentrated on my breathing as if I were on stage, balancing myself within the tunnel of sound.

At a table in the near corner, like a silver dollar above wooden nickels, sat Arden Mabry.

I froze. I had agreed to sit un-chaperoned with a fellow I didn't know. This was a bad choice. He could be a kidnapper who wanted to ransom me for every dollar I had earned. I turned to leave, praying he didn't look up.

"Watch it," barked a pallid man in a hat. I tried to apologize for stepping on his toe, but the man limped away as if he enjoyed making me feel bad.

Mr. Mabry waved. I was on stage. I waved back.

I'd already practiced sounding grown and calm, and pronounced my first line, "What a charming place," after the waiter, his hair shiny black, pulled my chair out for me. He presented me with a menu card, bowed, and vanished. White latticework woven with silk flowers framed the walls like a country fence. A string quartet played.

"Look at this selection," I said. "Once you've had possum, you ain't going back to squirrel."

That was crude. I blushed, and Mr. Mabry laughed. His pipe sat unlit in the ashtray. He was naturally considerate, not smoking in front of a lady.

"My father used to say that. I haven't eaten squirrel since I was little." My first lie of the day.

Squirrel was all right. Tender, if the squirrel was young and stewed with tomatoes and ramp. This was the wrong thing to say in a restaurant with a string quartet and daffodil-colored wallpaper. Discussing a recipe for squirrel was like picking my nose. I burned a hole in the menu from staring.

He had already ordered coffee. He sipped it before he spoke.

"What does it do to you?" Mr. Mabry asked, leaning forward across the table.

He wasn't talking about game. He was so close I felt his breath on my face. He smelled the way I remembered: soap. The something else was the smell of his difference from me. Whatever he was asking about seemed to mean life and death to him, but I wanted to touch his smooth cheek.

"What does what do to me, Mr. Mabry?" I asked, my face hot. He might be asking about what captivation felt like, alone.

He leaned back, and I was sorry. He spun his coffee cup in its saucer. The liquid never sloshed. I was still leaning in, so I arranged myself delicately in my seat, no longer so embarrassingly close. I was afraid to look up. People were probably staring.

"Call me Arden, please," he said. I had wounded him, and I was sorry. "When you're on that stage, you're all alone. Your father's off to the side, of course, but he comes in like a hawk the minute you take your hands away from your victim."

"Mark," I said. "The fellows or the ladies doing the tests are called marks. That's the professional word."

"And that's the thing," Arden said. His eyes lit up as they had on stage, before I knew his name, before we sat at a dining table like a man and a woman. "I want to know everything about the Magnetic Girl. You're fantastic, a damn miracle of deception!"

"Any person of a sound mind and body"—I thought of Leo and asked his forgiveness if I impugned him—"can learn a trick, Mr. Mabry. Arden." I liked the shape of his name, the ease with which I said it aloud. "No one's performing any miracles on stage, and there's no deception."

Arden left his cup alone and closed his eyes. I wondered if this was courting. I didn't know how to court: no one had told me. He seemed relieved to have asked his question, so I reached across the table to lay my hand over his. Arden opened his eyes, and I pretended I'd been reaching for the sugar, although I didn't yet have a cup.

"I'm sorry for the foul language," he said.

He didn't know one thing about opera houses. I heard worse than "damn" every day, although my parents pretended that I did not.

"People want miracles," I said. "They want promise that someone is enlightened or gifted enough to reach past the limits of the every day." Dale had called the very fact of my tests a miracle.

The waiter arrived. Without Momma ordering chamomile tea for me "in the best interests of your appearance," I ordered black tea, exotic and brave. The pastry cart had cakes with peaks of whipped cream, but hungry as I was, choosing a dessert was childish.

Arden saw straight through me. He ordered a plate of cookies and told the water to select what he thought "the young lady" would like. Maybe we *were* courting? I wound my reticule's strap through my fingers.

"For instance, you do your act with ladies, too," he said.

"Tests," I told him. "More scientific that way. And yes, we have ladies' shows."

And because of a plate of fancy cookies, or the wiry black hair on the backs of his slender fingers, or the radiance in his face when I spoke of miracles and promises, I explained the tests. I told him how iron filings get attracted to one end of a magnet and repelled from the other. Balancing a spoon across my wrist, I explained fulcrum and lever.

"I've read Isaac Newton," Arden said, and laughed.

I set the spoon down, embarrassed. If he knew all this, why ask me?

"I read, as well," I told him. *We have only broken hints of human-kind's true temperament*, Mrs. Wolf cautioned. I heard her clearly, there in the restaurant, a voice in my ear pausing the string quartet, the chatter around me, the clank of tableware. *The Truth of Mesmeric Influence* was my cherished friend. Even Daddy hadn't read it all the way through, dismissing the value in its words.

"I'm sure you do," Arden said. His smile was an invitation to confide.

He picked up his pipe and clenched his teeth around the black stem. The ivory bowl, burnished to the color of a nut hull, was an intricately curved man's face, its sharp nose, angular cheeks, and deep-set eyes below the elegant folds of a turban. The image itched my mind, a memory of something I couldn't place. The peculiar face protruded in front of Arden's own, young and sweet.

"There are science books," I said. "The *Modern Marvels of Alchemy* is one, or any schoolbook."

Arden dug in his pocket for a match and tobacco.

"My brother's not well," I told him. "Mesmerism—what I do— will help him."

"My condolences," Arden said. The liveliness in his eyes faded momentarily, and I nearly floated away. He had an ailing loved one, just as I did.

My tea arrived, a flowered cup on a flowered saucer, a spoon for a doll tucked into the folded napkin.

"Do you believe you have a unique power, Miss Hurst?" Arden peered at me over a sparkle of chocolate icing.

To myself, I said that I did. I can lift those fellows or throw them because they believe I can, and they believe I can because I hold their thoughts still for the seconds and minutes they're close by me. Mrs. Wolf had that power. In her pages, she confirmed for me that I did, too.

"Of course," I spoke aloud. Captivating was no humbug.

Arden's laugh sounded like bubbles popping. "It must be an impressive feeling to have everyone in your thrall. There must be nothing quite like that kind of power."

All these people in the restaurant, at their little round tables, listening to stuck-up music. I smiled at them, shining power their way. No one stopped their conversations, or even looked up to return my smile. Aggravation turned me into the silly schoolgirl I never could abide, yammering without sense.

"I don't know who you are, who your people are," I said. "We're from Georgia, near Tennessee. Just outside a beautiful place called Cedartown, south of Rome a little bit. Daddy goes up to Rome for the cotton brokers, we trade in cotton and corn."

Arden refilled his cup from the coffee pot. The cup was too feminine for him, and I wished, suddenly, he wouldn't drink from it.

"No, you don't, pardon me, ma'am. If you did like you make out, you wouldn't be here today, or on the stage yesterday and the day before or however long you've been at this. You'd be at home receiving sons of Confederate colonels and courting the lawyers and doctors and merchants in your town."

"Preachers." My voice was mine again. No more prattling.

"Not preachers." Arden mocked me. "They're not the ones with money. Pardon me for speaking plain, Lulu, but ever since your father met me up at the logging camp and brought me down to your show, I've been fixed on understanding The Magnetic Girl."

After Mr. Getty back in Rome warned Daddy away from selecting folks in advance, he picked from whomever we had in the seats. He'd never gone out into a town to fetch folks. That would mean he'd figured on our having a cold audience. That I'd fail. That I was no good.

"Miss Hurst?" Arden spoke softly, concerned. "Lulu?"

I bit into a cookie, tasting dirt. If I looked into Arden's eyes, he'd see that mine were wet.

"I assumed you knew. You're such a close team in the act, excuse me, the tests, that I never thought he didn't tell you how I'd come to be there."

You'd come to be there because you heard about me, read the newspapers, came along with a pal for the fun. Maybe you thought I was pretty. Daddy picked you from the audience because your fervor was all he could see.

Arden took the cookie from my hand with the same light touch I'd used on Sarah's egg. Carefully, he set the food on a napkin, and took both my hands in his. We had to be courting. He'd used my first name. That child I read about who was killed by touching an electrical wire must have felt this same fiery buzz in his skin before his life went up in smoke.

"You know it doesn't matter how I came to know you," Arden said. "The truth of the matter is that we know each other now, that you answered my letter, that you came here today. I'm going back to Pennsylvania for a bit, manage my father's concerns there while I see what comes next for me. I'd like it if you'd write me."

All my power sparked between his two warm hands.

Arden released me and extracted bills from his wallet the way I had unrolled money in my dreams. He arranged the payment for our meal in a fan on the table before he came around to hold my chair while I stood.

"We're heading to New York this week, and then Saratoga," I said. "I will write you. I would like that very much."

He took my hand and squeezed it just once. And then he let me go.

Dear Leo:

Why is it I never call you by your whole name, "Leo William?" I think I will start, so you can get used to how the girls will address you when you start courting.

Have I embarrassed you? Well good! I bought you a drawing of

*the Washington Monument, which is made to look like a statue
from ancient Egypt. I will read to you about Ancient Egypt when
I am home. Cousin Dale came to see me in Washington, DC, and
she and her school friends enjoyed the show very much, which was
for ladies.*

*Do you remember that blood oath we made? Please remember that
brothers and sisters are always better friends than anyone.*

*We will be in New York City next, where we have been told that
trains run on tracks over a person's head. I don't see how this can
last for very long. A train is too heavy for a trick like that to do
much good. I wish you were here to see it yourself.*

Love, your sister, Lulu

CHAPTER NINETEEN

New York City:
April 1884

DESPITE THE RUMORS OF AERIAL TRAINS, OUR TRAVEL to New York City was no different from any other. The tracks lay on solid ground, and the bridges were sturdy metal and brick. Only birds and sky arced over our heads.

Momma and I set out to stroll the famous Ladies Mile in Gotham as soon as we'd seen our bags installed at our hotel. Stylish women and men deep in conversation with each other, and occasionally with themselves, flowed up and down the Broadway. A sign as tall as me, reading "We Give Trading Stamps," filled a store window. There were stores for rugs, stores for tableware, stores for remedies, with nearly every window at least two stories high. The whole place clattered like a busy mind.

Even for someone with money to burn, there was no reason on earth any items should cost what they did. Spoons had names like "Eastlake" and "Orleans." Bars of soap from England cost more than a boxed lunch on a train. New Yorkers were gone suckers if they made a habit of spending that much. Mansions filled entire city blocks. One of these labyrinths of turrets and gables must have been where Mrs. Vanderbilt wore her electric light party dress. Somewhere in this city, maybe swarming around me this minute, were people who had been her guests. They were the same individuals who bought jewelry and silver tureens from stores that existed to sell only those things.

Momma took my hand.

We turned onto a side street in search of Sixth Avenue and the elevated train. One block, then two, and soon the two streets crossed, their rivers of people flowing together and separating again. In front of us stood a massive cage of iron struts, like the skeleton of a beast, and above, rail tracks crisscrossed the sky.

"We need to get back to the hotel," Momma warned, fingering the new gold watch pin on her dress.

Horse carts and carriages churned on Sixth Avenue, past six and seven stories of brick and stone. Between buildings pressed shoulder to shoulder, gold lettering juggled the sunlight over a recessed doorway. The gold spelled out "Gaiety Dime Museum."

Dime museums were all the rage with adventurous types. They purported to house living human oddities: mermaid tails and dancing aborigines, grizzly bear feet, relics of the Holy Land, and secrets of the deep. I'd learned this in Wilmington from Rosie the Four-Hundred-Pound Beauty, who dreamed of life as a mermaid with a merman husband.

"They have relics from the Bible," I said, pointing across the street to the gold letters. "Can we go in for just ten minutes?"

"I can't imagine where you learned that," Momma said, but she plucked the admission fee from her purse as we dodged traffic. At the door, a skeletal fellow unfolded himself like a mantis to accept her coins and usher us through a dim vestibule.

The overpowering smell of decayed mushrooms made me draw my sleeve to my nose. The place gave me the horrors in the best way possible. As my eyes adjusted to the darkness, a wall of glass-fronted cabinets took shape. While Momma bent low to read a wall card placed at the feet of a wax mannequin dressed as the Queen of

England, I went to the cabinets and tried to make out the contents of a jug half as big as a barrel. Roots from a monstrous turnip waved dreamily from milky fluid inside.

Looking closer, I counted twenty fat fingers, four fat hands, and four slender feet. One oversized head wobbled above the mass on a thick, yellow stem. Either side of the head had its own face. Two sets of closed eyes, two button-sized flat noses, and two tiny mouths poised to suckle. Two faces, one head. The card below the jar read, TWO-FACED BABY! ONE BODY ODDITY, TWO ENTIRE SETS OF LIMBS, TWO PERSONALITIES!

I stumbled backward into a chatty man and woman eyeing the next display. The shock of their skin against mine sent my flesh into a roll of twitches and ripples.

The fingers waving at me through the glass were real; the nails were like flecks of mica. The fat little arches of the feet were wrin-kled. They curled in like potato bugs. Two faces, one heart. How would someone make this object? Who would put it in a jar? Mrs. Voorhees could make a false canary out of a magnet, straw, and feathers, but she wouldn't create a baby.

I wondered if the baby had one brain or two. As repulsive as the thing was, my throat caught with the desire to help it. If this child were Leo, I would have smashed the glass and set him free. This baby might never have breathed a single minute, but what if I could captivate the thing until its eyes opened and it saw me? When I opened the baby's eyes, would its pain seep into me? *It was twenty minutes before the tumor was removed and another five before the stitches were complete, and all the while I showed and felt no more than a corpse.* Those were Mrs. Wolf's words after assisting a physician removing a growth. If an entire twin self was removed this way, the two baby faces would be forever lonely, unable to see each other no matter how much they wanted to look into the eyes of the one person on earth who truly knew them.

Weeping, I turned from the baby.

Six leathery black knots lay in a row along a worn straw mat. The card above them read, SHRUNKEN HUMAN HEADS FROM

THE AMAZON RIVER OF BRAZIL. I scrubbed my boot soles into the splintery wooden floor and looked down. No sparks. Those dead dark heads, pickled like tomatoes, the baby head in a jar. The whole place wanted to show me faces.

Momma came up beside me, tapping her watch. My rest hour was looming, but I didn't want it. Before I could form an argument for skipping a single afternoon's confinement, the mantis-man shouted, "Twelve o'clock show!" A hurdy-gurdy player with a gyrating monkey came from the darkness, cranking out a tune. I started to reach out my finger like I had with Pierre and his sailor suit, but this monkey snarled. His fangs were filed to nubs, but still.

A sparse crowd jostled us into a makeshift theater, their anticipation sparking like the moments before a Magnetic Girl test. The flow of bodies into the little room lifted my heart. Shrunken heads and pickled babies mattered not at all.

The gas was turned up enough to reveal a woman wrapped in blue robes. She looked bored. A blue and gold banner whimpered, MADAME PARNELL AND HER TAROT CARDS UNCOVER SECRETS OF THE ANCIENT EAST—SHE KNOWS WHAT LIES AHEAD! She had rimmed her eyes with lamp-black. A deck of tarot cards fanned out on the lace cloth before her. Incense in brass pots sent ribbons of spicy smoke toward the ceiling. No mark would notice how she crossed her eyes just enough to melt us all into a blur. I knew that routine like my own nose, and I did it one hundred times better. She was dressed so much like the drawing on the cover of *Modern Marvels of Alchemy* that I bit my knuckle to keep from laughing. Even her turban had a green jewel above her forehead, undoubtedly a chunk of glass or worse, a sticky piece of candy.

In the shadows, the tallest man I'd ever seen curled his upper body around two normal-sized people. The hurdy-gurdy man stopped cranking, and a very little man in a dirty jacket crossed in front of Madame Parnell.

"Who here is brave enough to allow Madame Parnell to see their future in her cards?" he shouted. He looked at each of us accusingly, pointing like a child. The midget didn't have Daddy's finesse in calling out marks. Daddy encouraged them, but this fellow aggravated people. He didn't seem to know that every member of an audience should *want* to be selected.

"You? Or you, sir?" A girl behind me whispered, "Go on," but her fellow hushed her. Were Arden here with me, his hand would be on my arm, an anchor in a churning sea. He wouldn't ask if I knew these tests. He would know that mine were well above this nonsense.

The talker pointed at me.

"You," he said. Arden's hand vanished from my arm. I drilled my gaze into the talker's eyes. He must have recognized me. He'd probably seen my face on a broadside or read about me in a newspaper. They always ran lithos showing me lifting a fellow or doing the cane test or something they'd simply made up, like that toothache cure.

"Madame Parnell's cards will reveal everything about you," the talker crooned. "Will your future be made from fire or water?"

If I were that two-faced baby, one pair of my eyes would see backward to the Ladies' Mile. The other pair would stare through Madame Parnell and her curtain of incense to look directly at myself tonight on the Wallack's Theater stage. I would have real curtains and a piano player, and every seat in the gilt-edged Opera House would be full. But I could only see the talker, and behind him, the embodiment of *Modern Marvels of Alchemy*.

All eyes in the theater burned into my back, my shoulders, my neck. I had taken the bait merely by coming in, making myself nothing more than any of the guileless, starry-eyed marks my father chose. I couldn't get out the door fast enough. The display room had gone completely dark except for a sign reading, SEE THE MAN-EATING CHICKEN under a window's light. I pressed my crawling back against the wall, holding myself in a safe place. I had no pin; I'd left it safely in the binding of *The Truth of Mesmeric Influence*, in my valise at the hotel. My fingers fluttered and grabbed at my arms.

Momma emerged from the theater, looking like she'd eaten something rotten.

"You know better than to make a scene that way, Lulu. People laughed."

If I opened my mouth to answer, I'd spit up. Focusing on putting one foot in front of the other, I accepted her grip on my wrist.

Outside in the bright afternoon, black electrical wires twisted above our heads, a contortionist act of their own. In some places, the wires interlaced so densely they obscured the blue sky.

CHAPTER TWENTY

New York City:
April 1884

AFTER SALLY AND LULU LEFT TO SEE THE SIGHTS,
Will ate a quick lunch of cold roast lamb, cauliflower in cream sauce,
and lemon pie. He could barely get it down. He had two errands to
get done before the afternoon show. The hotel clerk had given him
the address of a local game that never quit, and he wanted to get
into that garden before top-hatting on another stage. The first thing,
though, was the calling card. The clerk had seemed surprised when
he handed it over. Will had been taken aback by the high style, too,
but that was hardly anyone's business.

"Please call on a matter of mutual interest," the card read. The
name was Edgar Ellison, with an irritating "Esquire" at the end.

"Take Broadway south to Chambers Street," the clerk said. Will
pocketed the card, but the clerk was right that he didn't know his
way around Manhattan.

"Horse car." The clerk pointed to the street. "South."

Get the matter of mutual interest out of the way, whatever it was,
and roll into a game on the way back to the hotel. All the better for

his luck if he were on the clock. Pressure made him single-minded.

Will trotted alongside a southbound streetcar on Broadway. At the right moment in the tangle of horses and pedestrians, he leapt aboard, his youth returning for that airborne moment. Two decades before, he'd played the role of a mortally injured hero, engineering his passage on a vehicle that carried him to his future. Lately, as then, he had to have faith in his ability to turn events in his favor. Will found a place to stand in the crowded car. As casually as the folks around him, he held a leather strap and swayed with the movement. So many pockets so close at hand, but today was a different kind of business.

Maybe it was the power of memory, or his lapse into dreaming of easy picking, but an unmistakable flash of red hair stopped time. Will twisted for a view over a lady's massive hat as the Phaeton carrying Harmony jerked into northbound traffic. Will figured if he jumped out, he could outrun the horse car, but he'd never run fast enough to catch the carriage.

For so many years, he held on to the belief that when they met again, Harmony would embrace him and exclaim through manly tears how he'd been afraid Will had died that terrible day in 1862.

I had to get out of there, Will imagined he'd say, disgust at his own cowardice blessedly gone. *I didn't look back, I just ran.*

And Harmony would concede that he was the one who'd given him the idea about the ambulance in the first place, and then he'd laugh and say he'd been worried about ol' Force of Will.

I ain't heard from you since you hightailed it, he'd say.

And I ain't heard from you neither, Will would answer. *You're looking fine and dandy.*

Harmony would be aging, like him. He'd be worse, in fact: when Will was a sapling of nineteen, Harmony was already married, and to hear him tell it, a regular on the medicine show circuit. Will would pay for dinner, no questions asked. And then he would write Harmony a bank check for everything he owed from those long-ago games, with interest, and benevolently refuse his old friend's gratitude.

Will was so deep in thought that he nearly missed Chambers Street, and disembarked near the post office, a monstrous salt-cellar of a building. All of New York got on his nerves. Ugly. Loud. Will took another look at Ellison Esquire's card and went in search of Chambers Street.

At a brownstone on a street that led to the waterfront, Ellison himself answered Will's knock. He looked unpleasantly like a college man. Will followed Ellison past cases of boxed washing soda into a nest of an office. The electric chandelier sparkled, and sunlight streamed through massive windows where the shutters had been thrown open to the street. Ellison caught him looking and pointed to the light fixture.

"Like 'em? We cleaned every globe with Angeline's. Wanted to see how it would perform on the household items. Mighty fine, I'd say."

Will agreed and helped himself to a seat.

"Smoke?" Ellison held out a box of La Insular cigars. Will chose. Ellison snipped the tip, lit Will's, then his own. Tasting the smoke, Will watched the blue vapor drift upward. Then he looked to Ellison.

"I've got a humdinger of an idea," Ellison said, admiring his cigar. "These are imported from Manila. Yes, sir, as y'all like to say in the South. Like I said, I've done my research. So, you tell me. This Magnetic Girl stuff, she's got a Force, a Power, she lifts grown men, stops trains with her bare hands—"

"No one's stopped any train," Will said, relieved. This boy hadn't done any research into anything.

"She could if she wanted to, I'm thinking."

Will considered this. Ellison had bigger ideas than he had office space. He wasn't alone in his work. A typewriter pecked away down the hall, and he could hear a couple of men loading skids somewhere in the back.

"I imagine so," Will allowed. "She could stop a train if she felt the Force at that particular point in time."

"Exactly!" Ellison slapped his thigh, spraying ash onto his trousers. "Exactly! So, I'm thinking about Lulu Hurst, and I'm thinking about Angeline Washing Soda, and how your daughter looks sweet as an angel, and yet she's so strong, and how the ladies and their wash-women like a powerful cleaning product, and then it comes to me!"

Will waited for the slap of the card that a poor player believes will take the game.

"Comes to you?"

Ellison sketched a banner headline in the air with his finger. ANGELINE'S WASHING SODA. STRONG AS LULU HURST. Of course, the advertisements and the box would carry Miss Hurst's picture, maybe lifting a man in the air over her head? In the hall, a man hollered for someone to bring in another load. Boxes scraped the wooden floor. Sally would hate to see what's being done to these expensive floors.

"Strong as Lulu Hurst." Will tasted the words. "I like that. You're real smart."

He leaned closer to Ellison. "This could be a good arrangement for both of us. You sell more wash soap—"

"Washing soda," Ellison yipped.

"Washing soda, and Lulu gets what? We already got clean clothes." Will chuckled. Let Ellison take him for a fool.

"You get advertising, for one thing. Angeline Washing Soda's a top brand in New York, which includes Brooklyn and the Bronx as well as here in the City."

"We've got New York and the outliers in our hands, boy." Will stubbed the cigar out in the ashtray at his elbow. "Two straight weeks, double shows daily, sold out. We're on our way to Saratoga Springs after this, coming out of a week in Washington and Baltimore. Europe's in the works."

The last one was a lie, but Ellison bobbed slightly. Will took this as agreement and continued.

"What we'll want for your putting Lulu's name and picture on your washing soda boxes and your newspaper ads is plain and simple dollars. A thousand dollars for her likeness. And a percentage of your sales, paid quarterly to my bank back home."

"A thousand?"

"That's likeness and name, both, renegotiable after one year." Will had no idea what Max Berlin charged for putting a performer's name and image on a product. Maybe Berlin hadn't crossed this bridge. Will intended to pioneer this territory on his own. Berlin wasn't the man up there every night, dealing with the theater managers when time ran short or long, and making sure that Lulu was brimming with spit and vinegar every night and six afternoons a week.

Whether it was his indignation, the possibility of hooking a fish and letting it slip away, or if Ellison had been prepared to spend that kind of money all along, Will couldn't tell, but the college boy shook on it, and over brandy, they toasted the future of Angeline Washing Soda's new slogan, "As Strong as Lulu Hurst."

Will left with a bank check for one thousand dollars, made out to William J. Hurst, Esquire, "for the sole use of the image and name of Miss Lulu Hurst, known as The Magnetic Girl, by Angeline Washing Soda Company and Edgar Ellison, Esq."

CHAPTER TWENTY-ONE

New York City:
April 1884

DADDY TOOK HIS TIME SELECTING VOLUNTEERS FOR the chair test, despite his having been handed a slip from house management. We had officially been put on notice to keep things hopping. The cane tests always went fast and furious, but it looked like today Daddy was going to play the show his way, never mind if he irked another house manager.

I'd learned to keep myself busy counting hats in the audience or tallying the burnt-out gas lamps that looked like blind eyes. As Daddy pushed the edge of running long, I counted the yellow-lit faces, reminding myself that each was a higher class of person than those at Madame Parnell's.

Daddy brought me a man who looked like a goat. I told him the usual: sit with both feet firmly on the floor, hands on the side rails, make sure to hold on tight. Then I walked behind him, centered my weight, and cupped my hands over the chair splats. And I counted like always, disappearing into my breathing. I got to twelve and felt nothing. Any second now, the rain sound in my head would grow louder and become a blue glow behind my eyes. With it would come the excitation I loved. I would yank the chair onto its back legs just before I bent my knees to rock it forward. The goat-man sat immobile, waiting, barely breathing. I counted to fifteen. Eight was my usual. No rain, no glow, no thrill. Only hundreds of staring eyes in the audience, and the magnetic tug of their desire. Mrs. Voorhees's description swam in my mind. Bottomless need. She didn't know me. I yanked the chair, and again, it didn't move. I pushed her from my mind and pulled again. Nothing.

Perhaps I'd waited too long or not long enough. Maybe I'd been so lost in my thoughts that the single moment of rain and light came and went without my notice. I could go one more time, but the audience's mood had changed. The man in the chair turned and glared at me. He no longer resembled a goat, just an angry stranger. Daddy guided the man from the chair.

"The Power is unpredictable," Daddy bellowed to the audience as much as to the mark. "There are factors, equations in science that even we don't understand. No one can predetermine the Force."

My cheeks burned, and my palms were wet. Maybe perspiration was why I couldn't pull the chair. I wiped my hands on my skirt and closed my eyes. That bought and paid-for heckler in Atlanta laughed from below a snow-drifted stair. I had a reputation to uphold. The audience counted on me. My parents counted on me. And I couldn't even think about how much Leo counted on me, and him not even realizing it.

Failure in the performance, read that first contract. They'd always expected this to happen. Mr. Braunstein and now Mr. Berlin, lying in wait. My parents. Mrs. Voorhees. And Mrs. Wolf was not here to look me in the eye, massage my sore hands, or hold me to her breast until she had erased the sounds and smells and light that impaired me after every performance.

Tears salted the inside of my nose. Damn. I adored the precise thump that swear made in my mind. Damn Madame Parnell's talker calling me out like he knew me, damn that nasty museum, damn that poor little two-faced horror floating dead in its jar. Somebody's child, and they gave him up. Maybe he was dead already. Or maybe they gave him away when he was alive. How could you love someone with four arms, with a face that went two ways?

I opened my eyes to Daddy pushing a plump young man in a striped jacket into the chair.

"What is the Force but the Great Unknown?" Daddy hollered, not at the mark, but at me.

My job was to react as if I were a newborn baby, unable to make judgments, unable to think for myself. Babies, he'd said once, observe. Babyhood was fragile, like glass. Babies could do nothing for themselves.

I feared to move, Mrs. Wolf wrote. What had she done then, when she was afraid to move? Her words, my words, and my father's words slammed into one another, a wreck on the roadway of my mind. But she'd written *exhilaration,* too. Tentatively, I placed my hands on the back of the chair.

"Set your feet evenly on the floor," I began, and the fellow did as I told him.

NO ONE WAS PLEASED with me after that show. Heading to the dressing room in the shadows, I didn't see Daddy turn to me or pull back his arm. The minute we cleared the second set of curtains, his fist hit my chest. Disbelieving, gasping for breath, I fell onto a pulley, hitting my head on the metal winch.

"Mess up like that again and we're destroyed," he said. His voice was weirdly soft and empty of love. Struggling to right myself from the web of ropes and cables, I gingerly touched the back of my head, feeling for blood. My blood would make him sorry.

My hand came away clean.

"They were watching me so closely—" I started to say, but I knew how stupid that would sound. They were supposed to watch me.

"You wasted your rest today loitering in a dime museum. Don't think I wouldn't know," he said, and there was no point in saying that

I never intended to hide that from him. My mouth opened to say anything in self-defense, and he drew his hand back again. Damn.

Daddy railed at me, not so loud as to disrupt the act on the stage six feet to my left. *Save me*, I thought to the stage manager at the curtain, but he slipped away from us into the dark. *Look at me*, I telegraphed to the man whose act was to get hit in the stomach with cannonballs, but he pushed his cardboard weapon and hollow cork ammunition past us in a hurry.

"You cannot be trusted with the promise you made to your family," Daddy said. "All my dedication to teaching you these things and look at what you've done."

Something had broken loose in my father, and he couldn't, or wouldn't, hear me. *There are so many who cannot see what is before their eyes*, Mrs. Wolf wrote. All I wanted was to make Leo's life better. When I did, we could start over as if that moment when I tried to help baby Leo see the world had never happened.

"You are less responsible than your brother," Daddy said.

"Leo *is* responsible," I wailed. "He can't help what happened to him."

I hadn't meant to say it that way—what happened *to* him—but my soothing rain sound and blue glow were gone forever, replaced by a need to tell the truth. I hadn't stolen a book, I'd stolen my brother's future. Leo had twisted harder than a baby should, right out of my two hands, and I'd clutched his nightdress, but not enough, because what else was there to hold, and he slid out of it, of course he did, falling into what would be his life. I had intended only to show him the beauty of the world, but I lost my grip on his negligible weight. His head hit the floor with a cracking sound, loud as lightning, loud as breaking a glass jar with a baby inside, loud as a broken heart.

If I told the truth, my parents would leave me here in New York. They'd send me to Blackwell's Island, where I'd die in my own waste in the madhouse with the convicts. I would never see Leo again.

I was crying now, heartbroken.

"He was *sick*, Lulu," my father said. "Brain fever and aptha. He couldn't breathe, and then he could, but it was too late." He paused, his anger dipping and rising. "A child's not responsible for contracting a disease. He was a child, but you are not. And here we are, your mother and me, in cities where no right-minded person should ever be, relying on you day after day to make good on your sorry inheritance."

Daddy tried to put his arm around my shoulder. Torn between leaning into his embrace and pulling away, I stumbled, but he caught me and held me close. Weeping harder, leaving wet trails on his shirt, I breathed in his bitter dried sweat and something sweet, like caramel. Whiskey.

"That book you love so much," he said, as if he were dreaming. "That was my mother's. She wrote it."

I pushed away from him. He looked like someone I'd never seen before. He looked frightened.

"Your momma was Mrs. Wolf?"

"Her name before she married was Wolf. She kept it for her profession and added the Missus. The same way you can stare into someone's eyes and make them behave how you want, she could too."

My jaw ached. Pain blossomed in the bridge of my nose and behind my eyes. The back of my head stung. My chest ached, inside and out. My sorry inheritance. A grandmother who'd been speaking to me through the pages of a book, never once letting on who she really was. Daddy had known all along, and he'd never given so much as a hint.

"Never mind how I know this," he'd said, teaching me to rock a chair so a fellow would believe in my power. He just knew it, that was all. Every time I spoke her words to my father, every time I opened the book in his presence, he'd known whose words I was taking into my heart.

He'd never read past the first few pages. That's what he wanted me to believe. Maybe that was true. The skill I loved so much in myself he had seen in someone I never knew, but he kept that secret, a stone I couldn't touch.

"That time when I found you on the porch and you were waiting for dawn? That's when I knew you had my Momma in you," he said. "And I saw what you tried to do to your cousin at our table. You know you can't do it to me. You've tried, but I can see that coming from a mile."

Daddy let me go, and I sat, crumpled and weak, on a crate. The drum beat that signaled the cardboard cannon's explosions cued blurts of laughter from the audience. Not a one of them knew a thing, laughing at a sphere of cork, a cardboard tube, and a part-time strongman and sometime longshoreman doubling over his muscled torso, pretending to gasp in shock.

Daddy had called my skill a gift. I'd never asked where it came from. He'd pretended what made me special came from nowhere and anywhere. A child takes her father at his word, and like a child, I'd believed him.

"I can fix Leo," I said, my voice as disembodied as that laughing audience. "I learned from Mrs. Wolf's—"

What should I call her? Grandmother?

"You can't learn that from a book," Daddy said. He sat on the floor beside me, not caring that sawdust would dirty his trousers or how often the spittoon got missed. "You can stare at people, sure, like my mother did, and make them think they're confused, but it's me who trained you to put the ephemeral to tangible use."

"She didn't kill anyone, though," I ventured.

"Murder?" Daddy was startled. "Of course not. People in all states of desperation and illness sought her help. Whether she could give it was another matter, but she was no killer."

He was quiet for a moment, scraping at a fleck of something under his nail.

"Why on earth would you think that?"

Nowhere had she written that she'd taken a life. Perhaps the tragedy happened after she wrote her book. Perhaps it never happened, and she wasn't able to speak up. The wrong story outlived her.

"No reason," I said, keeping close a stone he couldn't touch.

Daddy shook his head. When he stood, he took a paper from his jacket pocket and handed it down to me.

It was a bank check for a thousand dollars, written to Colonel William Hurst, signed by someone named Edgar Ellison, Esquire.

Daddy mistook my inertia for ingratitude.

"For the image and likeness of Lulu Hurst on boxes of washing soda. Nothing trivial like boot insoles or electric undergarments. You won't have to do anything, missy, and after tonight, that seems our best choice. Some fellow with an easel will show up, and you'll sit nice and pretty while he makes you out to look like Sarah Bernhardt."

"Yes, sir," I said, and then, "thank you," which had to be the right thing to say. Daddy dipped a cup of water from a bucket and wiped his face with the graying towel that hung on a nail above it. The backstage commotion made it hard for me to think. While he drank, I went to the water closet and latched the door.

I had always known I was different. From the start, I was ahead of my schoolmates: the answer to a question often appeared in my head before the teacher had finished asking. And I'd captivated a fox, and Sarah, and Mr. Campbell, and Dale, and every fellow since then who stepped on stage to face me, the exception being this one today. Because of me, no one in my family struggled to eat.

Daddy and Momma didn't know they were wrong. Yes, Leo had taken ill, but that only compounded the damage I'd already done. I'd been a child myself that day, but I was responsible nonetheless, failing at the simple task of lifting my brother up to see the beauty of the world. The lamp over his head and the turpentine cloths across his chest didn't cure Leo. They couldn't. *Revitalization is enabled via the channels of Mesmerism.*

I unbuttoned the collar of my dress and wriggled myself free enough to touch the skin under my chemise. The dirty window didn't let in much daylight, giving me only a muted view of my pale skin and the black dress open to my white undergarment pulled aside. A red mark appeared when I touched the pain. It would bloom into a bruise. Momma didn't need to know. We were here, after all, because of me.

A pounding on the toilet door made me jump. I pressed the spot on my chest, watching it redden. The pounding on the door came again, angrier.

Closing my buttons, I hollered "Sorry!" and reached up, pulling the rusted chain and waiting for the rush of water to rattle the pipes and gurgle back to silence before I unlatched the door.

"Monthlies," I said to the angry woman in the hall. Let her be shocked. I didn't care.

Dear Leo:

Your sister will be immortalized like a painting in a book. Daddy made a business arrangement with a fellow who owns a soap fac‑tory. Can you imagine a factory just for making soap? Well, that soap will have my picture on the box with the words, "With the Power of The Magnetic Girl."
I'm happy to report that I do not have to clean anything with it, but instead sat in our hotel room for an entire day, dressed to the nines, while an artist with an easel and a box of pens and pencils sat across from me and drew my likeness. I tried to chat with him, but every time I did he moved his hand like he was cutting his throat.
How did I get an entire day just to sit, you wonder? I sometimes have an "off day," and that was the day the artist visited. He drew several likenesses of me, all of which we admired quite well. The final selection will be featured on the front of Ellison's Washing Soda boxes. We will ask Mrs. Hartnett to buy a few boxes in town so you can see your sister, but I will home by then, so you can see me in person, and I you!
The New York City shows have all gone very well. We are heading to Saratoga Springs, New York soon, which is close to Canada, so I hope we'll see some Esquimaux. I wish I could have the artist who drew me make a picture of a fur‑wrapped man for you. Instead, I have a steel button hook for your boots, engraved with the name of the store that gives them away for free. Can you imagine a place where objects are so plentiful that stores give them to you just for coming in?

Love, your sister, Lulu

CHAPTER
TWENTY-TWO

I PRETENDED TO SLEEP ON THE TRAIN OUT OF NEW YORK. At home, I could have disappeared into chores, a good time to get one thing done while thinking about another. But here on the train, nodding and smiling to passengers who recognized me, or at least acknowledged my elegant dress, my hat, and our luggage and trunks hauled by a porter, I had nothing but my hand exercises to occupy me while I pondered. Our seating arrangement was habit by now. Me at the window, Momma across, Daddy at my side. The fourth seat was taken up with the miscellany of travel; bought dinners, coats, newspapers. Why had this seating arrangement only now appeared to me as its own kind of container?

"I'm lucky," I'd told a reporter in Alabama or Pennsylvania or maybe both. "I've been blessed with a gift that captivates so many people, even though I never know how strong or weak my magnetic current will be. There's always a surprise for me." Another lie. This wasn't luck. Just *a blissful radiance,* Mrs. Wolf called it.

When I'd been unable to lift that fellow, I was alarmed, but there was a shadow of another feeling that I couldn't place. A day passed before I recognized the light-hearted feeling as happiness, but that's what it was. The Magnetic Girl had failed, but what Mrs. Wolf—my grandmother—could do was my inheritance, never mind chairs or canes. At home, with her true strength in my blood and no audience anticipating my faults, I would lay my hands upon Leo and I would not fail.

The sweet smell of whiskey surrounded my father like a cloud. I leaned into the window frame searching for a crack in the seam and a waft of fresh air. The bric-a-brac and curtains and woodwork around us in the train car smeared into ribbons of ugly color. I closed my eyes and eased myself lower into the cushioned seat. My joints hurt. My elbows creaked like hinges, my knees felt ballasted by stones. The motion of the train rocked me toward sleep.

"I told him two straight weeks, double shows daily, sold out, how we're on our way to Saratoga Springs coming out of a week in Washington and Baltimore. Been in Jersey City, too, and Bridgeport. Europe's in the works," Daddy was saying.

"We don't have Europe," Momma answered.

"Ellison doesn't know that," Daddy said. He was laughing. "Lulu's face on washing soap gets us to folks who will never see an opera house."

How is it that I could see Momma nodding, smiling, patting my father's cheek?

"She gets sick and worn out from all this stage work. Her picture on a commodity makes it so she doesn't have to keep handling strangers, standing in the limelights—"

"A thousand dollars," my father said, "lasts a while."

Sleeping, I melted away like soap.

No matter how I tired I was, the tracks stretching out ahead as they went around a bend, the crowded big city train stations and the lonely town stations with their wagons parked outside still made my heart kick. The train's steam blasts called the two syllables of "Lulu," cheering me on. Saratoga was ahead.

The artist for the soap company had been no fun at all. He introduced himself as Mr. Allan, but he said nothing about my dress, midnight blue with bows along the skirt and a good-sized bustle. I'd expected him to acknowledge how well I dressed, since Momma and I had inspected half a dozen dresses for my sitting. All he did was have me tilt my chin up to get clear of the corsage, the heavy yellow of sunflowers. He was quick with his easel, unfolding it in two shakes and setting himself up with the window at his back.

"I'll need the best light," he said, annoyed that he had to explain himself.

"That's fine," I told him. We'd be together the entire day, or at least until he captured the likeness he wanted.

I wasn't going back to the Dime Museum. The Ladies' Mile was off the ticket, too.

"Have you seen my tests?" I asked Mr. Allan.

"Don't move your mouth," he said, licking the tip of a pencil.

"I was just making conversation," I answered.

"Your mouth," he said, resting his foot on a brocade ottoman.

Your foot, I thought.

Mr. Allan drew me sitting, then standing. He drew me with my arms up as if I were juggling, then with my hands at my lap.

Momma and Daddy stayed within earshot the entire time. Daddy looked over Mr. Allan's shoulder now and again, nodding his approval, or pointing at one thing or another on the big sheets of paper. The artist's sour mood curdled the warmth I wanted to project in my smile.

After four hours, he said, "All right then," and put his pencils away. Sprung free, I rolled my neck and shoulders and cracked my wrists, until Momma threw me a look.

Unladylike. Not gentle. She didn't have to say a thing. I felt her words in my body.

Daddy shook Mr. Allan's hand, and Momma thanked him for his time and talent.

"Can I see?" I asked.

"Yes, please," Momma said to Mr. Allan.

He spread the drawings out on a table. The girl on the pages was a likeness of me, but she was better, she was more. My bangs were a perfect little curtain of black on my forehead, tight and groomed. The blue of my dress didn't show up; he drew in black and grey on white, but the ribbons and bows were there in detail. He had exaggerated the narrowness of my waist, making me all the more stylish, giving a subtle but ladylike strength to my big shoulders. I wondered, fleetingly, if Arden would buy the soap for his household.

"You, sir, are a rare talent," Daddy told him. Mr. Allan stared into the middle distance, unwilling to see how greatly he'd moved my parents.

His portraits were remarkable. But the smile I'd held all day was barely there. He had drawn a smirk on a hard little mouth. He had drawn my eyes too far apart and too small. True Mesmerists had big eyes.

The train was slowing, its wheels inside wheels churning. Distant houses and fields, blurry behind a curtain of snow, slid away like a curtain to reveal hulks of warehouses and factories. Daddy began to stir. Momma was ready for the porter, her coat buttoned and her hat on.

Mr. Allan hadn't captured me at all. I needed a new test of my own that went right to the heart of my skills as a *practical Mesmerist* like my grandmother. And then we would be ready for home. Tomorrow, The Magnetic Girl would take the stage at the Regal Opera House at eight in the evening. If I didn't slip up like I had in New York, and if I kept us moving fast enough that Daddy couldn't stop me, then there wasn't a single reason I couldn't chat oh-so-briefly with a mark while I seated him. And as I did, I would do something different on stage, something that was just mine. I would rest my hand on a pocket watch chain or the edge of a handkerchief as I held the mark's gaze. Sliding the object into my sleeve would be so simple and so enjoyable, no different than Sarah and her egg or Dale's scarf. I could put captivating and strength to real use on stage by bringing objects into my hands and making them mine, the same way forsaken buttons and pins found their safe home in a velvet-lined box.

My grandmother had written that when she touched people, a *sensation passed from the crown of her head to the soles of her feet*. If that sensation was electricity passing through one body to another, I was skilled enough to control it myself. My skin crawled. Nerves. Coming into a town was always more exciting than leaving one.

WE ARRIVED AT THE Regal an hour before curtain, bundled against the cold. The inside of my nose cracked and bled, and I'd rubbed cream into my hands every few minutes since we got off the train. Snow at home was gentle and soft, but here the flakes burned like match heads. The temperature wasn't much better inside the theater. The stove was lit in the dressing room, but it hadn't been going all day.

"We're all going to get catarrh," Momma said, unwinding her scarf.

Imagining the thunderous applause after my new tests was almost enough to warm me. Daddy would be angry that I added a new touch to the tests tonight, but he would come around once the audience was on their feet.

My travel trunk stood upright in the middle of the dressing room. I hated when the carter did that. Other *artistes* bad mouthed me about taking up space or winked extravagantly and asked me to show them how I could lift it out of the way.

Daddy, seeing the trunk was safely here, kissed Momma's cheek and left. He'd be gone until just before show time like always. Banking. Checking the posters. A father's job in a new town. Momma opened the trunk and got busy wiping a spot from a black dress and selecting a corsage. I hung my hat and coat and muffler and the rest of the protective gear on the coat rack, and started my preparations, flexing my fingers and wrists, playing pretend piano scales in the air. In the hallway, someone hollered for Margaret to lay off, for crying out loud. A pulley squealed, and I felt in the walls the drag of the heavy stage curtains bucking and stalling as someone tried to ease them across the boards.

While I did another round of deep knee bends, two petite women dressed to appear comically stout came in reciting lines to one another. The older one waved to me without breaking character. From the downside of a crouch, I waved back. When I stood, Momma was on me with a washrag. I was too old to let my mother bathe my face or help me dress, but she'd lately begun insisting, helping me into my heavy dress, buttoning the front from waist to throat. When I tried to make her quit, she got sentimental.

"You can't dress yourself for the tests," she said. "Your hands."

If I didn't change my chemise, she wouldn't see the mark on my chest from Daddy's knuckles, now purpling and green-tinged like the sky before a storm. I closed my eyes and held still, although I couldn't block out the sound of the women giggling at me. I could dress myself fine all damn day when I wasn't half an hour to being The Magnetic Girl. At home I washed Leo at the chamber pot and picked okra in all its spiny glory, and no one gave my hands a second thought.

Momma's fingers at my bosom made me twitchy. At my throat, they made me flat-out nervous. I pulled a breath in through my nose, and let it fill my arms and legs, my back and shoulders. When I opened my eyes, I was dressed, and Momma held open the dressing room door. In the hallway, five boys dressed as old Chinese men ran past, their fake black pigtails jouncing under their Coolie hats. The Thrilling Chinese Jugglers were leaving the stage. I heard the audience applaud, and someone in the back cheered, a little late. Probably a drunk. Daddy would be in the wings by now, ready to eye both me and his pocket watch at the same time. I'm carefree, and the audience is, too, I told myself. When I'm happy, they're happy.

The stage stank of lamp oil and liquor. Daddy chose the first fellow of the night. Like so many lately, the mark already knew what to do. He sat carefully in the wooden chair and waited. Daddy's watch ticked. I set my palms along the chair splats and the audience silenced in one breath. This fellow was plain, but the next would surely have a stickpin or a pocket watch that would come to rest in my palm before he sat.

My own breathing was loud in my ears, rhythmic and deep. Good. My tunnel hadn't failed me. I shifted slightly into the light. The audience in front would want to see for themselves that no gloves or rings diverted the magnetism in my fingers. This was my how do you do to any smart-mouthed reporter in the seats, too. Some of them thought I had buckshot in the canes. Setting my feet slightly apart and bending my knees barely an inch, I pressed my shins against the chair's rear legs. I counted silently, a last goodbye to any creeping thoughts of the fiasco back in New York City.

Three, two, one.

And then I pulled.

The mark was startled, just like he was supposed to be. They were always startled, even the ones who showed up night after night. His natural reaction was to lean back into the chair—we relied on it, and they always came through—which helped me lift the chair just a smidgen higher. Good boy. He yelped like a puppy, piercing my daze.

Time to let go.

Daddy sprang forward, leading a round of applause. I blinked and sucked air in through my nose. I'd done this test more than a thousand times, and never stopped feeling like I'd just emerged from underwater.

The crowd hollered "Lulu Hurst, Lulu Hurst," like always.

This time, though, a spot crawled at my upper back. The fellow must have been heavier than I figured. Maybe I strained something. The worry that I'd miss my internal cue again shook me and I focused my thoughts instead on ribbons of metal winding through stones, on strength in the flow of blood, on floating orbs, of my grandmother's *elated labor*. Daddy was full on with his patter, rounding up marks, and I put my hand to my forehead Hiawatha-style to scan the crowd.

A fellow ran by the curtain with his arm to his nose. Probably a backstage greenhorn spooked by a rat drowned in a barrel. My eyes stung. A good look at my father would put me back on track, but a curtain of mist separated us. The audience was on their feet. A woman screamed, "Fire!" and in a split second, every person in the two-hundred-seat opera house made for the aisles, running every which way, toward the lobby, toward the stage, up and down the aisle. Smoke, not mist, billowed from the purple curtain behind me. Someone knocked me in the back and my chin hit the floor. I tasted blood. Piano keys banged. People were climbing over the piano to rescue themselves. A sickening snap set off three hard crashes and out of habit I counted them the same way I counted my breaths before a lift, steam blasts from a train, migrating birds in formation. I tried to rise to my hands and knees, but heat like a mattress weighed me down, suffocating me beneath wilted feathers, a stolen scarf, an unlit pipe with a leering face. These objects hadn't jumped into my life on their own. I had pulled them here with my magnetic power.

The curtains ignited with a sizzle. Dirty boots, clean boots, a ladies' pair with worn heels stampeded past my head. A man's brown shoe stepped on my wrist and turned it like a rolling pin, twisting a muscle in my forearm all the way to my elbow. I screamed.

"Get up!" Daddy's voice, angry but with a vein of fear.

I curled into a ball, my head between my knees. I was going to die.

Daddy tugged me to my feet. We ran across the stage, passing weeping, pushing people. I tried to hold my hand out to them, to pull them along with us or shelter each of them in my pockets and keep them safe, but we kept running, past a flaming curtain and a beam from the ceiling dangling to the floor.

We ran into freezing night air.

As we ran through the door, I waved again, showing the frightened people our way out. Not one of them saw me.

CHAPTER
TWENTY-THREE

Saratoga, New York:
April 1884

DAWN CAME PINK AND SHINY LIKE NEW FLESH, SPILLING weak light on the divan in the hotel room. The banging of fire bells and the clatter of horses pulling fire wagons on the icy streets was gone, dire sounds of people trying to do something to help. Their absence told me that nothing could be done. My tongue tasted like old blood, even though I had cleaned my teeth and rinsed my mouth over and over again. *Cinders, singed, sorrow, stupid* counted out in my mind like a nursery rhyme. For close to the hundredth time that night, I hawked black-streaked mucus into a handkerchief, hating the rude sound.

Momma had run me a bath, and I'd washed the soot from my flesh, no longer enjoying the miracle of water that came hot and squealing from a spigot. My wrist throbbed. Momma wrapped clean cloths around my hands to protect the fat blisters on my palms. She had wanted the hotel to call for a doctor, but Daddy insisted we lie low until morning.

"Let her rest," he said, and Momma didn't argue.

Something around me smelled like cooked garbage despite the bath, and I wondered if the stench was my own skin, or if I had burned somewhere in my soul.

Daddy paced the carpet. His eyebrows were singed. Momma hadn't said a thing since he'd forbidden a doctor. When he announced he was going out to fetch a newspaper, she got his topcoat. After his footsteps had faded in the hall, Momma ordered broth for both of us, shooing me into the closet when the waiter knocked at the door. Nothing good would come from him spying a bloodshot-eyed Magnetic Girl stinking of ruin. From a crack at the closet door, I watched him set down the ramekins and soup pot. He glanced at the bloodied rags on the table and left before Momma could give him a coin.

We tried to drink our broth, unsure what to say, afraid to begin. I didn't want to see the newspaper. This was the wrong kind of fame, an Opera House destroyed. In a few days, the story would be embellished with drawings of fire horses, eyes wide and nostrils flared, water splashing from tanks in the wagons behind them.

Daddy returned with newspapers under each arm. He handed one to Momma and one to me. I scanned the headlines. Cholera rampaged through Europe, a band shell and park would be ready in time for summer, the weather in the West was officially a blizzard. They hadn't written a word about last night's fire. It couldn't have been as bad as I thought. Not newsworthy in the least. Lightheaded, I looked at Daddy. His expression stopped my heart.

"Go to the bottom of the page," he said. "Just keep reading."

Sick, I flipped the paper over and read below the fold.

Magnetism Torches Regal Opera House. One dead, five missing in the dramatic conflagration and total destruction to the city's finest theater at the start of the famous Magnetic Girl's opening night.

I nearly emptied my stomach onto the tablecloth. Someone was dead. Pressing my eyes closed wouldn't make today into yesterday. All the captivation in the world wouldn't un-print a newspaper.

Daddy said I was screaming when he pulled me from the flames.

Across the table, Momma turned the pages of her newspaper.

"A man here says sparks flew from your fingers and caught another man's jacket afire."

"You sound like you believe it!" My burned voice rasped. People would need an ear horn to listen to me. I cleared my throat; the flesh stung. I tasted fresh blood. That rumor in Savannah about sparks coming from my shoes. That woman in Ohio with the sparks in her fingers.

"Of course she doesn't believe it," Daddy said.

The emanation of power from the extremities. My grandmother had warned me. A real Mesmerist transmitted power through her hands, and her feet, too. I had not been careful with my strength. I had not, as Momma cautioned me in so many mundane things, been gentle.

I kept *The Truth of Mesmeric Influence* in my trunk, and my trunk was in the dressing room at the Opera House, same as any stop on any bill. My trunk, and everything in it, was a water-soaked smoldering corpse made of cardboard and leather and clothing. The book was the stilled heart in that dead pile.

Frantic, I clutched the newspaper to my chest as if it were a thing I could save.

Momma was busy staring into her bowl of broth.

I wanted to rip my bandages from my hands and fling them against the wall. I wanted to run until the urge to scream died in my lungs. Who knew what was right and true anymore? Look what I had done. Daddy took the newspaper from me and read aloud.

"The questionable safety of electricity and its natural parent, magnetism, has brought ruin to State Street's Regal Opera House last night."

I was shaking. "You know I can't set anything on fire with my bare hands!"

He continued. "Known to admirers nationwide as 'The Magnetic Girl,' Miss Lulu Hurst's power is said to have been the cause of a three-alarm fire at approximately eight p.m. yesterday that has, in the light of day, left an infant fatherless, a wife without a husband, and brought heartbreak and financial loss to many of our city's innocent fun seekers and their loved ones."

He handed the paper back to me as if it were something of mine he'd borrowed.

"There are people gathered outside the hotel looking for us," Daddy said. "I ducked them and came in the side."

He peered out the window to the sidewalk three floors below. When he opened the sash, the commotion below flew in with a drift of cinders. A man shouted, "Murderess," as if he were scolding a bad dog. "She started the Opera House fire," a newsboy sang out.

The crowds would only grow, ultimately rising to smother us if the hotel management didn't turn them out. The next knock on the door could be the police. I leapt forward, upending the soup, and reached to pull the window closed just as a rock grazed the glass and fell away, hurtling back down to the street. I flinched, imagining the rock landing solidly on the head of whoever threw it. What goes up. Newton's laws of motion. They were what had gotten us here.

"Someone's a good shot," Daddy said.

For the first time since the waiter left, Momma spoke.

"We need to go home."

CHAPTER
TWENTY-FOUR

WE BOARDED A TRAIN OUT OF SARATOGA AS THE WILSON family, a name Daddy made up as he bought the tickets. I thought about the name as we took our places on our wooden seats. Wilson. Will's son. The three of us were each like Leo now. Damaged.

We went west in our winter wear like a little herd of buffalo. The Wilson family didn't send a telegram to Mr. Berlin advising him that they'd absquatulated on the rest of The Magnetic Girl's nights in Saratoga or anywhere else. The Wilsons didn't tell him about heading home the long way, though Pennsylvania, down to Virginia, and into Georgia by way of Tennessee. We simply packed our valises and made for the station, settling the hotel bill by leaving a stack of cash on a bureau. We left my trunk of Richman's dresses at the hotel and my ruined on-stage dresses in the theater. I wept for them as if they were abandoned children, but we had no choice. The papers said a man was dead—a father, a husband. The police were certainly looking for us, ready to put us in jail. The theater management would be looking for us too, with Mr. Berlin leading the charge.

If I had Mrs. Voorhees's sleeping drops, I'd pour myself a tall glass. What was it the actors said? Sleep knitted up the raveled sleeve of care?

When the train was a few hours out of Saratoga, Daddy grew unnaturally cheerful. He made jokes about the fellow selling lunches from a pail, calling the food "a pale imitation of a meal." The Wilsons were happy people. To keep my father at bay, I forced a laugh. This Wilson daughter I had become hadn't heedlessly sabotaged her family's future. She had no "Will's son" in her life. She was no trouble at all.

Like the two-faced baby in its jar, or Mrs. Wolf's secret identity as my grandmother, I had become two people. Lulu Hurst became the Magnetic Girl. She was a version of me, only better. Her Mesmerizing skills were polished until they were top-notch, her voice gentle and warm, her height an attribute to admire rather than scorn. She could lift a man or enliven a cane until The Magnetic Girl became someone else yet again. Miss Wilson.

Like the two-headed baby, this Miss Wilson had no real name.

We arrived at a whistle stop long after dark, but Daddy pulled down the window and bought the evening papers from a newsboy. My knees trembled as he handed the paper through the window. I thought I might wet myself. I shut my eyes but couldn't obscure the sound Daddy made rattling the pages. No more building up The Magnetic Girl with foolish stories about curing toothache and tossing men high into the air. Every page could tear open the earth. The *Advertiser* in Albany, New York said the Regal had burned to the ground. The Rochester paper announced a charity drive for Mrs. Leora Schirmer and her newborn son, Abe, destitute after the tragic demise of the head of the family at his place of work. And what had happened to the Five Chinese Brothers? I would go to jail forever, and who would tell the actual Will's son what had become of me? Leo's little face swam before me. I wished the newsboy hadn't been at the window, that we had slept through this station, that the paper Daddy was shaking out to read would be smeared and illegible beyond use.

He rattled the pages again. I wanted to jump out of my skin.

"What is it?" I whispered, my eyes squeezed closed. The train was starting up again, and the conductor's shout grated on my last nerve. I opened one eye. New passengers settled in. A mother cooed at a baby, a man excused himself to the smoker. Daddy was looking at the newspaper like it was a wormy ear of corn.

"There's a girl performing as 'Dixie's Darling Magnet.' She filled the opera house in Savannah three nights running, and Macon for a week. Her people have her booked into Atlanta next month."

"Is she playing at DeGive's?" I asked. Jealousy was absurd, but DeGive's was *my* opera house, my first real theater.

I opened both eyes and looked at the floor. My boot toes were peeled. These were the same boots I'd worn on stage last night. We must reek of smoke and regret.

"The Georgia Magnet sounds too much like Lulu's name," Momma said. "That girl can't just take it. She's stealing."

"She's *Dixie's* Magnet," Daddy said. "Her management's come up with enough of a difference in the name." He shook the newspaper out, and I thought he might wave it like a battle flag. Momma took the paper from him.

"Her real name is Amiracle Marshall," she read. "A fellow named Arden Mabry manages her, and it says here he named her after the song, 'Dixie.'"

She must have misread. I must have misheard. The name wasn't Mabry. I snatched the newspaper from her hands and scanned the page. The words made no sense, piling up and spreading out like marching ants. I stared, trying to captivate the unruly alphabet, until a phrase formed.

Management, Arden Mabry, Esquire.

That pretentious string quartet from the McGill Dining Room played savagely in my head. What had I told him? Fulcrum and lever. He had laughed over that, teased me about my reading habits. "Anyone can learn a trick," I'd said.

Had we spoken about Mrs. Wolf? I felt sick, but I was sure I wouldn't have spoken about her. I wouldn't have told him how captivating made me strong inside, or that I had learned to call what I'd always known by the name Mesmerism.

But here on the page was Arden Mabry Esquire's own Magnet.

Momma reached for the paper, *tsk*ing at my rudeness. I couldn't meet her eyes or Daddy's. My face would show that I had created this duplicate. Arden's letter to me was charred to ruin within the pages of *The Truth of Mesmeric Influence*, but even without that proof that we'd met, it was clear that he had learned from me what he needed to know. At the very least, he'd assembled enough to get started. Arden wasn't having this child captivate. She couldn't do it. He'd made off with the terminology, the basic parts of what Dorcas Edwards rightly called a game.

Where he met this Miss Marshall, I didn't know. Pennsylvania, or New York, or maybe he'd gone to Georgia or Mississippi and found a girl who could—what? The book was gone, but the power lived on in me. That was my true inheritance. Mrs. Voorhees, for all her caution to me about forebears, was right. A person had to understand the responsibility in magnetism.

I was not weak inside. I was strong. I turned my calm gaze toward my parents. Daddy looked pained.

WE STAYED IN ROOMING houses when we didn't sleep sitting up on an overnight train. Miss Wilson couldn't show off and have a porter carry her bags. We ate whatever a boarding house was serving. I felt like an immigrant, and as if I didn't comprehend English, I barely spoke. In a boarding house in Erie, Momma found someone's left-behind old-fashioned bonnet for me to wear, hiding most of my face. There wasn't any need to disguise Daddy, but he enjoyed the subterfuge. He let his beard grow out and talked like a bumpkin, getting in all the "might coulds" and "aint's" that he normally disparaged.

We checked the newspapers in every city. Some papers had the Regal destroyed. Others wrote that the stage was merely scorched, and the curtains demolished. The Opera House would be rebuilt, "newer and up to date," said the Cleveland paper. The theater management was even putting in electric lights. When Daddy joked that the Magnetic Girl had brought electrical power to the Opera House after all, I wanted to tear my hands off. As if my hands could start fires, I kept them pinned underneath my thighs. When I gathered my valise or accepted a drink of water, my hands were numb. I kept my fingers away from the needle hidden in my stays.

We would have to make good on the property damage in Saratoga Springs. Momma said so. Their loss, Daddy said. That money I'd counted in my head when I couldn't sleep was as good as gone. As we traveled southward toward home, my dates as The Magnetic Girl in Massachusetts and Connecticut and Rhode Island went unfulfilled. Worry flattened us like a sickness, but none of us spoke about it.

Each passing mile brought fewer news stories about the Regal Opera House fire, and more about Arden's Magnet. Her standing ovation at DeGive's. Her upcoming week at the City Hall Theater in Chattanooga, which I knew seated two hundred and fifty. Daddy threw the local newspapers, already soiled, to the floor of one train car after another.

"Amiracle Marshall is taking up your space in the papers," Daddy growled after tossing a two-day-old Louisville *Courier* to yet another gummed-up floor.

"Hush, Will," Momma said, staring into the same needlepoint green leaves and yellow roses she'd been poking at since Lockport.

As days passed, my longing to captivate began to grow, tentative as a green shoot. I tried my power on a lone cow that approached my window while our train chuffed on the tracks at a mail stop. The heifer's big eyes didn't glaze as I counted ten, fifteen, and then twenty. The muscles around my eyes tightened as I stared hard, then harder. After more than a minute of me staring and her chewing, she ambled away, bored. In the depot in Paducah, I caught a woman's eye and stared her down until her baby's cries vexed me so much I gave up. The young mother paled and busied herself with her infant. She did not applaud.

There was no applause for me on the train, no beautiful clothing
to protect me, no Miss Marie or Fyodor Dubrovsky or little Pierre
the monkey to befriend me. My own face, scowling and sad, flick-
ered in the train's window as we gained speed again. If she were a
stranger, I would captivate that moon-faced girl. With a town clicking behind her and her face floating like a tintype image over the
warehouses and roads, she looked weak enough to fall for anything.
I narrowed my eyes at her, and of course she narrowed hers back at
me. She looked—I looked—aching for a fight.

Daddy held stripped chicken bones from his boxed lunch out the
train window. The wind sucked them from his fingers.

"Amiracle Marshall will fill their minds for a while, and then we'll
come back with a bang," Daddy said.

The fried chicken smell made my stomach crawl.

"There's nothing in the papers about the fire anymore," he said,
satisfied. "Idiots gyrating about conflagrations wore themselves out."

Closing my eyes wouldn't make him disappear, and I never could
fully block out the sound of his voice.

"This girl doesn't have 'Luluism,'" he said.

Someone along the way had coined the phrase, and the papers
picked it up. Luluism brought us the washing soda arrangement. I
read about a fad at parties for three and four or more people to pile
together on chairs. Luluism. A man in Virginia had named his mule
Lulu. A fellow asking for my autograph told me.

"But not 'cause of her looks," he'd said. "She's just real strong and
sweet tempered."

The thought that a mule with my name was a jibe at my appearance hadn't crossed my mind, but once he mentioned it, the idea
stuck. Daddy was mad that he couldn't collect on the mule's name.
We named you, he said. We ought to have gotten a cut.

Daddy pointed a chicken leg in my face. "We'll lie low at home
for a while, change up the tests to make it new, and then see what
we can see."

Changing up the tests was exactly what had started the problem.
I was weak, the living embodiment of the wavering image in the

train's window. Daddy upended the decimated contents of the lunch box out the window. Chicken bones, gray and greasy, fluttered down to the ground behind us, leaving mysterious remnants on a railroad track between cities I'd never see.

"And besides," Daddy said. "You look like you could use a rest."

At nearly every stop, Daddy jumped down from the train and hurried into the station, returning with yet another newspaper, a gallant kiss for Momma, and a weak smile for me. He smelled of whiskey, the same burnt sugar odor that trailed half the stagehands we'd met. Whiskey for my father, drops for Mrs. Voorhees, medicine for Leo. Insulation from the real and true.

NO ONE GREETED US in Cedartown. We practically crept through the nearly empty station.

"Colonel!" A man's voice at our backs.

I crumpled. Daddy turned, all smiles, as if his shabby coat and untrimmed beard wouldn't raise questions. The telegraph operator, impatient, signaled from his window. Momma began to tremble. I took her hand, but we were clearly done for. It didn't matter that I hadn't intentionally killed Abner Schirmer in a fire I'd started with my hands: a policeman would be waiting on our porch, his face dour and sagging like an old hound's, the key to my prison cell in his hand.

At the telegraph window, Daddy leaned down to the fellow behind the cage, but I couldn't hear what they said. I was Miss Wilson still, powerless. But Daddy was smiling when he turned to us. His step was lighter than it had been in weeks. I felt faint.

"I knew it," he said, handing the telegram to Momma like a bouquet of flowers. Sweating into my gloves, I read over her shoulder.

BREACH OF CONTRACT. FAILURE TO PERFORM headed a list of the cities we'd abandoned. REGAL OPERA HOUSE FIRE DEEMED LAMP ACCIDENT. NO LEGAL CHARGES. NO FURTHER BUSINESS.

Mr. Berlin's telegram had been there for three weeks. The Magnetic

Girl was home, a place that anyone in New York or Washington, DC would call the back of beyond.

OUR PORCH STEPS HAD soft, rain-soaked patches, wounds gone rotten with neglect. In the three months we'd been gone, Mr. Hartnett hadn't swept away the leaves and snow. I walked backward away from the house to see the mountains rise behind the roofline. My home sky was a blue dome, uninterrupted by smoke, steam, wires, brick, or stone. Applause would be strange here, but the breeze made a sound, and the birds, too. A cricket jumped in the grass. A few weeks earlier, the sound would not have resembled that of a striking match.

I bent to the early spring grass and pressed my hands into the green, taking in the cold, fertile smell of dirt. Staying right here forever would be perfect, but Momma would come looking for me to help peel the sheets off the furniture, or rain would fall, or I'd get hungry, or have to go around back to the outhouse.

The clattering of the wagon on the road roused me. Leo called to me without words from the wagon.

I see you! Lulu, I see you! Yoohoo!

Captivated, I waved.

CHAPTER TWENTY-FIVE

Cedartown, Georgia:
May 1884

SO LITTLE HAD CHANGED. SUNLIGHT POURED FROM the open front door in a great wash, lifting my heart. No electricity illuminated corners beside the stove or parlor chairs that I would never have to lift. I didn't need it. Momma and carried the sheets from the furniture and hung them in the sun. We opened every window and unrolled every carpet. Sunlight sparkled on the dust mites and cobwebs we swept out. Leo took on tasks gleefully: cleaning our valises of so many weeks on trains and in boarding houses. When I saw Momma getting nowhere trying to pull the furniture aside, I didn't have the urge to say, "Be gentle," to watch her hackles rise. My poor Momma had lost her dreams of a better house, finer clothes, and who knew what for her son.

I tried not to think of my trunk and my dresses abandoned in Saratoga. My armor, burned to a crisp or stolen. Nothing was usual. The middle of the day with the fields overgrown and Daddy gone to town, me not in school, Leo telling stories to himself and laughing, and Momma, despite our great losses, happy as I'd seen her in a long time.

The money I'd earned until Saratoga would be waiting for us in the bank. Here on our shaded porch, the green valley spread around me, I could barely conjure an image of the damaged theater. NO CHARGES FILED, Mr. Berlin's telegraph said. I swept the floor and watched the dust dance in the air. Saratoga was as far as the moon.

Daddy went into Cedartown every few days. At least once a week he brought home the Atlanta papers. Their writers called Dixie's Darling Magnet "heavy as a Roman column." Arden's Magnet reversed my tests by offering marks the chance to try and lift *her*, and of course they couldn't. If I'd been anywhere near her act, I'd have walked onto her stage and torn her boot soles open to show off the metal weights I knew were inside. Arden clearly had that figured out. Newspaper artists depicted her as impossibly delicate, and of course they didn't show if she lined her stays with lead.

According to the Cedartown *Appeal*, I was officially unimpeachable.

"Furman owes me, for once," Daddy said to Momma when he thought I had left the room. He had forgotten how distinctly I could hear, how deeply I could feel. But we had chicken for dinner, and not just on Sunday. New seats for the wagon, the planks smooth and smelling of fresh pine. Fabric for Momma to make dresses for her, for me. Trousers and shirts for Leo, store-bought. Leather braces to hold his trousers up. New shoes for everyone. The dry goods just kept coming, every time Daddy went into town. Stick candy for Momma, wrapped like birthday presents.

"You're going to use that money up," Momma said, scolding Daddy. She took a peppermint from the box. I chose clove. Daddy kissed the top of her head. Embarrassed, I went for another candy. Wintergreen. The candy burned like a cold spark on my tongue.

ON A MONDAY MORNING, Daddy handed me a letter. The postmark was Chattanooga, the sender the Tennessee Spiritualist Society. He nodded as I read aloud.

We have reached the understanding among our members that Miss Lulu Hurst, The Magnetic Girl, is a bona fide example of the finer attributes of the psychically sensitive. We are pleased to invite her to Chattanooga as soon as you are able to arrange it.

"We'll treat this like a split week," Daddy said. "Bringing The Magnetic Girl directly to the eager Spiritualists in Chattanooga will introduce you to a new circle."

I'd end up eyeball to eyeball with dry ladies and fusty uncles wearing amulets, looking to spend one more moment with their very dead loved ones. Spiritualists were old women who'd lost their husbands and sons in a war over before I was born. They were ghost chasers, without the gumption that a mark showed in getting on stage with me. She hadn't taken her own life in the standard dramatic way, no knife, no gun, no *louche* poison as Mrs. Voorhees was slowly doing. The woman who called herself Mrs. Wolf when she Mesmerized had been worn through from the strain of giving, eaten alive from the inside.

Perhaps my grandmother had looked at my father when he was young the same way he looked at me now. Perhaps she had barely looked at him at all. What was in balance now wasn't magnetic fluid, but the truth of our own lives, mine, and Leo's.

"She took sick and died," Daddy had said.

Captivating was true as true could be. Ask that fox in our field, or the tens of dozens of fellows who lost their stuffing in the moments I held their gaze on stage. Lifting a fellow sprawled in a parlor chair or electric-shocking him through a walking stick was merely a trick, fulcrum and lever, or a kind of sleight of hand. They wanted to be humbugged and convinced themselves. The idea that had come to me since I'd been home—that some fellows desired close proximity to a young girl—made me shudder. Others were what Mrs. Voorhees predicted. A wall of people radiating need.

I could do nothing for them.

I could hear Mrs. Wolf. *Be attentive to the blessing and remain openhanded in imparting it to souls.*

Like the two heads on a single-bodied baby, I was weighted with a curse and a blessing. That child in the jar hadn't been a blessing, except perhaps to his mother before she saw him squalling double-time as he was pulled from her body. Or maybe she loved him— them—for the days or weeks they lived. Maybe she loved the idea of him, even now.

What my grandmother left me was both a blessing and a curse. *Insight and dominion over one's own nature.* My natural observation of shifts in sound and light, the humors in the world around me that I'd had as a child had been masked by my desire for fame. What I truly wanted was recognition for who I was. Not a tall tree, or an ungentle girl. Just Lulu Hurst. What I believed Leo needed, what Daddy wanted, what I presumed Arden wanted in me obscured my view.

The reverse face of a blessing is a curse. I needed to hear not a sunrise, but my own voice, clear and true.

No Chattanooga, no Spiritists. To my father, I said, "I can't do it."

Daddy lay his hand against my cheek, his touch gentle.

"You know that wasn't your fault. A person tripped over a lamp and the next thing you know the newspapers say it's you. This is a *good* outcome, Lulu."

How could he believe that? The bruises on my chest from his blow were long healed, but they throbbed a warning.

His mind was made up. The lost clothing and the lost tests had blown away like smoke. He was building something new, and like last time, he was building it on me.

"Your audience is temporarily diverted by this new Magnet, but she'll be old news soon enough. And don't you worry, Missy. She's got nothing on you. You're through with that lifting and throwing stuff. We're going all in with the Mesmerism."

This time he didn't say the word like "hoodoo," howling like a ghost.

"Don't make fun," I said, protecting my blessing and curse. "Your own Momma believed—"

"And that's why I know exactly what these folks are after, and the audience after them, and the audiences beyond that," Daddy said.

He took the letter from me and slapped it against his hand, keeping time to some hidden tune. "This is my bailiwick, Missy. It's a shame how your grandmother had those people convinced."

"Of what?" I asked, holding my invisible grandmother close.

"That she knew best."

Outdoors with the washtub, I slammed the metal against a tree until the tub buckled. Turning the cistern handle, I squeezed hard enough to cut my palm. To hell with The Magnetic Girl, and to hell with her precious hands. *Bona fide attributes*, the letter said. The Spiritualists would make me into a toy, a glue and feather bird hopping in a parlor while a demented person waited for me to bring back an old general and a dear major.

A disgraceful amusement for the ignorant, my grandmother wrote.

I cranked a wet dress through the wringer. It looked like a dead person—like the empty clothes arranged across my bed so many months ago. I had stepped into that dress and become someone else, a person deluded by avarice and shame. Water sloshed into my boots. Flecks of dead skin spun in the water. I dunked Leo's nightclothes into the dingy water, rubbing the striped cotton with Angeline's Washing Soda. We had an endless supply of the stuff, each box with that empty-headed drawing of me on the label, where my bosoms jutted out like Miss Marie's.

Look what I had done. Magnets push against opposite poles. When they do that, they can't come close or unite. I let this happen the day I went into his study. I let this happen when I held that ruined broomstick. I let this happen every time I stepped onto a stage, night after night, day after day.

The person who had betrayed me was not my father, and it wasn't Arden.

"Damn," exploded from my mouth. Saying the word out loud at home felt evil and free, and if I were bound for hell, then make way. "Damn it all to hell," I hollered.

CHAPTER TWENTY-SIX

THE IDEA CAME WHILE I THREW OUT THE KITCHEN slop water at night and thought about clean water gone dirty. Slicing carrots, I watched one object separate into two. One baby tears into two. One Lulu peels in half. The Magnetic Girl had loomed from broadsides, and now she posed rudely on boxes of laundry soap. When I looked in a mirror, there she was. With our "new circle" expecting miracles, I would never break free of her.

In a schoolbook, I drew a line down the center of a blank page at the back. I named the left-side column, *For*. The right-hand column was *Against*. Under *For*, I wrote *Travel*. Once a positive, but a scrim of laughing faces in a dark opera house changed my mind. *Disturbing*, I put in the matching *Against* column. *Intellectual growth* went on the *For* side. The paid heckler scurrying away in the snow went in the *Against* side. *Fine dresses and high style* went under *For*. On the *Against* side, I wrote *burned*. The theaters rumbling with stomping feet and cheers had flung my stomach into my throat and made me want to dance my way onto a stage. *For*. But fields and towns rushing past train windows signaled that I lived nowhere. *Against*.

I closed the book. Through the window, I saw Leo making his way to the house. He used canes now, one under each arm. "Like a veteran," Daddy said, proud, as if Leo, like him, had weathered the Battle of Murfreesboro.

Leo leaned his canes against the wall and sat in a kitchen chair.

"He's won, Leo," I said. "I can't go out again, but I can't not go. I am trapped."

Trapped? My brother had a different idea of trapped than I did.

"I am more trapped than you," I said, although I knew I shouldn't have.

Leo cut his eyes at me the same way Momma did, disapproval that punched me deeper inside than merely my stomach. His eyes were as grey as Daddy's. Both parents disdained me in his eyes.

Just because I don't want to go anywhere doesn't make me trapped. His sigh rippled the tablecloth.

Leo was just fine where he was. I was the one who had wanted to run away.

Do you remember?

"I remember all kinds of things," I said. "Which do you mean?"

Leo kicked me on purpose. When I went to rub my shin, he laughed just enough so I knew he was teasing.

When I was born. You were there, helping.

Leo being born was Momma biting down on a cloth in the bed, me by the door for so long, hours and hours after I'd thought she was dying, after she had me run for Daddy.

"You don't remember being born. No one does," I said.

You told me about it. You sang me a song about how I was a baby no bigger than a kitty cat. Leo giggled. The baby talk made us laugh, but we feared letting it go. Leo was no longer a baby. "Itty bitty kitty cat," I teased, because I would run from the room if I let myself remember Momma crying because he wouldn't take her breast. He doesn't know how, she said, her voice small and sick. Daddy refused to dig a grave, although he thought he might have to. At six years old, I could do nothing to help any of them.

Just tell Daddy you don't want to go.

I said nothing. You are the favored child, Leo, the one we watch and worry over, the child for whom any desire is delivered, hands open, supplicant, to stave off the darkness lurking around every corner.

"Momma would say I made my bed, and now I have to lie in it," I told him.

Suit yourself, Leo said, because there was nothing else to say.

THAT NIGHT, I WISHED my parents good night just as I always did, and went upstairs, lamp in hand.

I changed into my nightdress and hung up my clothes. I brushed my hair with the stiff-bristled brush, my own hands on my own head, not Momma handling me while eager strangers counted the minutes until they could witness The Magnetic Girl. I got into bed and waited. No more imaginary shopping trips. I'd lost dresses more extravagant than I could have dreamed up. Another hour dripped by, and I lay still, imagining the number of train timetables Momma had collected, city after city, rail line after rail line, from that first trip up to Rome through this last one home. I counted how many cities I had shared a bill with Miss Marie. In my head, I followed the barrel-rolling terrier act, turning the dogs' figure eight to the right and the left, rolling backward and forward while they danced on their hind legs.

All the while, I questioned Daddy's motives. His anger at his mother smoldered even with her dead in the ground. I loved Leo so much that my heart hurt when he smiled. How hard did a person have to be to break themselves off from love?

Outside, a barred owl called. The night was soft and sweet with the early spring smell of green things unfurling. My family slept. I left my bedroom and descended the stairs as if I were walking a tight wire, step after careful step.

At the parlor door, I watched the vision of a girl in a pink sash counting out a stranger's years by surreptitiously tapping the back of a chair. She counted, over and over, and I left her there to heel-toe my way to Daddy's study. Phantom images performed wherever I looked: The Magnetic Girl bending her knees inside the safety of her skirts, waving in the endless echo of applause from a crowd, helping a woman in a green dress to her feet on stage in a ladies' matinée.

The door popped open when I pressed it with my shoulder. We'd left our home alone so long that the doors were sticking. Even in the gloom the disorder was overwhelming. Papers sprawled across my father's desk. An overturned chair lay broken in a corner. His anger was alive here, and I recoiled, but I'd given myself a task. I lit the lamp and turned the wick low. Books lay strewn on the floor as if wounded. An open ledger on a desk stared at the ceiling. Another lay face down beside it. A desk drawer hung open like a busted lip. The sound in the air was the whine of wasps or an animal keening in a trap. Nothing and no one was there but me.

I steadied myself the same way I would on a stage. Count my breath, let my vision go into a tunnel, focus on traversing this wreckage and deliver myself safely to my destination.

Scraps of paper littered the desktop, shining like pale scars in the lamplight. I wire-walked to the desk and reached for one.

IOU five dollars. William Hurst.

Another. *IOU two dollars. William Hurst.*

Another. *IOU ten dollars. William Hurst.*

Torn-out pages from his People's Regulator notebooks, each made out to a different man. Some signatures were scrawls, others effortful printing. Several were only an "X" with my father's handwriting alongside the letter, noting a Mr. Ivory in Baltimore, a Mr. Sayres in Norfolk.

My money. Those coins we rolled across a rooming house floor had rolled into the bank, they rolled into a department store to buy dresses, and some—too many, how many was too many, any was too many—had rolled into stranger's pockets. He wrote out little pages of promises. Every scrap of paper on this desk was made by my father before a show, when he was "at the telegraph office," or "out for a stroll" in a new city. Every scrap of paper was a piece of me.

Another piece of me torn deliberately in two was buried in the pages of a book in this room. The book I'd come for was on the highest shelf. He'd moved it since our practice sessions. On my tiptoes, I reached up, but only grazed the book with my pinky nail.

The desk could support me like a little stage. I moved the inkwell and a small mountain of ledgers, taking care not to touch the tiny paper promises. Hiking my nightdress up as if I were a child, I listened to the house again. Only the nighttime sighs of people and bricks and wood at rest. On the desk, I went from hands and knees to standing, bowing my head to keep from bumping the ceiling. *Modern Marvels of Alchemy* was at eye level. I slid the book neatly into my hand and rifled the pages. Back when we started, Daddy put my letter away as a threat. That day he tore it in half, we made a pact. He would protect me from the trouble I'd started if I'd learn to make my talent serve his vision. Put the ephemeral to good use, he'd said.

"She lifted the loan right off the house," he'd told a reporter. The first time I'd heard that, I was proud. The aftermath of the fire wasn't the first time I'd wanted to run from The Magnetic Girl, but it was the strongest. The Magnetic Girl had become a bird made of straw, a trinket proving how well my father could bend fools to his will. It was me, not The Magnetic Girl, who earned all that money, paid for the dresses, the train tickets, the hotel rooms, and the games of chance. Those IOUs on the desk were no different from my pinpricks that raised beads of blood on my skin. They were promises, and they only caused harm.

If Daddy looked for this letter one day and didn't find it, he might doubt himself. Had he moved it? Thrown it away? He would never do such a thing. And when he found only half of the whole, he would know that I'd been here, on my own, healing my wound.

I flipped through the pages again. In two neat strips, I found what I came for.

One half of the page read:

Dear Dale:
I am sorry to tell
My hands in our house
I am afraid
Better of me
Bedroom were from electrical
Tell you that I neglected
Make a false statement
No electricity
I pushed
Allowed everyone to believe
Other than my own hand
Forgive me
Lulu

The other half read:

you this but there was no work of the Lord from
In Cedartown when you were our guest.
You know how much I like to play pranks and
that I let my poor nature get the
and make a prank of you. My mother said then that the noises
in orbs, and I regret to
to speak up and so let my mother.
There was
or work of the Lord, I am sorry to say that
a pin through the mattress to make a noise and
in causes
The scarf was also my doing.
I pray that you will understand me, and I remain,
Your cousin

THE FIRST PALE WASHES of dawn lit the window, but the thin light was silent. The whole world itself, not light, made the sounds, the birds and animals waking under the sun. I tucked half of the letter inside my sleeve, turned the lamp down, and returned *Modern Marvels of Alchemy* to the shelf. We will study this one, Daddy had said. But never in our practice did he open the book. That glowing, fiendish turbaned head on the cover flustered me that first day, but with the passage of time he was nothing more than an ancestor to Madame Parnell.

I didn't wake the sleepers in my house. By now, this *was* my house. I had earned tens of thousands of dollars, a sum I wouldn't have believed existed before I made The Magnetic Girl, no matter how often I counted.

I could have swiped my arm across my father's books, hurtling them into a defeated heap on the floor. Instead, I closed his door behind me and wondered if sorrow can be cured.

CHAPTER
TWENTY-SEVEN

PRACTICE FOR THE SPIRITUALIST AUDIENCE MEANT breaking Momma's one good end table. No scraping the floor with my boot heel or cracking my toes inside my stockings. In the parlor, Daddy leafed through *The Philosophy of Mysterious Agents* like he wasn't watching my fingers move across the table's walnut surface. When I was Leo's age, I jumped my fingers from one light-colored wooden square to another, pretending one finger man was dodging another. The finger men weren't dodging anything today, though. After ten miserable minutes of touching the tabletop and feeling for something loose, wiggling the side of my foot against the table leg, and digging my elbow into the trim at the edge and the parquet in the middle, I gave up trying the top surface and crouched beneath, to see what was what. The table was more tightly made than the parlor chair I'd toyed with once upon a time. Every pin and screw was flush against the wood. When I reached in to touch them, just one was loose enough that a few turns released the table. I felt as if I had undone a corset. I exhaled as if my own stays had been loosened. My fingertips were warm.

I nearly hit my head getting out from under the table. Daddy didn't look up.

"It's in the screws," I said. "We find a loose one, and when I put pressure on the table above it, the wood squeaks."

Daddy put the book down and looked me over. He asked me how many wings were on a chicken. With the table, I answered with creaks and pops. Two. He asked how many legs on a mule, and I made the table squeak four times.

He tapped on Momma's good table.

"We won't 'find' a loose screw in the table, Lulu. We only find it if I put it there."

How many heads on a baby, I silently asked the table. *How many drops of medicine guarantee sleep without dreams?*

WHEN THE REPORTER FROM *the Appeal* knocked at the door, I welcomed him, even though Daddy had told Colonel Furman that a newspaper story about my return to the stage would challenge Dixie's Darling Magnet. If Arden came to a test I might cry, or I might slap his face. Or both. Daddy didn't want him there either, despite his boasting, but he couldn't stop himself from playing to the newspapers.

Daddy reached past me at the door and pumped the reporter's hand. Momma fussed and led him to her good chair, and I seated myself facing him. He flipped open his notebook and licked his pencil tip. As if I were an electric light, I turned on my stage smile.

Leo came around the corner unaided, his steps measured, his hand steady on the wall. A mixture of pride and the urge to rush to his aid rose in me, but his confidence kept me still.

How do you do? he asked the reporter.

The reporter, notepad in hand, answered him directly.

"Hello."

Leo sat by me. I reached for him, but he closed his hand in his lap.

I can tell you all about my sister, he said.

The reporter furrowed his brow but didn't turn away.

"I'm sorry," the reporter said. "Say again?"

Lulu. Leo said. *Me and her made an oath.*

The sun went behind a cloud, and I went cold with dread. *Don't you dare tell them how I dropped you* flew from my mind, even while I wanted to leap up and shout to the reporter, "You're hearing him like there's not one thing wrong."

Momma laughed.

The reporter leaned closer to Leo. "You made a boat?"

Leo scowled. *An oath!* In my head he was nearly yelling.

"Oh!" The reporter laughed. "An oath. Like a promise."

Leo nodded, satisfied.

"What did you promise?" the reporter asked him.

This, I thought. I promised this. Daddy spoke up.

"She promised to lift the loan off our backs. She's as good as done it, too."

While Daddy talked, I observed the greening field out the window. My father narrated The Magnetic Girl's creation story: how composed I had been in front of ever-growing crowds, the power—magnetism, a fluid in our bodies that turned like the tides—enabling his young daughter to lift grown men as they sat, to turn canes into objects of force with a touch of her finger. Did the reporter know about the laundry soap, and that a plow bearing my image would be available before fall? The Magnetic Girl's power has only continued to grow. This Darling Dixie person about whom your readers have been informed? No match for our Lulu.

I counted away the seconds until he'd quit invoking the girl who represented Arden's deceit. Every time I bent my knees behind a mark's chair or offered up a cane, I was inviting complicity in a falsehood. But I'd never considered how many times had I fallen for a lie.

I looked at Leo. He grinned. The gaps left by his baby teeth's departure had filled in. This time, he let me take his hand. The reporter had finished writing Daddy's words. He looked at me, and Leo, our hands enjoined.

"Miss Hurst, I hope you'll tell the *Appeal*'s readers your impressions of visiting so many of our county's grandest cities these past few months?"

"Lulu has been invited to meet a prominent civic group in the beautiful city of Chattanooga," Daddy said. Momma made an approving noise.

"That so?" The reporter smiled at me like I was his favorite little sister.

"We received a letter asking if I'd take time to meet them," I said. I was long past requiring any cues. I'd send this fellow all to pieces if I could levitate his pencil or overturn a table by staring at it.

I could tell him that the Spiritualist society had decided that I was ripe with the ability to raise their dead. I could throw that whole act right this minute and tell this lackluster fellow that only my father's inability to get a Blue Book, the semi-secret compendium of followers of Spiritualism, had prevented him from arranging something like this earlier in my career. The reporter would have his story then. I'd be Lulu Hurst, revealer of secrets.

"So, of course we've planned a visit to Tennessee," I said, smiling so hard my face hurt. That smile was, he would have to write it, like a magnet.

The reporter scribbled in his pad. The mantel clock ticked, and a cow lowed in the pasture.

"Please tell your readers, our friends and neighbors," I added, "how pleased I am to be back in our precious hometown again, if only for a little while. The Force is a gift, and it's my honor to bear it, but please know that I am merely your own Lulu Hurst."

CHAPTER
TWENTY-EIGHT
Atlanta, Georgia
May 1884

FOUR OF US WAITED ON THE PLATFORM FOR THE
morning train to Atlanta. Momma, Daddy, me, and Mr. Starnes,
the *Appeal*'s man. The rails didn't dance this time. They seized and
bucked.

"Phrenology," Momma had said, "is all the rage."

She'd heard from Mrs. Hartnett that a Doctor Walter in Atlanta
was taking appointments to see new patients. They had picked up
their sewing circle where they'd left off, mostly as a chance for Mrs.
Hartnett to pump Momma for every detail about our glamorous
theater life. Momma gladly told her, and then some. Mrs. Hartnett
had dreamy predictions about her future and did her best to drop
heavy hints in front of me about curing this ailment or the other
tormenting her extended family. I wasn't going to make up some
story about who her unattractive niece would marry, or if her cousin
would leave them money in a will. I had no idea. What I wanted to
know was why Mr. Hartnett had let our house go to the dogs.

"We had a phrenologist on a bill," I told Momma when she brought it up. "Remember, the fellow who toted the model of a head under his arm? He called her Anne Boleyn."

Momma made a face.

"This one in Atlanta's not a joker, Lulu. What he says goes straight to the opinions of the right people."

I hadn't realized the fellow with the head was making fun.

"We'll write to Dr. Walter and get you a visit with him."

I was far from sick.

"Once he assesses your character, we can let everyone know that a physician recommends you."

Dr. Walter's medical practice was on the second floor of a bank building on Whitehall Street, one door in a warren of dentist offices and closed-door business along a corridor of polished brass and waxed dark wood. We let ourselves in, Momma clutching his appointment letter like a lucky charm. White ceramic models of heads and necks stared at nothing from a table, each bare scalp mapped in blue lines and solemn words. *Combatitiveness* curved in a crescent shape behind an ear, over a figure of two pugilists the size of bees. *Language* hung under an eye socket. A square called *Conscientiousness* was depicted by a figure carrying buckets from either end of a stick, and a rectangle labeled *Acquisitiveness* showed a miser at his counting.

A man with the palest blue eyes I'd ever seen emerged from behind a lace curtain. He extended his hand and introduced himself. Daddy, Momma, and I each shook Dr. Walter's hand.

"This is Mr. Starnes," Daddy said. "He'll be telling the world about your judgment of our Magnetic Girl."

My skin itched for a pin or a needle.

"It's no trouble at all," Dr. Walter replied. "A young lady with your daughter's characteristics will be a unique study for me, a pleasure."

He guided me to a chair, and like one of my own marks, I sat upright, feet apart, hands at my sides.

"Imagine knowing a person's deepest nature better than they do, just from the shape of their skull," Momma said, trying make conversation.

The doctor pulled the lace curtain aside, revealing a windowless chamber with a settee. At his direction, my parents made themselves comfortable there. Mr. Starnes loomed at my side, his pencil poised to create a story.

Dr. Walter addressed me as if we were old friends.

"I'll need you to take your hair down, or it will interfere with the measuring. When I step out, kindly do so. I'll need to get as near to your plain skull as I can." He signaled to Mr. Starnes, who followed him to the anteroom.

Arranging my hairpins on the table beside me, I formed a kind of map, Cedartown to New York and back to Cedartown again. These pins were tortoiseshell and silver, proof of all I'd earned and how changed I was—we all were—since last autumn. I arranged the pins in a row, friends, weapons, deceivers. I ignored the urge to slide a sharp tip into my flesh and pull it away, anticipating that one drop of dark blood. Hairpins were simply what their name implied; pins for hair. Objects to hold something in its place.

Instead of piercing me open, Dr. Walter held me motionless. With my hair loose down the back of the chair, I felt as risqué as Miss Marie. He cradled my head as if I were an invalid, a metal clamp open near my face. Slowly, the way I approached a mark, he applied the calipers to my skull, stopping every few turns to write notes onto a pad. Sometimes he said, "Hmmmm," which caused the reporter to ask "What?"

What, indeed? When I tried to ask, the doctor held up his hand to stop me from speaking. Moving my jaw could affect a calculation.

Moving my jaw hadn't been to anyone's liking when I sat for my washing soda portrait. Moving my jaw on stage meant speaking only the simplest directions: how to sit, where a mark should place his hands and feet. The Magnetic Girl was a woman who did not speak. My grandmother expressed what she believed. *My story*, she wrote, *speaks for itself. My duty is to express the truth.*

Although I wasn't permitted to speak, the doctor labored under no such limitations. He chattered about his love of theater, the famous patients he'd measured, and the science of phrenology's value in understanding humankind's future. All the while, he skimmed instruments along my head. I read the charts on the wall over and over (KNOW THYSELF in bold lettering arcing across the top, a numbered list of the brain's twenty-seven organs beneath) until he removed his hands from my head and pushed the instrument table away. The reporter looked pleased. Dr. Walter rose to fetch my parents. They took their places on either side of the chair from which I hadn't yet been permitted to rise. Dr. Walter consulted his findings.

"I'm always happy to find a female patient whose vanity area is diminutive. That's unusual for the fairer sex," he told my parents. "Your daughter is that rare breed, a girl with a modest vanity trait. Miss Hurst's skull area for poetics, her architecture or talent for the building trades, are oddly large for a lady, but then again, we already know she's blessed with some supremacy in that field."

He winked at them before he turned to me.

"You've got a remarkable memory for faces, for learning your facts and figures, for language. In fact, the benevolence area," he reached out and poked his finger under my bangs, "is truly well-developed."

Wishing I could scrub away his touch, I smoothed my bangs.

"In the end, then," he said, "this is wonderful news for you all, but it's nothing we didn't already know from Miss Hurst's fine reputation. I'm pleased that phrenology can tell us how true a person is to himself." He patted my shoulder. "Or herself, as the case may be."

DR. WALTER'S GOOD TIDINGS, touted in the *Appeal* by Mr. Starnes, and telegrammed by Daddy to theaters from Knoxville to Bowling Green, assured The Magnetic Girl's return to the stage. This time, she had the clairvoyant's touch.

Daddy decided that planning a tour didn't take special brains. Any good soldier who'd ever marched could manage an opera house tour without breaking a sweat. Anyway, Mr. Berlin had been stealing from us, Daddy said. He'd taken our money for no work at all. We didn't need Mr. Getty, either.

But you stole from us, too, formed in my mouth. I swallowed it back, a sour lump. The slips of paper on his desk were surely put away by now. He'd have tabulated them in a ledger, who owed him, and who he owed.

He owed me so much, but I owed him, too.

I said nothing. To my father, I was nothing more than soap. Shake me from a box and make yourself clean with the Power of the Magnetic Girl.

THE *APPEAL* WAS NO longer my atlas. The sight of a newspaper turned my stomach. The narrow, rutted road to Cedartown shimmered dusty yellow brown in the heat. So much waited just beyond that road.

One warm afternoon, I sat with Leo, who was engrossed in the mail order catalogue from Montgomery Ward. While he looked at the pictures and made up stories, I looked out at our hills. Leo had vanished into piggy banks and fur hats. Telling him I'd be right back, I went inside, banging the door behind me. He didn't look up. From the drawer in Momma's good table, I took a pen, an ink bottle, and a sheet of paper. And then I joined my brother on the porch.

Dear Mrs. Voorhees, I wrote.

She had a first name, but I didn't know it. We weren't friends of that kind. We weren't friends at all, even with her residing in my thoughts since the day she captivated me in her sickroom. *This thing we do,* she'd called it, as if she owned Mesmerism, as if she'd invented it.

Dear Mrs. Voorhees. When we met, you kindly told me about the women you called my forebears, women like you and me who can hold a moment of time in their gaze, in their hands, and for that brief instant make circumstances go their way. Thank you for the lesson, as my only knowledge before our meeting was of our shared mentor, Mrs. Wolf.

Rolling the pen between my fingers, I examined the nib. Not as sharp as a pin or needle, and bubbling with noxious-looking black ink besides. This didn't belong in my skin. Nothing of its kind did.

Since our encounter, I learned that Mrs. Wolf is truly my prede-
cessor in the most literal sense. I am her granddaughter, on my
father's side. This means that Mesmerism—captivation—truly
lives in my blood.
You proposed then the question of my curing you and answered
yourself. You determined that I could not but denied me the oppor-
tunity to try. Perhaps you were right, as I was inexperienced
beyond my natural skill.
I was naïve.

The minute the word *naïve* hit the page, relief took wing inside me.
Here was my voice, telling the truth.

May I pay a call to you next month when I am again in Knoxville?
I believe I know the route to a cure if you will put your faith in me.

Best wishes,
Lulu Hurst

Best wishes. Wishes were what brought anyone to my tests, the
same way that wishes sold toy canaries. The Mesmerist is herself an
object. The sufferer brings the wishes. My grandmother knew this.
She'd as much as told me, except my own wishes made me deaf to
her words. The moment of first recognition of a sufferer's desire to be
cured alleviated my own qualms. I was half of a correlation.

We Mesmerists couldn't cure a person of their tumor or their
palsy, or their drinking, or their broken heart, but in coming to us, the
sufferer lifts his own fear or pain. He cures himself, if only for those
moments he believes. My grandmother and I and Mrs. Voorhees
could hold a stranger's gaze long enough to stop time for a fleeting
instant. We could float gloriously in that suspended space, and that
was indeed our gift, offering freedom from the sorrow and pain that
roared and clanked and stank around us. The sick and scared were
drawn to that power, and we gave them what we could. And then we
found ourselves empty, until the next person arrived at our door or
we stepped out onto to the next opera house stage.

I sealed the letter to Mrs. Voorhees, and addressed it with her name, her street, in Knoxville, Tennessee. I asked my father to send it for me the next time he was in town.

"A thank you letter," I told him.

I was telling the truth.

CHAPTER TWENTY-NINE

Knoxville, Tennessee:
May 1884

I STOPPED BY THE HOTEL DESK IN KNOXVILLE casually, as if asking for my messages was a tiresome addition to an already full day. Daddy did it countless times in every hotel. While the desk clerk sorted through cards in the pigeonhole cabinet, I soothed my hands against the cool marble counter and surveyed the lobby. A fellow with a gut like a melon crossed his legs in a chair. He would be almost impossible to lift. A frail woman with chapped lips and red nostrils that telegraphed "head cold" would be an easy mark for her purse if I ever surrendered to raw thievery.

"There's a card for you, Mrs. Hurst."

The desk clerk slid a cream and yellow calling card across the counter.

"Came in this morning's mail."

The card bore the legend PROFESSOR HARMONY'S MAGNETIC BIRDS. in old-fashioned engraving over the name *Therese Voorhees*. On the back, in careful handwriting, *Please telephone*.

She'd read my card. And her name was Therese. Oh, I could just see her, taking the mail from Ouida, setting her drops aside in surprise at a word from me. As if I used a telephone every day, I asked the clerk where I might place a call. Knowing that Mrs. Voorhees chose to see me again guided me through the doorway into a closet-sized room. The telephone itself, a miracle I'd seen but never used, squatted alone on a desk.

"You pick up the earpiece there, and tell Central who you're wanting," the boy said before he left. I was sorry to be alone with it: I wanted a witness to my ease with the device. The brass earpiece was unexpectedly heavy in my hand, a palm-sized telescope for the ear. At first, nothing happened. A memory of Arden taunting me about places I had no business being rose in my mind. Waiting for something to happen, I browsed the desk drawers. Spare inkwells, pen nibs, a ball of twine, and an India-rubber eraser. Then a voice came through, far away like a ghost, gaining strength through crackling air.

"Therese Voorhees, please," I said, calm and certain as a Sunday school recitation. Asked and answered, then take your seat, well done.

Far down the hole of the earpiece came metallic chirping and clicking, and then a girl's voice saying hello. Of course Ouida would be at the other end. A telephone was nothing more than a chore at Mrs. Voorhees's house.

"Hello," I called out, not sure how loudly to speak if I couldn't be seen. "This is Miss Lulu Hurst. I received a calling card?" Too strident. I would have to speak normally.

Ouida's voice was even. I was jealous. A mere child, but comfortable enough with a telephone to modulate her voice easily.

"Thank you for calling, Miss Hurst. We have sorrowful news." Ouida's voice wavered like an actress's in a melodrama.

The earpiece was smooth in my hands. I looked at it as if the wood and brass would remake themselves into Ouida's pinched, serious face. Sorrowful news without a telling glance and the touch of a kind hand was inhumane.

"Are you there?" Ouida asked.

"Yes, sorry," I said. "Please tell me."

"Mrs. Voorhees has died," Ouida said, as matter-of-fact as telling the time. "Three weeks ago. We didn't get your card until just this week, and I thought you ought to know, since you'd written her."

Without Mrs. Voorhees to hear me, would my truth flutter from my mouth like a feather and lie here on the carpet, discarded in the sweepings at the end of the day? I'd written "understand me" in my letter to Dale, but until I'd torn one paper into two, the words hadn't stood out on their own.

I had been so ready to stand before her in that room and say the truth: that the means to a cure began with knowing that I wasn't the one who *had* the cure. Mesmerism, captivating, or a toy bird wasn't the answer. There might be no cure at all but putting the medicine bottle away and leaving Ouida to her own wits. Stand and walk if those blankets and *chaise longue* are props for your act. If they're not, live as if you are standing.

Every person in an audience wanted me to cure them of something. They radiated need that I couldn't satisfy. Fame was like a fire. Before I knew better I loved its light, but soon enough, I got burned. That bottomless need was my own.

"My condolences," I told Ouida, my voice breaking. The earpiece went back into the cradle.

THE GOLD AND RED patterned carpets in the Staub Theater lobby were threadbare, as worn and tired as when I played here the first time. This world was new to me then, and I observed so little. An hour before curtain, the lobby was nearly empty. I rarely ventured to the front of the house, but I wanted a stranger's view of my life. At the ticket booth, an old man gabbed at the early buyers.

"She's not the same as some shyster in a ten-in-one, no sir. She ain't playing for the cake eaters, neither. This one, Magneto Gal, she's played all the big towns, New York, Chicago, Washington DC."

Bending my knees to hide my height, I studied an easel card and kept my back to the room.

"Wanna know how I know she's the real thing?"

I did want to know. What had I gotten them to believe, these strangers who would never know me? I leaned away from the easel, brushing my hand through my hair to lift my hat from my ear.

"I worked as a first-of-May one season for the Serafini-Sula show, out of Astoria, near Manhattan. I melted down heads from the waxworks when they got wore out, so they could make new ones. I gaffed a bit, filled in for the talkers. I know my marks, and I know my talent. I seen the Dixie Darlin', too, but this Lulu Magneto, she ain't kidding around. This here girl's *bona fide* guided by the beyond."

The double doors into the theater opened, an entryway into a black maw. I had to slip away quickly, into the street and back in through the stage door. I wanted to hear how I was guided by the beyond, why he believed.

"Why'd you leave?" a fellow asked. I nodded my thanks, if only to the easel-card.

"I'm upstanding now. I ended up here after too many stops in one Bumfuck, Egypt after another. Now I'm working for the gas light people. We're installin' in fancy residences. Down in Atlanta, they got Peachtree Street lit up like Paris, France."

Backstage reeked of nerves and desperation. The door handles, the window glass, even the wooden stairs were tarnished like a cheap copper bracelet when the gold plate flakes off. In the dressing room mirror's mottled glass, I didn't quite look like me. The girl in the mirror raised her hand to her mouth. One twin stays in the bottle, while the other gets torn loose.

The Chattanooga Spiritualists had swooned and fawned over The Magnetic Girl, and I did all kinds of tricks that put worn-out table rapping to shame. Daddy had gotten hold of the Blue Book. A week of half hours before bedtime spent memorizing choice names from the pages made the afternoon with the Spiritualists effortless. Some of the names had "dead easy" written next to them in a woman's hand, a promise from whomever had worked the book before me that they were believers. Call out Mrs. Milton and tell her that her son George, buried on a battlefield, misses her. Mention Miss Parker's brother, Floyd, who, dead of a suppurating wound in a field hospital, greets her painlessly from heaven. I was sorry, I'd said to Mrs. White, making myself well up with tears, but there was still no word from her son, missing now twenty years. The Magnetic Girl really went to work then, patting their hands while dabbing at my eyes with a handkerchief doused with the scent of orange blossoms. Momma had read about that in the *Spirit Messenger*. The ladies closed their eyes, held hands in a circle, thought hard about their beloveds. Yes, The Magnetic Girl was there in full force, gracious and mysterious, but I was merely the body carrying her. I was the captive twin. After the grateful kisses and thanks as we left the Society's meeting, Daddy counted our payment. He tucked the money in his vest pocket. Momma nibbled from the gift basket of candy they'd given us, but I had no appetite.

In the dressing room mirror in Knoxville, The Magnetic Girl watched me fumble with my bangs. My memory of a female voice shrilling from some crowd, "Her power's in her hair" stopped me. The site of benevolence, Dr. Walter had said. I smiled The Magnetic Girl's magnetic smile and plumped the accordion folds at my shoulders. I arranged my pleated collar away from scratching my chin.

This was my first dressing room without *The Truth of Mesmeric Influence* in my hands. Would she cheer me on today, my grandmother, my Mrs. Wolf? From habit, I turned to the corner where my trunk would have stood.

My strongest power, she'd written. *I find my strongest power in making two into one.*

Applause from the theater rumbled through the walls. The first act, a slapstick comedy, had started, which meant I should get my exercises started. Deep knee bends, arms out ahead like railroad tracks. They used to be so important. Pivot my shoulders in their sockets. Swinging my arms, loosening my muscles and increasing my heartbeat before the act. I flexed my fingers, and as I did before every show, focused on feeling the perfect moment in my elbows, knees, deep inside my being. Mrs. Wolf had handed me the truth without my knowing.

The stronger nature. I have the stronger nature.

The knock on the dressing room door was my father's, sure as the sun set in the evening. Sounding like a stage manager, he told me, "In five." Five minutes until show time. Momma was waiting to wet my hair and smooth it out after dipping her handkerchief in the water bucket by the door. She would straighten some ribbon or sleeve that she'd say had gone awry.

"I'm on my way, Daddy." I sang it out. With one last look in the mirror, I blew The Magnetic Girl a kiss.

My father and I went purposefully and quickly to the stage, my heart racing. For a moment, black spots floated before my eyes. Easy as pie, I reminded myself, pacing my steps.

Six months ago, I was a little girl, too naïve to understand the deep hole of my father's need. He relied on me more than he did anyone, and it was so easy for me to fool crowds simply by bending my knees and staring into a stranger's eyes.

My parents would be frail someday, and then gone. Leo would grow into a man. People other than me will hear him speak. I would miss the joy of lifting a man, feeling his weight balanced on two chair legs and the weightlessness that came to me when I set him down. No one would applaud for me after today, unless I did for myself, and maybe someday a husband, a son, a daughter. Perhaps I would entertain them at home with little tests, a scarf in a sleeve, a wild animal paused as if in thought. Perhaps I never would again.

The pianist began "I'll Be Ready When the Great Day Comes" as the Fortenberry Comedy Company left the stage, all four of them waving to the cheering audience and bowing as they went. The third Fortenberry, the one with the wandering eye, licked his lips at me as he ran by. If I'd had a pin, he would have gotten it in the leg but I had no more need for pins in that way.

The stage was empty, ready for me. The audience's stomping chant, "Magnetic Girl, Magnetic Girl," had already begun. My father waited for their excitement to crest before he bounded out toward the lights. No matter if I performed a chair test or threw a fellow across a cane, if I told the time without consulting a clock or conveyed a message from the heaven of Summerland, rumors would fly again. The Magnetic Girl can cure a toothache, lift a grand piano. Burn a man to death. Strangers wouldn't bother to pretend that they weren't watching my boots, waiting for sparks to fly.

Alone in the dark, I touched the paper scroll I'd put in my waistband. No need to read it again. What mattered most was memorized. Easy as pie.

I am sorry to tell
No electricity
Forgive me
Lulu

My words.

The pianist launched into another round. I was taking too long. No one expected anything more shocking than my lifting men and chair, sending canes flying across the stage with my eyes on you—yes, you—or the thrilling, surging electrical touch when I bested you. My magnetism could reach your lost loves, too, and hear what they needed you to know.

I'd imagined what I would say tonight but hadn't yet said the words aloud. Once I did, I could never take them back. On stage, Daddy launched into his warm-up patter.

"The greatest of all living human problems remains unsolved. Science and skepticism are confounded by the power of The Magnetic Girl. Community leaders and the common man alike are changed forever by her mere touch."

In the suspended moments before I took the stage, I turned again and looked over my shoulder. Once my words took flight from my mouth, I would never see this backstage view again. If I didn't say them tonight, I would say them on another stage, soon. My words would cause a kind of death, a thing broken in my deliberate hands.

Bowing deeply to the audience, Daddy removed his top-hat and swept it grandly in my direction. As he straightened, he began to applaud, and the audience, as always, followed his lead.

I had my fill. I pulled aside the heavy curtain and walked into the light.

AUTHOR NOTE

LULU HURST WAS A REAL PERSON. HER BROTHER, AS written here, was not, and neither was the character of her paternal grandmother. The "tests," as she called her performances, are depicted here largely as she described them in her 1897 autobiography, *Lulu Hurst (The Georgia Wonder) Writes Her Autobiography and for the First Time Explains and Demonstrates the Great Secret of her Marvelous Power*, which she dedicated to her beloved parents and friends. Her actual tour dates covered several periods beginning in the late months of 1883 and ending in the early months of 1885.

Lulu retired from the stage in 1885 at the age of sixteen. She never performed again. She attended college, married, and had two sons. Lulu Hurst Atkinson died in Madison, Georgia in 1950.

The Truth of Mesmeric Influence is inspired by British author Harriet Martineau's 1844 book, *Letters on Mesmerism*. Lulu herself may never have seen this book.

The Magnetic Girl is fiction. Although some of the circumstances are inspired by real life, my interest lies in exploring what makes us want to turn away from the people and places we love, why we return, and the ways we learn to understand who we really are.

When The Beatles' song, "Being For the Benefit of Mr. Kite," came out in 1967, I was eight years old. That song was alive with spectacle, and I was captivated. Suddenly, I was in love with the idea of carnivals and vaudeville. (I was already in love with The Beatles.) Follow that with Randy Newman's poignant "Simon Smith and the Amazing Dancing Bear," in 1972, and the heartbreak and bravado in tales of gas-lit stages and street corner performances became clear: daring feats can mask sorrow, no matter if we are on stage or off.

No book that dips into history can be written without predecessors. For me, some of those invaluable resources include Lulu Hurst's own book, as well as Barry Wiley's important compilation, *The Georgia Wonder: Lulu Hurst and the Secret That Shook America*, which contains, among other fascinating items, a reprint of that autobiography.

My thanks to the Kenan Research Center at the Atlanta History Cente, and *The New Georgia Encyclopedia*. Terri Callahan's master's thesis opened my eyes to possibility. A standing ovation goes to Katharine Weber for the space to write and the laying on of healing hands, to Joshilyn Jackson for the map of wants, and to Sam Starnes for the dual alchemy of insight and cheerleading. Hours of applause for Walter Biggins, Eileen Drennen, Beth Gylys, Sheri Joseph, Alison Law, Kathryn Rhett, Anna Schachner, Gray Stewart, Suzanne Van Atten, Susan Rebecca White, and Susan Woodring. A spotlight shines on Peter McDade for insisting on fun. Thanks to *Tin House*, *Digital Americana*, and *The Bitter Southerner* for providing homes for essays and early ventures. The generous citizens of Cedartown who sat with me for interviews and the Polk Couny Historical Society were clear lenses. Eli Arnold, Director of the Oglethorpe University Library, gets a curtain call for pulling a research rabbit out of his hat when I needed it most. There's not enough applause in the world for Betsy Teter, Meg Reid, Kate McMullen, and C. Michael Curtis at Hub City Press. You are my dream team. And always, gratitude to Mickey Dubrow, without whom I can make no journey large or small.

The COLD MOUNTAIN *Fund*

S E R I E S

NATIONAL BOOK AWARD WINNER Charles Frazier generously supports publication of a series of Hub City Press books through the Cold Mountain Fund at the Community Foundation of Western North Carolina. Beginning in 2019, the Cold Mountain Series spotlights works of fiction by new and extraordinary writers from the American South.

HUB CITY PRESS has emerged as the South's premier independent literary press. Focused on finding and spotlighting new and extraordinary voices from the American South, the press has published over eighty high-caliber literary works. Hub City is interested in books with a strong sense of place and is committed to introducing a diverse roster of lesser-heard Southern voices. We are funded by the National Endowment for the Arts, the South Carolina Arts Commission and hundreds of donors across the Carolinas.

RECENT HUB CITY PRESS TITLES